Bernhard Tauchnitz

The life of Charles Dickens by John Forster

Bernhard Tauchnitz

The life of Charles Dickens by John Forster

ISBN/EAN: 9783742854971

Manufactured in Europe, USA, Canada, Australia, Japa

Cover: Foto ©Andreas Hilbeck / pixelio.de

Manufactured and distributed by brebook publishing software
(www.brebook.com)

Bernhard Tauchnitz

The life of Charles Dickens by John Forster

THE LIFE

OF

CHARLES DICKENS.

BY

JOHN FORSTER.

COPYRIGHT EDITION.

VOL. II.

LEIPZIG
BERNHARD TAUCHNITZ
1872.

TABLE OF CONTENTS.

VOLUME II.

CHAPTER XIII. 1840.

Pages 17-35.

DEVONSHIRE TERRACE AND BROADSTAIRS. ÆT. 28.

	Page
A good saying	17
Landor mystified	18
The mirthful side of Dickens	18
Extravagant flights	19
Humorous despair	19
Riding exercise	20
First of the Ravens	21
The groom Topping	21
The smoky chimneys	22
Juryman at an inquest	23
Practical humanity	23
Publication of *Clock's* first number	24
Transfer of *Barnaby* settled	25
A true prediction	26
Revisiting old scenes	26
C. D. to Chapman and Hall	27
Terms of sale of *Barnaby*	28
A gift to a friend	28
Final escape from bondage	29
Published libels about him	30
Said to be demented	30
To be insane and turned Catholic	31
Begging-letter-writers	31
A donkey asked for	32
Mr. Kindheart	32
Friendly meetings	33

	Page
Social talk	33
Reconciling friends	34
Hint for judging men	35

CHAPTER XIV. 1841.
Pages 36-55.
BARNABY RUDGE. ÆT. 29.

Advantage in beginning *Barnaby*	36
Birth of fourth child and second son	37
The Raven	38
A loss in the family	38
Grip's death	39
C. D. describes his illness	39
Family mourners	41
Apotheosis by Maclise	42
Grip the second	43
The inn at Chigwell	43
A *Clock* dinner	44
Lord Jeffrey in London	45
The *Lamplighter*	45
The *Pic Nic Papers*	45
Character of Lord George Gordon	46
A doubtful fancy	47
Interest in new labour	48
Constraints of weekly publication	49
The prison-riots	49
A serious illness	50
Close of *Barnaby*	50
Character of the tale	50
Defects in the plot	51
The No-Popery riots	52
Descriptive power displayed	52
Leading persons in story	53
Mr. Dennis the hangman	55

CHAPTER XV. 1841.
Pages 56-74.
PUBLIC DINNER IN EDINBURGH. ÆT. 29.

His son Walter Landor	56
Dies in Calcutta (1863)	57

	Page
C. D. and the new poor-law	57
Moore and Rogers	58
Jeffrey's praise of Little Nell	59
Resolve to visit Scotland	59
Edinburgh dinner proposed	59
Sir David Wilkie's death	60
Peter Robertson	61
Professor Wilson	61
A fancy of Scott	62
Lionization made tolerable	63
Thoughts of home	63
The dinner and speeches	63
Wilson's eulogy	65
His reception	66
Home yearnings	67
Freedom of city voted to him	67
Speakers at the dinner	68
Politics and party influences	68
Whig jealousies	69
At the theatre	70
Hospitalities	70
Moral of it all	71
Proposed visit to the Highlands	71
Maclise and Macready	72
Guide to the Highlands	73
Mr. Angus Fletcher (Kindheart)	73

CHAPTER XVI. 1841.

Pages 75-93.

ADVENTURES IN THE HIGHLANDS. ÆT. 29.

A fright	75
Fletcher's eccentricities	76
The Trossachs	77
The travellers' guide	77
A comical picture	77
Highland accommodation	78
Grand scenery	79
Changes in route	80

	Page
A waterfall	80
Entrance to Glencoe	81
The pass of Glencoe	82
Loch Leven	82
A July evening	82
Postal service at Loch-carn-head	83
The maid of the inn	84
Impressions of Glencoe	84
An adventure	85
Torrents swollen with rain	86
Dangerous travelling	87
Incidents and accidents	87
Broken-down bridge	88
A fortunate resolve	88
Post-boy in danger	89
The rescue	90
Narrow escape	90
A Highland inn and inmates	91
English comfort at Dalmally	91
Dinner at Glasgow proposed	92
Eagerness for home	93

CHAPTER XVII. 1841.

Pages 94-103.

AGAIN AT BROADSTAIRS. ÆT. 29.

Peel and his party	94
Getting very radical	95
Thoughts of colonizing	95
Political squib by C. D.	96
Fine old English tory times	96
Mesmerism	98
Metropolitan prisons	98
Book by a workman	98
An August day by the sea	99
Another story in prospect	100
Clock discontents	100
New adventure	100
Agreement for it signed	101

	Page
The book that proved to be *Chuzzlewit*	102
Peel and Lord Ashley	102
Visions of America	103

CHAPTER XVIII. 1841.

Pages 104-113.

EVE OF THE VISIT TO AMERICA. ÆT. 29.

Greetings from America	104
Reply to Washington Irving	104
Difficulties in the way	105
Resolve to go	106
Wish to revisit scenes of boyhood	106
Proposed book of travel	107
Arrangements for the journey	107
Impatience of suspense	108
Resolve to leave the children	109
Mrs. Dickens reconciled	119
A grave illness	110
Domestic griefs	110
The old sorrow	111
At Windsor	112
Son Walter's christening	112
At Liverpool with the travellers	113

CHAPTER XIX. 1842.

Pages 114-142.

FIRST IMPRESSIONS OF AMERICA. ÆT. 30.

Rough passage	114
A steamer in a storm	114
Resigned to the worst	115
Of himself and fellow-travellers	116
The Atlantic from deck	116
The ladies' cabin	117
Its occupants	117
Card-playing on Atlantic	118
Ship-news	119
A wager	120
Halifax harbour	121

	Page
Ship aground	121
Captain Hewitt	122
Speaker of house of assembly	122
Ovation to C. D.	123
Arrival at Boston	124
Incursion of editors	124
At Tremont-house	125
The welcome	125
Deputations	126
Dr. Channing to C. D.	126
Public appearances	128
A secretary engaged	128
Bostonians	129
General characteristics	129
Personal notices	130
Perils of steamers	131
A home thought	131
American institutions	132
How first impressed	133
Reasons for the greeting	133
What was welcomed in C. D.	134
Old world and New world	134
Daniel Webster as to C. D.	135
Channing as to C. D.	136
Subsequent disappointments	136
New York invitation to dinner	137
Facsimiles of signatures	138
Additional facsimiles	139
New York invitation to ball	140
Facsimiles of signatures	141
Additional facsimiles	142

CHAPTER XX. 1842.

Pages 143-175.

SECOND IMPRESSIONS OF AMERICA. ÆT. 30.

Second letter	143
International copyright	144
Third letter	144
The dinner at Boston	145
Worcester, Springfield, and Hartford	146

	Page
Queer travelling	146
Levees at Hartford and Newhaven	147
At Wallingford	147
Serenades	148
Cornelius C. Felton	149
Payment of personal expenses declined	149
At New York	150
Irving and Colden	150
Description of the ball	151
Newspaper accounts	152
A phase of character	153
Opinion in America	153
International copyright	154
American authors in regard to it	154
Outcry against the nation's guest	155
Declines to be silent on copyright	155
Speech at dinner	156
Irving in the chair	156
Chairman's breakdown	157
An incident afterwards in London	158
Results of copyright speeches	159
A bookseller's demand for help	159
Suggestion for copyright memorial	160
Henry Clay's opinion	160
Life in New York	161
Distresses of popularity	161
Intentions for future	162
Refusal of invitations	162
Going south and west	163
As to return	163
Dangers incident to steamers	164
Slavery	165
Ladies of America	166
Party conflicts	166
Non-arrival of Cunard steamer	166
Copyright petition for Congress	167
No hope of the Caledonia	168
A substitute for her	169
Anxiety as to letters	170
Of distinguished Americans	170

	Page
Hotel bills	171
Thoughts of the children	171
Acadia takes Caledonia's place	172
Letter to C. D. from Carlyle	172
Carlyle on copyright	173
Argument against stealing	173
Rob Roy's plan worth bettering	174
C. D. as to Carlyle	175

CHAPTER XXI. 1842.

Pages 176-205.

PHILADELPHIA, WASHINGTON, AND THE SOUTH. ÆT. 30.

At Philadelphia	176
Rule in printing letters	176
Promise as to railroads	177
Experience of them	178
Railway cars	178
Charcoal stoves	179
Ladies' cars	179
Spittoons	180
Massachusetts and New York	180
Police-cells and prisons	181
House of detention and inmates	182
Women and boy prisoners	184
Capital punishment	185
A house of correction	186
Four hundred single cells	186
Comparison with English prisons	187
Inns and landlords	188
At Washington	188
Hotel extortion	188
Philadelphia penitentiary	189
The solitary system	189
Solitary prisoners	190
Talk with inspectors	191
Bookseller Cary	192
Changes of temperature	192
Henry Clay	192
Proposed journeyings	193
Letters from England	194

	Page
Congress and Senate	194
Leading American statesmen	195
The people of America	196
Englishmen "located" there	196
"Surgit amari aliquid"	197
The copyright petition	197
At Richmond	198
Irving appointed to Spain	198
Experience of a slave city	199
Incidents of slave-life	199
Discussion with a slave-holder	200
Feeling of South to England	201
Levees at Richmond	201
One more banquet accepted	202
My gift of *Shakespeare*	203
Home letters and fancies	203
Self-reproach of a noble nature	204
Washington Irving's leave-taking	205

CHAPTER XXII. 1842.

Pages 206-235.

CANAL BOAT JOURNEYS: BOUND FAR WEST. ÆT. 30.

Character in the letters	206
The *Notes* less satisfactory	207
Personal narrative in letters	207
The copyright differences	208
Social dissatisfactions	208
A fact to be remembered	209
Literary merits of the letters	210
Personal character pourtrayed	211
On board for Pittsburgh	211
Choicest passages of *Notes*	211
Queer stage-coach	212
Something revealed on the top	213
At Harrisburgh	213
Treaties with Indians	214
Local legislatures	215
A levee	215
Morning and night in canal-boat	216
At and after breakfast	217

	Page
Making the best of it	218
Hardy habits	218
By rail across mountain	219
Mountain scenery	220
New settlements	220
Original of Eden in *Chuzzlewit*	220
A useful word	221
Party in America	222
Home news	223
Meets an early acquaintance	224
"Smallness of the world"	224
Queer customers at levees	225
Our anniversary	226
The Cincinnati steamer	226
Frugality in water and linen	227
Magnetic experiments	228
Life preservers	229
Bores	230
Habits of neatness	230
Wearying for home	231
Another solitary prison	232
New terror to loneliness	232
Arrival at Cincinnati	233
Two judges in attendance	233
The city described	234
On the pavement	235

CHAPTER XXIII. 1842.

Pages 236-269.

THE FAR WEST: TO NIAGARA FALLS. ÆT. 30.

Descriptions in letters and in *Notes*	236
Outline of westward travel	237
An Arabian-Night city	238
A temperance festival	238
A party at Judge Walker's	239
The party from another view	239
Young lady's description of C. D.	240
Mournful results of boredom	241
Down the Mississippi	242
Listening and watching	242

	Page
A levee at St. Louis	243
Compliments	243
Lord Ashburton's arrival	244
Talk with a judge on slavery	245
A negro burnt alive	246
Feeling of slaves themselves	246
American testimony	247
Pretty little scene	247
A mother and her husband	247
The baby	247
St. Louis in sight	250
Meeting of wife and husband	251
Trip to a prairie	251
On the prairie at sunset	252
General character of scenery	253
The prairie described	253
Disappointment and enjoyment	254
Soirée at Planter's-house-inn	255
Good fare	255
No grey heads in St. Louis	255
Duelling	256
Mrs. Dickens as a traveller	257
From Cincinnati to Columbus	258
What a levee is like	258
From Columbus to Sandusky	259
The travellers alone	260
A log-house inn	261
Making tidy	261
A monetary crisis	261
Americans not a humorous people	263
The only recreations	263
From Sandusky to Buffalo	264
On Lake Erie	264
Reception and consolation of a mayor	265
From Buffalo to Niagara	266
Nearing the Falls	266
The Horse-shoe	267
Effect upon him of Niagara	267
The old recollection	268
Looking forward	269

CHAPTER XXIV. 1842.
Pages 270-283.
NIAGARA AND MONTREAL. ÆT. 30.

	Page
Last two letters	270
Dickens vanquished	270
Obstacles to copyright	271
Two described	272
Value of literary popularity	273
Substitute for literature	274
The secretary described	274
His paintings	275
The lion and ——	275
Toryism of Toronto	277
Canadian attentions	277
Proposed theatricals	278
Last letter	279
The private play	279
Stage manager's report	280
The lady performers	281
Bill of the performance	282
A touch of Crummles	283
HOME	283

	Page
Apotheosis of Grip the Raven, by Maclise, R.A.	42
Facsimile of C. D.'s autograph signature Boz (1841)	93
Facsimile of Invitation to the Public Dinner in New York, with the signatures	137
Facsimile of Invitation to the Public Ball in New York, with the signatures	140
Facsimile of the Bill of the Private Play in Canada	282

THE

LIFE OF CHARLES DICKENS.

CHAPTER XIII.

DEVONSHIRE TERRACE AND BROADSTAIRS.

1840.

IT was an excellent saying of the first Lord Shaftesbury, that, seeing every man of any capacity holds within himself two men, the wise and the foolish, each of them ought freely to be allowed his turn; and it was one of the secrets of Dickens's social charm that he could, in strict accordance with this saying, allow each part of him its turn: could afford thoroughly to give rest and relief to what was serious in him; and, when the time came to play his gambols, could surrender himself wholly to the enjoyment of the time, and become the very genius and embodiment of one of his own most whimsical fancies.

A good saying.

Turning back from the narrative of his last piece of writing to recall a few occurrences of the

LONDON: 1840.

year during which it had occupied him, I find him at its opening in one of these humorous moods, and another friend, with myself, enslaved by its influence. "What on earth does it all "mean," wrote poor puzzled Mr. Landor to me, enclosing a letter from him of the date of the 11th of February, the day after the royal nuptials of that year. In this he had related to our old friend a wonderful hallucination arising out of that event, which had then taken entire possession of him. "Society is unhinged here," thus ran the letter, "by her majesty's marriage, and I am sorry "to add that I have fallen hopelessly in love with "the Queen, and wander up and down with vague "and dismal thoughts of running away to some "uninhabited island with a maid of honor, to be "entrapped by conspiracy for that purpose. Can "you suggest any particular young person, serving "in such a capacity, who would suit me? It is "too much perhaps to ask you to join the band "of noble youths (Forster is in it, and Maclise) "who are to assist me in this great enterprise, but "a man of your energy would be invaluable. I "have my eye upon Lady . . . , principally because "she is very beautiful and has no strong brothers. "Upon this, and other points of the scheme, how-"ever, we will confer more at large when we

Landor mystified.

The mirthful side of Dickens.

A bold proposal.

"meet; and meanwhile burn this document, that "no suspicion may arise or rumour get abroad." LONDON: 1840.

Extravagant flights.

The maid of honor and the uninhabited island were flights of fancy, but the other daring delusion was for a time encouraged to such whimsical lengths, not alone by him, but (under his influence) by the two friends named, that it took the wildest forms of humorous extravagance; and of the private confidences much interchanged, as well as of the style of open speech in which our joke of despairing unfitness for any further use or enjoyment of life was unflaggingly kept up, to the amazement of bystanders knowing nothing of what it meant, and believing we had half lost our senses, I permit myself to give from his letters one further illustration. "I am utterly lost in "misery," he writes to me on the 12th of February, "and can do nothing. I have been reading *Oliver*, "*Pickwick*, and *Nickleby* to get my thoughts to-"gether for the new effort, but all in vain:

C. D. to J. F.

"My heart is at Windsor,
"My heart isn't here;
"My heart is at Windsor,
"A following my dear.

Despairing thoughts.

"I saw the Responsibilities this morning, and "burst into tears. The presence of my wife ag-

LONDON: 1840.

C. D. to J. F.

"gravates me. I loathe my parents. I detest my "house. I begin to have thoughts of the Serpen-"tine, of the regent's-canal, of the razors upstairs, "of the chemist's down the street, of poisoning "myself at Mrs.——'s table, of hanging myself "upon the pear-tree in the garden, of abstaining "from food and starving myself to death, of being "bled for my cold and tearing off the bandage, "of falling under the feet of cab-horses in the "New-road, of murdering Chapman and Hall and "becoming great in story (SHE must hear some-"thing of me then—perhaps sign the warrant: or "is that a fable?), of turning Chartist, of heading "some bloody assault upon the palace and saving "Her by my single hand——of being anything "but what I have been, and doing anything but "what I have done. Your distracted friend, C. D." The wild derangement of asterisks in every shape and form, with which this incoherence closed, cannot here be given.

Riding exercise.

Some ailments which dated from an earlier period in his life made themselves felt in the spring of the year, as I remember, and increased horse exercise was strongly recommended to him. "I find it will be positively necessary to go, for "five days in the week at least," he wrote to me in March, "on a perfect regimen of diet and exer-

"cise, and am anxious therefore not to delay "treating for a horse." We were now in consequence, when he was not at the seaside, much on horseback in suburban lanes and roads; and the spacious garden of his new house was also turned to healthful use at even his busiest times of work. I mark this, too, as the time when the first of his ravens took up residence there; and as the beginning of disputes with two of his neighbours about the smoking of the stable-chimney, which his groom Topping, a highly absurd little man with flaming red hair, so complicated by secret devices of his own, meant to conciliate each complainant alternately and having the effect of aggravating both, that law proceedings were only barely avoided. "I shall give you," he writes, "my latest report of the chimney in the form of "an address from Topping, made to me on our "way from little Hall's at Norwood the other night, "where he and Chapman and I had been walking "all day, while Topping drove Kate, Mrs. Hall, "and her sisters, to Dulwich. Topping had been "regaled upon the premises, and was just drunk "enough to be confidential. 'Beggin' your pardon, "'sir, but the genelman next door sir, seems to "'be gettin' quite comfortable and pleasant about "'the chim'ley.'—'I don't think he is, Topping.'—

Grip: the first of his ravens.

Groom Topping.

C. D. to J. F.

LONDON: 1840.

"'Yes he is sir I think. He comes out in the "'yard this morning and says, *Coachman* he says' "(observe the vision of a great large fat man "called up by the word) '*is that your raven* he "'*says, Coachman? or is it Mr. Dickens's raven?* "'he says. My master's sir, I says. *Well*, he "'says, *It's a fine bird. I think the chimley 'ill* "'*do now Coachman,—now the jint's taken off the* "'*pipe* he says. I hope it will sir, I says; my "'master's a genelman as wouldn't annoy no genel- "'man if he could help it, I'm sure; and my "'missis is so afraid of havin' a bit o' fire that o' "'Sundays our little bit o' weal or wot not, goes "'to the baker's a purpose.—*Damn the chimley,* "'*Coachman*, he says, *it's a smokin' now.*—It a'nt "'a smokin your way sir, I says; *Well* he says "'*no more it is, Coachman, and as long as it smokes* "'*anybody else's way, it's all right and I'm agree-* "'*able.*' Of course I shall now have the man "from the other side upon me, and very likely "with an action of nuisance for smoking into his "conservatory."

The smoky chimneys.

A graver incident, which occurred to him also among his earliest experiences as tenant of Devonshire-terrace, illustrates too well the always practical turn of his kindness and humanity not to deserve relation here. He has himself described it, in one of his minor writings, in setting down what he remembered as the only good that ever came of a beadle. Of that great parish functionary, he says, "having newly taken the lease of a "house in a certain distinguished metropolitan "parish, a house which then appeared to me to "be a frightfully first-class family mansion involv-"ing awful responsibilities, I became the prey." In other words he was summoned, and obliged to sit, as juryman at an inquest on the body of a little child alleged to have been murdered by its mother; of which the result was, that, by his persevering exertion, seconded by the humane help of the coroner, Mr. Wakley, the verdict of himself and his fellow-jurymen charged her only with concealment of the birth. "The poor desolate "creature dropped upon her knees before us with "protestations that we were right (protestations "among the most affecting that I have ever heard "in my life), and was carried away insensible. I "caused some extra care to be taken of her in "the prison, and counsel to be retained for her "defence when she was tried at the Old Bailey; "and her sentence was lenient, and her history "and conduct proved that it was right." How much he felt the little incident, at the actual time of its occurrence, may be judged from the few

LONDON: 1840.

Juryman at an inquest.

Practical humanity.

London: 1840.

lines written to me next morning: "Whether it "was the poor baby, or its poor mother, or the "coffin, or my fellow-jurymen, or what not, I can't "say, but last night I had a most violent attack "of sickness and indigestion which not only pre-"vented me from sleeping, but even from lying "down. Accordingly Kate and I sat up through "the dreary watches."

Birmingham. Publication of the *Clock's* first number.

The day of the first publication of *Master Humphrey* (Saturday, 4th April) had by this time come, and, according to the rule observed in his two other great ventures, he left town with Mrs. Dickens on Friday the 3rd. With Maclise we had been together at Richmond the previous night; and I joined him at Birmingham the day following with news of the sale of the whole sixty thousand copies to which the first working had been limited, and of orders already in hand for ten thousand more! The excitement of the success somewhat lengthened our holiday; and, after visiting Shakespeare's house at Stratford and Johnson's at Lichfield, we found our resources so straitened in returning, that, employing as our messenger of need his younger brother Alfred, who had joined us from Tamworth where he was a student-engineer, we had to pawn our gold watches at Birmingham.

A holiday.

BROADSTAIRS. 1840.

At the end of the following month he went to Broadstairs, and not many days before (on the 20th of May) a note from Mr. Jerdan on behalf of Mr. Bentley opened the negotiations formerly referred to,* which transferred to Messrs. Chapman and Hall the agreement for *Barnaby Rudge*. I was myself absent when he left, and in a letter announcing his departure he had written: "I "don't know of a word of news in all London, "but there will be plenty next week, for I am "going away, and I hope you'll send me an ac-"count of it. I am doubtful whether it will be a "murder, a fire, a vast robbery, or the escape of "Gould, but it will be something remarkable no "doubt. I almost blame myself for the death of "that poor girl who leaped off the monument "upon my leaving town last year. She would "not have done it if I had remained, neither "would the two men have found the skeleton in "the sewers." His prediction was quite accurate, for I had to tell him, after not many days, of the potboy who shot at the queen. "It's a great pity," he replied very sensibly, "they couldn't suffocate "that boy, Master Oxford, and say no more about "it. To have put him quietly between two

Transfer of *Barnaby Rudge* settled.

C. D. to J. F.

The potboy traitor.

* See Vol. I. p. 204.

BROADSTAIRS: 1840.

A true prediction.

"feather-beds would have stopped his heroic "speeches, and dulled the sound of his glory very "much. As it is, she will have to run the gauntlet of many a fool and madman, some of whom "may perchance be better shots and use other "than Brummagem firearms." How much of this actually came to pass, the reader knows.

From the letters of his present Broadstairs visit, there is little further to add to their account of his progress with his story; but a couple more lines may be given for their characteristic expression of his invariable habit upon entering any new abode, whether to stay in it for days or for years. On a Monday night he arrived, and on the Tuesday (2nd of June) wrote to me: "*Before* "I tasted bit or drop yesterday, I set out my "writing-table with extreme taste and neatness, "and improved the disposition of the furniture "generally." He stayed till the end of June; when Maclise and myself joined him for the pleasure of posting back home with him and Mrs. Dickens, by way of his favourite Chatham and Rochester and Cobham, where we passed two agreeable days in revisiting well-remembered scenes. I had meanwhile brought to a close the treaty for repurchase of *Oliver* and surrender of *Barnaby*, upon terms which are succinctly stated

Habits of order.

Revisiting old scenes.

in a letter written by him to Messrs. Chapman and Hall on the 2nd of July, the day after our return.

LONDON: 1840.

C. D. to Chapman and Hall.

"The terms upon which you advance the money "to-day for the purchase of the copyright and "stock* of *Oliver* on my behalf, are understood "between us to be these. That this 2250*l.* is to "be deducted from the purchase-money of a work "by me entitled *Barnaby Rudge*, of which two "chapters are now in your hands, and of which "the whole is to be written within some con-"venient time to be agreed upon between us. "But if it should not be written (which God for-"bid!) within five years, you are to have a lien "to this amount on the property belonging to me "that is now in your hands, namely, my shares "in the stock and copyright of *Sketches by Boz*, "*The Pickwick Papers*, *Nicholas Nickleby*, *Oliver* "*Twist* and *Master Humphrey's Clock;* in which

* By way of a novelty to help off the stock he had suggested (17th June): "Would it not be best to print new title-"pages to the copies in sheets and publish them as a new "edition, with an interesting Preface? I am talking about "all this as though the treaty were concluded, but I hope "and trust that in effect it is, for negotiation and delay are "worse to me than drawn daggers." See my remark Vol. I. p. 153.

LONDON: 1840.

"we do not include any share of the current profits of the last-named work, which I shall remain at liberty to draw at the times stated in "our agreement. Your purchase of *Barnaby* "*Rudge* is made upon the following terms. It is "to consist of matter sufficient for ten monthly "numbers of the size of *Pickwick* and *Nickleby*, "which you are however at liberty to divide and "publish in fifteen smaller numbers if you think "fit. The terms for the purchase of this edition "in numbers, and for the copyright of the whole "book for six months after the publication of the "last number, are 3000*l*. At the expiration of "the six months the whole copyright reverts to "me." The sequel was, as all the world knows, that Barnaby became successor to little Nell, the money being repaid by the profits of the *Clock*; but I ought to mention also the more generous sequel that my own small service had, on my receiving from him, after not many days, an antique silver-mounted jug of great beauty of form and workmanship, but with a wealth far beyond jeweller's chasing or artist's design in the written words that accompanied it.* I accepted them to

Terms of sale of *Barnaby*.

A gift.

* "Accept from me" (July 8th, 1840), "as a slight memorial of your attached companion, the poor keepsake

commemorate, not the help they would have far overpaid, but the gladness of his own escape from the last of the agreements that had hampered the opening of his career, and the better future that was now before him.

BROADSTAIRS: 1840.

Escape from bondage.

At the opening of August he was with Mrs. Dickens for some days in Devonshire, on a visit to his father, but he had to take his work with him; and, as he wrote to me, they had only one real holiday, when Dawlish, Teignmouth, Babbicombe, and Torquay were explored, returning to Exeter at night. In the beginning of September he was again at Broadstairs.

C. D. to J. F.

"which accompanies this. My heart is not an eloquent one "on matters which touch it most, but suppose this claret jug "the urn in which it lies, and believe that its warmest and "truest blood is yours. This was the object of my fruitless "search, and your curiosity, on Friday. At first I scarcely "knew what trifle (you will deem it valuable, I know, for "the giver's sake) to send you; but I thought it would be "pleasant to connect it with our jovial moments, and to let "it add, to the wine we shall drink from it together, a flavor "which the choicest vintage could never impart. Take it "from my hand—filled to the brim and running over with "truth and earnestness. I have just taken one parting look "at it, and it seems the most elegant thing in the world to "me, for I lose sight of the vase in the crowd of welcome "associations that are clustering and wreathing themselves "about it."

BROADSTAIRS: 1840. C. D. to J. F.

"I was just going to work," he wrote on the 9th, "when I got this letter, and the story of the "man who went to Chapman and Hall's knocked "me down flat. I wrote until now (a quarter to "one) against the grain, and have at last given it "up for one day. Upon my word it IS intolerable.

Published libels about him.

"I have been grinding my teeth all the morning. "I think I could say in two lines something about "the general report with propriety. I'll add them "to the proof" (the preface to the first volume of the *Clock* was at this time in preparation), "giving "you full power to cut them out if you should "think differently from me, and from C and H, "who in such a matter must be admitted judges." He refers here to a report, rather extensively circulated at the time, and which through various channels had reached his publishers, that he was

Stated to be insane.

suffering from loss of reason and was under treatment in an asylum.* I would have withheld

* Already he had been the subject of similar reports on the occasion of the family sorrow which compelled him to suspend the publication of *Pickwick* for two months (Vol. I. p. 148), when, upon issuing a brief address in resuming his

C. D. *loq.*

work (30th June, 1837), he said: "By one set of intimate "acquaintances, especially well-informed, he has been killed "outright; by another, driven mad; by a third, imprisoned "for debt; by a fourth, sent per steamer to the United-

from him the mention of it, as an absurdity that must quickly pass away—but against my wish it had been communicated to him, and I had difficulty in keeping within judicious bounds his extreme and very natural wrath.

BROADSTAIRS: 1840.

Other similar reports.

A few days later (the 15th) he wrote: "I have "been rather surprised of late to have applica-"tions from roman-catholic clergymen, demanding "(rather pastorally, and with a kind of grave au-"thority) assistance, literary employment, and so "forth. At length it struck me, that, through some "channel or other, I must have been represented "as belonging to that religion. Would you be-"lieve, that in a letter from Lamert at Cork, to "my mother, which I saw last night, he says "'What do the papers mean by saying that Charles "'is demented, and further, *that he has turned* "'*roman-catholic?'—!*" Of the begging-letter-writers, hinted at here, I ought earlier to have said something. In one of his detached essays he has described, without a particle of exaggeration, the extent to which he was made a victim

Begging-letter-writers.

"States; by a fifth, rendered incapable of mental exertion "for evermore; by all, in short, represented as doing any-"thing but seeking in a few weeks' retirement the restoration "of that cheerfulness and peace of which a sad bereavement "had temporarily deprived him."

BROAD-STAIRS: 1840.

by this class of swindler, and the extravagance of the devices practised on him; but he has not confessed, as he might, that for much of what he suffered he was himself responsible, by giving so largely, as at first he did, to almost every one who applied to him. What at last brought him to his senses in this respect, I think, was the request made by the adventurer who had exhausted every other expedient, and who desired finally, after describing himself reduced to the condition of a travelling Cheap Jack in the smallest way of crockery, that a donkey might be left out for him next day, which he would duly call for. This I perfectly remember, and I much fear that the applicant was the Daniel Tobin before mentioned.*

A donkey asked for.

Many and delightful were other letters written from Broadstairs at this date, filled with whimsical talk and humorous description relating chiefly to an eccentric friend who stayed with him most of the time, and is sketched in one of his published papers as Mr. Kindheart; but all too private for reproduction now. He returned in the middle of October, when we resumed our almost daily ridings, foregatherings with Maclise at Hampstead and elsewhere, and social entertainments with

Mr. Kindheart.

* See Vol. I. p. 98-99.

LONDON: 1841.

Friendly meetings.

Macready, Talfourd, Procter, Stanfield, Fonblanque, Elliotson, Tennent, d'Orsay, Quin, Harness, Wilkie, Edwin Landseer, Rogers, Sydney Smith, and Bulwer. Of the genius of the author of *Pelham* and *Eugene Aram* he had, early and late, the highest admiration, and he took occasion, to express it during the present year in a new preface which he published to *Oliver Twist*. Other friends became familiar in later years; but, disinclined as he was to the dinner invitations that reached him from every quarter, all such meetings with those whom I have named, and in an especial manner the marked attentions shown him by Miss Coutts which began with the very beginning of his career, were invariably welcome.

Social talk.

To speak here of the pleasure his society afforded, would anticipate the fitter mention to be made hereafter. But what in this respect distinguishes nearly all original men, he possessed eminently. His place was not to be filled up by any other. To the most trivial talk he gave the attraction of his own character. It might be a small matter; something he had read or observed during the day, some quaint odd fancy from a book, a vivid little outdoor picture, the laughing exposure of some imposture, or a burst of sheer mirthful enjoyment; but of its kind it would be something

London: 1841.

unique, because genuinely part of himself. This, and his unwearying animal spirits, made him the most delightful of companions; no claim on good-fellowship ever found him wanting; and no one so constantly recalled to his friends the description Johnson gave of Garrick, as the cheerfullest man of his age.

Of what occupied him in the way of literary labour in the autumn and winter months of the year, some description has been given; and, apart from what has already thus been said of his work at the closing chapters of *The Old Curiosity Shop*, nothing now calls for more special allusion, except that in his town-walks in November, impelled thereto by specimens recently discovered in his country-walks between Broadstairs and Ramsgate, he thoroughly explored the ballad literature of Seven-dials, and took to singing himself, with an effect that justified his reputation for comic singing in his childhood, not a few of these wonderful productions. His last successful labour of the year was the reconciliation of two friends; and his motive, as well as the principle that guided him, as they are described by himself, I think worth preserving. For the first: "In the midst of "this child's death, I, over whom something of "the bitterness of death has passed, not lightly

Ballads of Seven-dials.

Reconciling friends.

"perhaps, was reminded of many old kindnesses, "and was sorry in my heart that men who really "liked each other should waste life at arm's "length." For the last: "I have laid it down as a "rule in my judgment of men, to observe narrowly "whether some (of whom one is disposed to think "badly) don't carry all their faults upon the sur- "face, and others (of whom one is disposed to "think well) don't carry many more beneath it. "I have long ago made sure that our friend is in "the first class; and when I know all the foibles "a man has, with little trouble in the discovery, "I begin to think he is worth liking." His latest letter of the year, dated the day following, closed with the hope that we might, he and I, enjoy together "fifty more Christmases, at least, in this "world, and eternal summers in another." Alas!

C. D. to J. F.

Hint for judging men.

CHAPTER XIV.

BARNABY RUDGE.

1841.

LONDON: 1841.

THE letters of 1841 yield similar fruit as to his doings and sayings, and may in like manner first be consulted for the literary work he had in hand.

C. D. to J. F.

He had the advantage of beginning *Barnaby Rudge* with a fair amount of story in advance, which he had only to make suitable, by occasional readjustment of chapters, to publication in weekly portions; and on this he was engaged before the end of January. "I am at present" (22nd January, 1841) "in what Leigh Hunt would "call a kind of impossible state—thinking what "on earth Master Humphrey can think of through "four mortal pages. I added, here and there, to "the last chapter of the *Curiosity Shop* yesterday, "and it leaves me only four pages to write." (They were filled by a paper from Humphrey introductory of the new tale, in which will be found a striking picture of London, from midnight to the break of day.) "I also made up, and wrote "the needful insertions for, the second number of "*Barnaby*—so that I came back to the mill a "little." Hardly yet: for after four days he writes, having meanwhile done nothing: "I have been "looking (three o'clock) with an appearance of extraordinary interest and study at *one leaf* of the "*Curiosities of Literature* ever since half-past ten "this morning—I haven't the heart to turn over." Then, on Friday the 29th, better news came. "I "didn't stir out yesterday, but sat and *thought* all "day; not writing a line; not so much as the "cross of a t or dot of an i. I imaged forth a "good deal of *Barnaby* by keeping my mind "steadily upon him; and am happy to say I have "gone to work this morning in good twig, strong "hope, and cheerful spirits. Last night I was un-"utterably and impossible-to-form-an-idea-of-ably "miserable. . . . By the bye don't engage yourself "otherwise than to me, for Sunday week, because "it's my birthday. I have no doubt we shall have "got over our troubles here by that time, and I "purpose having a snug dinner in the study." We had the dinner, though the troubles were not over; but the next day another son was born to him. "Thank God," he wrote on the 9th, "quite "well. I am thinking hard, and have just written "to Browne enquiring when he will come and "confer about the raven." He had by this time

LONDON: 1841.

Hard work.

At work on *Barnaby*.

A fourth child and second son born: 8 Feb.

LONDON: 1841.

resolved to make that bird, whose accomplishments had been daily ripening and enlarging for the last twelve months to the increasing mirth and delight of all of us, a prominent figure in *Barnaby;* and the invitation to the artist was for a conference how best to introduce him graphically.

The raven.

The next letter mentioning *Barnaby* was from Brighton (25th February), whither he had flown for a week's quiet labour. "I have (it's four "o'clock) done, a very fair morning's work, at "which I have sat very close, and been blessed "besides with a clear view of the end of the "volume. As the contents of one number usually "require a day's thought at the very least, and "often more, this puts me in great spirits. I think "—that is, I hope—the story takes a great stride "at this point, and takes it WELL. Nous verrons. "Grip will be strong, and I build greatly on the "Varden household."

A loss in the family.

Upon his return he had to lament a domestic calamity, which, for its connection with that famous personage in *Barnaby*, must be mentioned here. The raven had for some days been ailing, and Topping had reported of him, as Shakespeare of Hamlet, that he had lost his mirth and foregone all customary exercises: but Dickens paid no great heed, remembering his recovery from an illness of the previous summer when he swallowed some white paint; so that the graver report which led him to send for the doctor came upon him unexpectedly, and nothing but his own language can worthily describe the result. Unable from the state of his feelings to write two letters, he sent the narrative to Maclise, under an enormous black seal, for transmission to me; and thus it befell that this fortunate bird receives a double passport to fame, so great a humorist having celebrated his farewell to the present world, and so great a painter his welcome to another.

LONDON 1841.

"You will be greatly shocked" (the letter is dated Friday evening, March 12th, 1841) "and "grieved to hear that the Raven is no more. He "expired to-day at a few minutes after twelve "o'clock at noon. He had been ailing for a few "days, but we anticipated no serious result, con-"jecturing that a portion of the white paint he "swallowed last summer might be lingering about "his vitals without having any serious effect upon "his constitution. Yesterday afternoon he was "taken so much worse that I sent an express for "the medical gentleman (Mr. Herring), who "promptly attended, and administered a powerful "dose of castor oil. Under the influence of this "medicine, he recovered so far as to be able at "eight o'clock p.m. to bite Topping. His night

Death of the raven 12 March.

C. D. describes his illness.

LONDON: 1841.

"was peaceful. This morning at daybreak he appeared better; received (agreeably to the doctor's directions) another dose of castor oil; and partook plentifully of some warm gruel, the flavor of which he appeared to relish. Towards eleven o'clock he was so much worse that it was found necessary to muffle the stable-knocker. At half-past, or thereabouts, he was heard talking to himself about the horse and Topping's family, and to add some incoherent expressions which are supposed to have been either a foreboding of his approaching dissolution, or some wishes relative to the disposal of his little property: consisting chiefly of half-pence which he had buried in different parts of the garden. On the clock striking twelve he appeared slightly agitated, but he soon recovered, walked twice or thrice along the coach-house, stopped to bark, staggered, exclaimed *Halloa old girl!* (his favourite expression), and died.

Disposal of his property.

"He behaved throughout with a decent fortitude, equanimity, and self-possession, which cannot be too much admired. I deeply regret that being in ignorance of his danger I did not attend to receive his last instructions. Something remarkable about his eyes occasioned Topping to run for the doctor at twelve. When they returned together our friend was gone. It was the

The doctor sent for.

LONDON: 1841.

"medical gentleman who informed me of his de-"cease. He did it with great caution and delicacy, "preparing me by the remark that 'a jolly queer "'start had taken place;' but the shock was very "great notwithstanding. I am not wholly free "from suspicions of poison. A malicious butcher "has been heard to say that he would 'do' for "him: his plea was that he would not be molested "in taking orders down the mews, by any bird "that wore a tail. Other persons have also been "heard to threaten: among others, Charles Knight, "who has just started a weekly publication price "fourpence: *Barnaby* being, as you know, three-"pence. I have directed a post-mortem examina-"tion, and the body has been removed to Mr. "Herring's school of anatomy for that purpose.

Suspicions.

"I could wish, if you can take the trouble, "that you could inclose this to Forster imme-"diately after you have read it. I cannot discharge "the painful task of communication more than "once. Were they ravens who took manna to "somebody in the wilderness? At times I hope "they were, and at others I fear they were not, or "they would certainly have stolen it by the way. "In profound sorrow, I am ever your bereaved "friend C.D. Kate is as well as can be expected, "but terribly low as you may suppose. The

Family mourners.

LONDON: 1841.

Death of raven.

"children seem rather glad of it. He bit their "ancles. But that was play."

Maclise's covering letter was an apotheosis, to be rendered only in facsimile.

Apotheosis by Maclise.

In what way the loss was replaced, so that *Barnaby* should have the fruit of continued study of the habits of the family of birds which Grip had so nobly represented, Dickens has told in the preface to the story; and another, older, and larger Grip, obtained through Mr. Smithson, was installed in the stable, almost before the stuffed remains of his honoured predecessor had been sent home in a glass case, by way of ornament to his master's study. **LONDON: 1841.** **Grip the second.**

I resume our correspondence on what he was writing. "I see there is yet room for a few lines," (25th March) "and you are quite right in wishing "what I cut out to be restored. I did not want "Joe to be so short about Dolly, and really wrote "his references to that young lady carefully—as "natural things with a meaning in them. Chig-"well, my dear fellow, is the greatest place in the "world. Name your day for going. Such a de-"licious old inn opposite the churchyard—such a "lovely ride—such beautiful forest scenery—such "an out of the way, rural, place—such a sexton! "I say again, name your day." The day was named at once; and the whitest of stones marks it, in now sorrowful memory. His promise was exceeded by our enjoyment; and his delight in the double recognition, of himself and of *Barnaby*, **C. D. to J. F.** **The inn at Chigwell.** **Reception there.**

LONDON: 1841. by the landlord of the nice old inn, far exceeded any pride he would have taken in what the world thinks the highest sort of honour.

Working alone. "I have shut myself up" (26th March) "by "myself to-day, and mean to try and 'go it' at the "*Clock;* Kate being out, and the house peacefully "dismal. I don't remember altering the exact part "you object to, but if there be anything here you "object to, knock it out ruthlessly." "Don't fail" (April the 5th) "to erase anything that seems to "you too strong. It is difficult for me to judge "what tells too much, and what does not. I am "trying a very quiet number to set against this "necessary one. I hope it will be good, but I am "in very sad condition for work. Glad you think "this powerful. What I have put in is more relief, "from the raven." Two days later: "I have done "that number and am now going to work on an-"other. I am bent (please Heaven) on finishing "the first chapter by Friday night. I hope to "look in upon you to-night, when we'll dispose of "the toasts for Saturday. Still bilious—but a "good number, I hope, notwithstanding. Jeffrey "has come to town and was here yesterday." The toasts to be disposed of were those to be given

A "Clock" dinner. at the dinner on the 10th to celebrate the second volume of *Master Humphrey:* when Talfourd presided, when there was much jollity, and, according to the memorandum drawn up that Saturday night now lying before me, we all in the greatest good humour glorified each other: Talfourd proposing the *Clock*, Macready Mrs. Dickens, Dickens the publishers, and myself the artists; Macready giving Talfourd, Talfourd Macready, Dickens, myself, and myself the comedian Mr. Harley, whose humorous songs had been the not least considerable element in the mirth of the evening.

LONDON: 1841.

Five days later he writes: "I finished the number yesterday, and, although I dined with Jeffrey, "and was obliged to go to Lord Denman's afterwards (which made me late), have done eight "slips of the *Lamplighter* for Mrs. Macrone, this "morning. When I have got that off my mind, "I shall try to go on steadily, fetching up the "*Clock* lee-way." The *Lamplighter* was his old farce,* which he now turned into a comic tale; and this, with other contributions given him by friends and edited by him as *Pic Nic Papers*, enabled him to help the widow of his old publisher in her straitened means by a gift of £300. He had finished his work of charity before he next wrote of *Barnaby Rudge*, but he was fetch-

Lord Jeffrey in London.

The *Lamplighter*.

Pic Nic Papers.

* See Vol. I. pp. 154 and 229.

LONDON: 1841.

ing up his leeway lazily. "I am getting on" (29th of April) "very slowly. I want to stick to the "story; and the fear of committing myself, be-"cause of the impossibility of trying back or "altering a syllable, makes it much harder than it "looks. It was too bad of me to give you the "trouble of cutting the number, but I knew so "well you would do it in the right places. For "what Harley would call the 'onward work' I "really think I have some famous thoughts."

C. D. to J. F.

There is an interval of a month before the next allusion. "Solomon's expression" (3rd of June) "I meant to be one of those strong ones to which "strong circumstances give birth in the com-"monest minds. Deal with it as you like. . . . .

Character of Lord George Gordon.

"Say what you please of Gordon" (I had objected to some points in his view of this madman, stated much too favourably as I thought), "he must have "been at heart a kind man, and a lover of the "despised and rejected, after his own fashion. "He lived upon a small income, and always "within it; was known to relieve the necessities "of many people; exposed in his place the corrupt "attempt of a minister to buy him out of Parlia-"ment; and did great charities in Newgate. He "always spoke on the people's side, and tried "against his muddled brains to expose the pro-

"fligacy of both parties. He never got anything "by his madness, and never sought it. The "wildest and most raging attacks of the time, "allow him these merits: and not to let him have "'em in their full extent, remembering in what a "(politically) wicked time he lived, would lie upon "my conscience heavily. The libel he was im-"prisoned for when he died, was on the queen "of France; and the French government interested "themselves warmly to procure his release—which "I think they might have done, but for Lord "Grenville." I was more successful in the counsel I gave against a fancy he had at this part of the story, that he would introduce as actors in the Gordon riots three splendid fellows who should order, lead, control, and be obeyed as natural guides of the crowd in that delirious time, and who should turn out, when all was over, to have broken out from Bedlam: but though he saw the unsoundness of this, he could not so readily see, in Gordon's case, the danger of taxing ingenuity to ascribe a reasonable motive to acts of sheer insanity. The feeblest parts of the book are those in which Lord George and his secretary appear.

LONDON: 1841.

Unprofitable madness.

A doubtful fancy.

He left for Scotland after the middle of June, but he took work with him. "You may suppose," he wrote from Edinburgh on the 30th, "I have

From Edinburgh: C. D. to J. F.

LONDON: 1841.

C. D. to J. F.

"not done much work—but by Friday night's "post from here I hope to send the first long "chapter of a number and both the illustrations; "from Loch-earn on Tuesday night, the closing "chapter of that number; from the same place on "Thursday night, the first long chapter of an-"other, with both the illustrations; and, from "some place which no man ever spelt but which "sounds like Ballyhoolish, on Saturday, the "closing chapter of that number, which will "leave us all safe till I return to town." Nine days later he wrote from "Ballechelish:" "I "have done all I can or need do in the way of "*Barnaby* until I come home, and the story is "progressing (I hope you will think) to good "strong interest. I have left it, I think, at an "exciting point, with a good dawning of the riots. "In the first of the two numbers I have written "since I have been away, I forget whether the "blind man, in speaking to Barnaby about riches, "tells him they are to be found in *crowds*. If I "have not actually used that word, will you in-"troduce it? A perusal of the proof of the fol-"lowing number (70) will show you how, and "why." "Have you," he wrote, shortly after his return (29th July), "seen no. 71? I thought there "was a good glimpse of a crowd, from a window

Interest in his new labour.

"—eh?" He had now taken thoroughly to the interest of his closing chapters, and felt more than ever the constraints of his form of publication. "I am warming up very much" (on the 5th August from Broadstairs) "about *Barnaby*. "Oh! If I only had him, from this time to the "end, in monthly numbers. *N'importe!* I hope "the interest will be pretty strong—and, in every "number, stronger." Six days later, from the same place: "I was always sure I could make a "good thing of *Barnaby*, and I think you'll find "that it comes out strong to the last word. I "have another number ready, all but two slips. "Don't fear for young Chester. The time hasn't "come——there we go again, you see, with the "weekly delays. I am in great heart and spirits "with the story, and with the prospect of having "time to think before I go on again." A month's interval followed, and what occupied it will be described shortly. On the 11th September he wrote: "I have just burnt into Newgate, and am "going in the next number to tear the prisoners "out by the hair of their heads. The number "which gets into the jail you'll have in proof by "Tuesday." This was followed up a week later: "I have let all the prisoners out of Newgate, "burnt down Lord Mansfield's, and played the

LONDON: 1841.

Constraints of weekly publication.

C. D. to J. F.

The prison-riots.

LONDON: 1841.

"very devil. Another number will finish the fires, "and help us on towards the end. I feel quite "smoky when I am at work. I want elbow-room "terribly." To this trouble, graver supervened at his return, a serious personal sickness not the least; but he bore up gallantly, and I had never better occasion than now to observe his quiet endurance of pain, how little he thought of himself where the sense of self is commonly supreme, and the manful duty with which everything was done that, ailing as he was, he felt it necessary to do. He was still in his sick-room (22nd October) when he wrote: "I hope I shan't leave off "any more, now, until I have finished *Barnaby*." Three days after that, he was busying himself eagerly for others; and on the 2nd of November the printers received the close of *Barnaby Rudge*.

Serious illness.

Close of *Barnaby*.

This tale was Dickens's first attempt out of the sphere of the life of the day and its actual manners. Begun during the progress of *Oliver Twist*, it had been for some time laid aside; the form it ultimately took had been comprised only partially within its first design; and the story in its finished shape presented strongly a special purpose, the characteristic of all but his very earliest writings. Its scene is laid at the time when the incessant execution of men and women, com-

Character of the book.

paratively innocent, disgraced every part of the country; demoralizing thousands, whom it also prepared for the scaffold. In those days the theft of a few rags from a bleaching ground, or the abstraction of a roll of ribbons from a counter, was visited with the penalty of blood; and such laws brutalized both their ministers and victims. It was the time, too, when a false religious outcry brought with it appalling guilt and misery. These are vices that leave more behind them than the first forms assumed, and they involve a lesson sufficiently required to justify a writer in dealing with them. There were also others grafted on them. In Barnaby himself it was desired to show what sources of comfort there might be, for the patient and cheerful heart, in even the worst of all human afflictions; and in the hunted life of the outcast father, whose crime had entailed not that affliction only but other more fearful wretchedness, we have as powerful a picture as any in his writings of the inevitable and unfathomable consequences of sin. But, as the story went on, it was incident to these designs that what had been accomplished in its predecessor could hardly be attained here, in singleness of purpose, unity of idea, or harmony of treatment; and other defects supervened in the management of the plot. The

LONDON: 1841.

Lessons of *Barnaby Rudge.*

Defects in the plot.

LONDON: 1841.

interest with which the tale begins, has ceased to be its interest before the close; and what has chiefly taken the reader's fancy at the outset, almost wholly disappears in the power and passion with which, in the later chapters, the great riots are described. So admirable is this description, however, that it would be hard to have to surrender it even for a more perfect structure of fable.

The No-Popery riots.

There are few things more masterly in any of his books. From the first low mutterings of the storm to its last terrible explosion, this frantic outbreak of popular ignorance and rage is depicted with unabated power. The aimlessness of idle mischief by which the ranks of the rioters are swelled at the beginning; the recklessness induced by the monstrous impunity allowed to the early excesses; the sudden spread of this drunken guilt into every haunt of poverty, ignorance, or mischief in the wicked old city, where the rich materials of crime lie festering; the wild action of its poison on all, without scheme or plan of any kind, who come within its reach; the horrors that are more bewildering for this complete absence of purpose in them; and, when all is done, the misery found to have been self-inflicted in every cranny and corner of London, as if a plague

Descriptive power.

had swept over the streets: these are features in the picture of an actual occurrence, to which the manner of the treatment gives extraordinary force and meaning. Nor, in the sequel, is there anything displayed with more profitable vividness, than the law's indiscriminate cruelty at last, in contrast with its cowardly indifference at first; while, among the casual touches lighting up the scene with flashes of reality that illumine every part of it, may be instanced the discovery, in the quarter from which screams for succour are loudest when Newgate is supposed to be accidentally on fire, of four men who were certain in any case to have perished on the drop next day.

Vivid touches.

Principal characters.

The story, which has unusually careful writing in it, and much manly upright thinking, has not so many people eagerly adopted as of kin by everybody, as its predecessors are famous for; but it has yet a fair proportion of such as take solid form within the mind, and keep hold of the memory. To these belong in an especial degree Gabriel Varden and his household, on whom are lavished all the writer's fondness, and not a little of his keenest humour. The honest locksmith with his jovial jug, and the tink-tink-tink of his pleasant nature making cheerful music out of steel and iron; the buxom wife, with her plaguy tongue

London: 1841.

that makes every one wretched whom her kindly disposition would desire to make happy; the good hearted plump little Dolly, coquettish minx of a daughter, with all she suffers and inflicts by her fickle winning ways, and her small self-admiring vanities; and Miggs the vicious and slippery, acid, amatory, and of uncomfortable figure, sower of family discontents and discords, who swears all the while she wouldn't make or meddle with 'em

Social satire.

"not for a annual gold mine and found in tea "and sugar": there is not much social painting anywhere with a better domestic moral, than in all these; and a nice propriety of feeling and thought regulates the use of such satire throughout. No one knows more exactly how far to go with that formidable weapon; or understands better that what satirizes everything, in effect satirizes nothing.

Another excellent group is that which the story opens with, in the quaint old kitchen of the Maypole; John Willett and his friends, genuinely

Barnaby and his raven.

comic creations all of them. Then we have Barnaby and his raven: the light-hearted idiot, as unconscious of guilt as of suffering, and happy with no sense but of the influences of nature; and the grave sly bird, with sufficient sense to make himself as unhappy as rascally habits will make the human animal. There is poor brutish Hugh, too, loitering lazily outside the Maypole door, with a storm of passions in him raging to be let loose; already the scaffold's withered fruit, as he is doomed to be its ripe offering; and though with all the worst instincts of the savage, yet not without also some of the best. Still farther out of kindly nature's pitying reach lurks the worst villain of the scene: with this sole claim to consideration, that it was by constant contact with the filthiest instrument of law and state he had become the mass of moral filth he is. Mr. Dennis the hangman is a portrait that Hogarth would have painted with the same wholesome severity of satire which is employed upon it in *Barnaby Rudge.*

LONDON: 1841.

Dennis the hangman.

CHAPTER XV.

PUBLIC DINNER IN EDINBURGH.

1841.

LONDON: 1841.

AMONG the occurrences of the year, apart from the tale he was writing, the birth of his fourth child and second son has been briefly mentioned. "I mean to call the boy Edgar," he wrote the day after he was born (9th February), "a good honest Saxon name, I think." He changed his mind in a few days, however, on resolving to ask Landor to be godfather. This intention, as soon as formed, he announced to our excellent old friend; telling him it would give the child something to boast of, to be called Walter Landor, and that to call him so would do his own heart good. For, as to himself, whatever realities had gone out of the ceremony of christening, the meaning still remained in it of enabling him to form a relationship with friends he most loved: and as to the boy, he held that to give him a name to be proud of was to give him also another reason for doing nothing unworthy or untrue when he came to be

Son Walter.

a man. Walter alas! only lived to manhood. He obtained a military cadetship through the kindness of Miss Coutts, and died at Calcutta on the last day of 1863, in his 23rd year. LONDON: 1841. Dies in Calcutta 1863.

The interest taken by this distinguished lady in him and in his had begun, as I have said, at an earlier date than even this; and I remember, while *Oliver Twist* was going on, his pleasure because of her father's mention of him in a speech at Birmingham, for his advocacy of the cause of the poor. Whether to the new poor-law Sir Francis Burdett objected as strongly as we have seen that Dickens did, as well as many other excellent men, who forgot the atrocities of the system it displaced in their indignation at the needless and cruel harshness with which it was worked at the outset, I have not at hand the means of knowing. But certainly this continued to be strongly the feeling of Dickens, who exulted in nothing so much as at any misadventure to the whigs in connection with it. "How often used Black and I," he wrote to me in April, "to quarrel about the effect of the "poor-law bill! Walter comes in upon the cry. "See whether the whigs go out upon it." It was the strong desire he had to make himself heard upon it, even in parliament, that led him not immediately to turn aside from a proposal, now Sir F. Burdett C. D. and the new poor-law

London: 1841.

privately made by some of the magnates of Reading, to bring him in for that borough; but the notion was soon dismissed, as, on its revival more than once in later times, it continued very wisely to be. His opinions otherwise were extremely radical at present, as will be apparent shortly; and he did not at all relish Peel's majority of one when it came soon after, and unseated the whigs. It was just now, I may add, he greatly enjoyed a quiet setting-down of Moore by Rogers at Sir Francis Burdett's table, for talking exaggerated toryism. So debased was the house of commons by reform, said Moore, that a Burke, if you could find him, would not be listened to. "No such "thing, Tommy," said Rogers; "*find yourself*, "and they'd listen even to you."

Moore and Rogers.

This was not many days before he hinted to me an intention soon to be carried out in a rather memorable manner. "I have done nothing to-day" (18th March: we had bought books together, the day before, at Tom Hill's sale) "but cut the *Swift*, "looking into it with a delicious laziness in all "manner of delightful places, and put poor Tom's "books away. I had a letter from Edinburgh this "morning, announcing that Jeffrey's visit to Lon- "don will be the week after next; telling me that "he drives about Edinburgh declaring there has

C. D. to J. F.

"been 'nothing so good as Nell since Cordelia,' "which he writes also to all manner of people; "and informing me of a desire in that romantic "town to give me greeting and welcome. For "this and other reasons I am disposed to make "Scotland my destination in June rather than Ire-"land. Think, *do* think, meantime (here are ten "good weeks), whether you couldn't, by some effort "worthy of the owner of the gigantic helmet, go "with us. Think of such a fortnight—York, Car-"lisle, Berwick, your own Borders, Edinburgh, "Rob Roy's country, railroads, cathedrals, country "inns, Arthur's-seat, lochs, glens, and home by "sea. DO think of this, seriously, at leisure." It was very tempting, but not to be.

LONDON: 1841.

Jeffrey's praise of little Nell.

Resolve to visit Scotland.

Early in April Jeffrey came, many feasts and entertainments welcoming him, of which he very sparingly partook; and before he left, the visit to Scotland in June was all duly arranged, to be initiated by the splendid welcome of a public dinner in Edinburgh, with Lord Jeffrey himself in the chair. Allan the painter had come up meanwhile, with increasing note of preparation; and it was while we were all regretting Wilkie's absence abroad, and Dickens with warrantable pride was saying how surely the great painter would have gone to this dinner, that the shock of his sudden

Edinburgh dinner proposed.

London: 1841.

Sir David Wilkie's death.

death * came, and there was left but the sorrowful satisfaction of honouring his memory. There was one other change before the day. "I heard "from Edinburgh this morning," he wrote on the 15th of June. "Jeffrey is not well enough to take "the chair, so Wilson does. I think under all "circumstances of politics, acquaintance, and *Edin-"burgh Review*, that it's much better as it is— "Don't you?"

Edinburgh: 23rd June.

His first letter from Edinburgh, where he and Mrs. Dickens had taken up quarters at the Royal-hotel on their arrival the previous night, is dated the 23rd of June. "I have been this morning "to the Parliament-house, and am now introduced "(I hope) to everybody in Edinburgh. The hotel "is perfectly besieged, and I have been forced to "take refuge in a sequestered apartment at the "end of a long passage, wherein I write this letter. "They talk of 300 at the dinner. We are very "well off in point of rooms, having a handsome "sitting-room, another next to it for *Clock* pur-"poses, a spacious bed-room, and large dressing-"room adjoining. The castle is in front of the

C. D. to J. F.

* Dickens refused to believe it at first. "My heart as-"sures me Wilkie liveth," he wrote. "He is the sort of "man who will be VERY old when he dies"—and certainly one would have said so.

EDINBURGH: 1841.

"windows, and the view noble. There was a "supper ready last night which would have been "a dinner anywhere." This was his first practical experience of the honours his fame had won for him, and it found him as eager to receive as all were eager to give. Very interesting still, too, are those who took leading part in the celebration; and, in his pleasant sketches of them, there are some once famous and familiar figures not so well known to the present generation. Here, among the first, are Wilson and Robertson.

Peter Robertson.

"The renowned Peter Robertson is a large, "portly, full-faced man with a merry eye, and a "queer way of looking under his spectacles which "is characteristic and pleasant. He seems a very "warm-hearted earnest man too, and I felt quite "at home with him forthwith. Walking up and "down the hall of the courts of law (which was "full of advocates, writers to the signet, clerks,

Professor Wilson.

"and idlers) was a tall, burly, handsome man of "eight and fifty, with a gait like O'Connell's, the "bluest eye you can imagine, and long hair— "longer than mine—falling down in a wild way "under the broad brim of his hat. He had on a "surtout coat, a blue checked shirt; the collar "standing up, and kept in its place with a wisp "of black neckerchief; no waistcoat; and a large

EDINBURGH: 1841.

C. D. to J. F.

"pocket-handkerchief thrust into his breast, which "was all broad and open. At his heels followed "a wiry, sharp-eyed, shaggy devil of a terrier, "dogging his steps as he went slashing up and "down, now with one man beside him, now with "another, and now quite alone, but always at a "fast, rolling pace, with his head in the air, and "his eyes as wide open as he could get them. I "guessed it was Wilson, and it was. A bright, "clear-complexioned, mountain-looking fellow, he "looks as though he had just come down from "the Highlands, and had never in his life taken "pen in hand. But he has had an attack of "paralysis in his right arm, within this month. "He winced when I shook hands with him; and "once or twice when we were walking up and "down, slipped as if he had stumbled on a piece "of orange-peel. He is a great fellow to look at, "and to talk to; and, if you could divest your "mind of the actual Scott, is just the figure you "would put in his place."

A fancy of Scott.

Nor have the most ordinary incidents of the visit any lack of interest for us now, in so far as they help to complete the picture of himself. "Allan has been squiring me about, all the morn-"ing. He and Fletcher have gone to a meeting "of the dinner-stewards, and I take the opportunity "of writing to you. They dine with us to-day, "and we are going to-night to the theatre. M'Ian "is playing there. I mean to leave a card for "him before evening. We are engaged for every "day of our stay, already; but the people I have "seen are so very hearty and warm in their man-"ner that much of the horrors of lionization gives "way before it. I am glad to find that they pro-"pose giving me for a toast on Friday the Me-"mory of Wilkie. I should have liked it better "than anything, if I could have made my choice. "Communicate all particulars to Mac. I would to "God you were both here. Do dine together at "the Gray's-inn on Friday, and think of me. If I "don't drink my first glass of wine to you, may "my pistols miss fire, and my mare slip her "shoulder. All sorts of regard from Kate. She "has gone with Miss Allan to see the house she "was born in, &c. Write me soon, and long, &c."

EDINBURGH: 1841. C. D. to J. F.

Lionization made tolerable.

Thoughts of home.

His next letter was written the morning after the dinner, on Saturday the 26th June. "The "great event is over; and being gone, I am a man "again. It was the most brilliant affair you can "conceive; the completest success possible, from "first to last. The room was crammed, and more "than seventy applicants for tickets were of neces-"sity refused yesterday. Wilson was ill, but

The dinner

EDINBURGH: 1841.

"plucked up like a lion, and spoke famously.* I "send you a paper herewith, but the report is

The speeches.

* The speeches generally were good, but the descriptions in the text by himself will here be thought sufficient. One or two sentences ought however to be given to show the tone of Wilson's praise, and I will only preface them by the remark that Dickens's acknowledgments, as well as his tribute to Wilkie, were expressed with great felicity; and that Peter Robertson seems to have thrown the company into convulsions of laughter by his imitation of Dominie Sampson's PRO-DI-GI-OUS, in a supposed interview between that worthy schoolmaster and Mr. Squeers of Dotheboys. I now quote from Professor Wilson's speech:

Dominie Sampson and Mr. Squeers.

"Our friend has mingled in the common walks of life; he "has made himself familiar with the lower orders of society. "He has not been deterred by the aspect of vice and wicked-"ness, and misery and guilt, from seeking a spirit of good "in things evil, but has endeavoured by the might of genius "to transmute what was base into what is precious as the "beaten gold . . . . But I shall be betrayed, if I go on much "longer—which it would be improper for me to do—into "something like a critical delineation of the genius of our "illustrious guest. I shall not attempt that; but I cannot but "express in a few ineffectual words, the delight which every "human bosom feels in the benign spirit which pervades all "his creations. How kind and good a man he is, I need "not say; nor what strength of genius he has acquired by that "profound sympathy with his fellow-creatures, whether in "prosperity and happiness, or overwhelmed with unfortunate "circumstances, but who yet do not sink under their miseries, "but trust to their own strength of endurance, to that prin-

Professor Wilson's speech.

"dismal in the extreme. They say there will be "a better one—I don't know where or when. "Should there be, I will send it to you. I *think* "(ahem!) that I spoke rather well. It was an ex-"cellent room, and both the subjects (Wilson and "Scottish Literature, and the Memory of Wilkie)

EDINBURGH. 1841.

C. D. to J. F.

"ciple of truth and honour and integrity which is no stranger "to the uncultivated bosom, and which is found in the lowest "abodes in as great strength as in the halls of nobles and the "palaces of kings. Mr. Dickens is also a satirist. He sa-"tirizes human life, but he does not satirize it to degrade it. "He does not wish to pull down what is high into the neigh-"bourhood of what is low. He does not seek to represent "all virtue as a hollow thing, in which no confidence can be "placed. He satirizes only the selfish, and the hard-hearted, "and the cruel. Our distinguished guest may not have given "us, as yet, a full and complete delineation of the female "character. But this he has done: he has not endeavoured "to represent women as charming merely by the aid of ac-"complishments, however elegant and graceful. He has not "depicted those accomplishments as their essentials, but has "spoken of them rather as always inspired by a love of do-"mesticity, by fidelity, by purity, by innocence, by charity, "and by hope, which makes them discharge, under the most "difficult circumstances, their duties; and which brings over "their path in this world some glimpses of the light of heaven. "Mr. Dickens may be assured that there is felt for him all "over Scotland a sentiment of kindness, affection, admira-"tion, and love; and I know for certain that the knowledge "of these sentiments must make him happy."

Professor Wilson *loq.*

Edinburgh: 1841.

C. D. to J. F.

"were good to go upon. There were nearly two "hundred ladies present. The place is so con- "trived that the cross table is raised enormously: "much above the heads of people sitting below: "and the effect on first coming in (on me, I mean) "was rather tremendous. I was quite self-pos- "sessed however, and, notwithstanding the en- "thoosemoosy, which was very startling, as cool "as a cucumber. I wish to God you had been "there, as it is impossible for the 'distinguished "'guest' to describe the scene. It beat all natur"....

His reception.

Here was the close of his letter. "I have been "expecting every day to hear from you, and not "hearing mean to make this the briefest epistle "possible. We start next Sunday (that's to-mor- "row week). We are going out to Jeffrey's to- "day (he is very unwell), and return here to- "morrow evening. If I don't find a letter from "you when I come back, expect no Lights and "Shadows of Scottish Life from your indignant "correspondent. Murray the manager made very "excellent, tasteful, and gentlemanly mention of "Macready, about whom Wilson had been asking "me divers questions during dinner." "A hundred "thanks for your letter," he writes four days later. "I read it this morning with the greatest pleasure "and delight, and answer it with ditto, ditto.

"Where shall I begin—about my darlings? I am "delighted with Charley's precocity. He takes "arter his father, he does. God bless them, you "can't imagine (*you!* how can you!) how much I "long to see them. It makes me quite sorrowful "to think of them. . . . Yesterday, sir, the lord "provost, council, and magistrates voted me by "acclamation the freedom of the city, in testimony "(I quote the letter just received from 'James For- "'rest, lord provost') 'of the sense entertained by "'them of your distinguished abilities as an author.' "I acknowledged this morning in appropriate terms "the honour they had done me, and through me "the pursuit to which I was devoted. It *is* hand- "some, is it not?"

EDINBURGH: 1841.

Home yearnings.

Freedom of the city voted to him.

The parchment scroll of the city-freedom, recording the grounds on which it was voted, hung framed in his study to the last, and was one of his valued possessions. Answering some question of mine he told me further as to the speakers, and gave some amusing glimpses of the party-spirit which still at that time ran high in the capital of the north.

C. D. to J. F.

"The men who spoke at the dinner were all "the most rising men here, and chiefly at the "Bar. They were all, alternately, whigs and "tories; with some few radicals, such as Gordon,

EDINBURGH: 1841. C. D. to J. F.

"who gave the memory of Burns. He is Wilson's "son-in-law and the lord advocate's nephew—a "very masterly speaker indeed, who ought to be-"come a distinguished man. Neaves, who gave "the other poets, a *little* too lawyer-like for my "taste, is a great gun in the courts. Mr. Primrose "is Lord Rosebery's son. Adam Black, the pub-"lisher as you know. Dr. Alison, a very popu-"lar friend of the poor. Robertson you know. "Allan you know. Colquhoun is an advocate. "All these men were selected for the toasts as "being crack speakers, known men, and opposed "to each other very strongly in politics. For this "reason, the professors and so forth who sat "upon the platform about me made no speeches "and had none assigned them. I felt it was very "remarkable to see such a number of grey-headed "men gathered about my brown flowing locks; "and it struck most of those who were present "very forcibly. The judges, solicitor-general, lord-"advocate, and so forth, were all here to call, "the day after our arrival. The judges never go "to public dinners in Scotland. Lord Meadow-"bank alone broke through the custom, and none "of his successors have imitated him. It will give "you a good notion of *party* to hear that the so-"licitor-general and lord-advocate refused to go,

Speakers.

Politics and party.

The Judges.

"though they had previously engaged, *unless* the "croupier or the chairman were a whig. Both "(Wilson and Robertson) were tories, simply be-"cause, Jeffrey excepted, no whig could be found "who was adapted to the office. The solicitor "laid strict injunctions on Napier not to go if a "whig were not in office. No whig was, and he "stayed away. I think this is good?—bearing in "mind that all the old whigs of Edinburgh were "cracking their throats in the room. They give "out that they were ill, and the lord-advocate did "actually lie in bed all the afternoon; but this is "the real truth, and one of the judges told it me "with great glee. It seems they couldn't quite "trust Wilson or Robertson, as they thought; and "feared some tory demonstration. Nothing of "the kind took place; and ever since, these men "have been the loudest in their praises of the "whole affair."

EDINBURGH: 1841.

The law-officers.

Whig jealousies.

The close of his letter tells us all his engagements, and completes his grateful picture of the hearty Scottish welcome given him. It has also some personal touches that may be thought worth preserving. "A threat reached me last night (they "have been hammering at it in their papers, it "seems, for some time) of a dinner at Glasgow.

Rumours from Glasgow.

Edinburgh: 1841. C. D. to J. F.

"But I hope, having circulated false rumours of "my movements, to get away before they send "to me; and only to stop there on my way home, "to change horses and send to the post-office.... "You will like to know how we have been living. "Here's a list of engagements, past and present. "Wednesday, we dined at home, and went incog.

At the theatre.

"to the theatre at night, to Murray's box: the "pieces admirably done, and M'Ian in the *Two "Drovers* quite wonderful, and most affecting. "Thursday, to Lord Murray's; dinner and even-"ing party. Friday, *the* dinner. Saturday, to "Jeffrey's, a beautiful place about three miles off" (Craig-crook, which at Lord Jeffrey's invitation I afterwards visited with him), "stop there all night. "dine on Sunday, and home at eleven. Monday, "dine at Dr. Alison's, four miles off. Tuesday,

Hospitalities.

"dinner and evening party at Allan's. Wednes-"day, breakfast with Napier, dine with Black-"woods seven miles off, evening party at the trea-"surer's of the town-council, supper with all the "artists (!!). Thursday, lunch at the solicitor-"general's, dine at Lord Gillies's, evening party "at Joseph Gordon's, one of Brougham's earliest "supporters. Friday, dinner and evening party at "Robertson's. Saturday, dine again at Jeffrey's;

EDINBURGH: 1841. C. D. to J. F.

"back to the theatre, at half-past nine to the moment, for public appearance;* places all let, &c. "&c. &c. Sunday, off at seven o'clock in the "morning to Stirling, and then to Callender, a "stage further. Next day, to Loch-earn, and pull "up there for three days, to rest and work. The "moral of all this is, that there is no place like "home; and that I thank God most heartily for "having given me a quiet spirit, and a heart that "won't hold many people. I sigh for Devonshire-"terrace and Broadstairs, for battledore and "shuttlecock; I want to dine in a blouse with "you and Mac; and I feel Topping's merits more "acutely than I have ever done in my life. On "Sunday evening the 17th of July I shall revisit "my household gods, please heaven. I wish the "day were here. For God's sake be in waiting. "I wish you and Mac would dine in Devonshire-"terrace that day with Fred. He has the key of "the cellar. *Do*. We shall be at Inverary in the "Highlands on Tuesday week, getting to it "through the pass of Glencoe, of which you may "have heard! On Thursday following we shall

Moral of it all.

Proposed visit to the Highlands.

* On this occasion, as he told me afterwards, the orchestra did a double stroke of business, much to the amazement of himself and his friends, by improvising at his entrance *Charley is my Darling*, amid tumultuous shouts of delight.

EDINBURGH: 1841.

"be at Glasgow, where I shall hope to receive "your last letter before we meet. At Inverary, "too, I shall make sure of finding at least one, "at the post-office. . . . Little Allan is trying hard "for the post of queen's limner for Scotland, va- "cant by poor Wilkie's death. Every one is in "his favor but——who is jobbing for some one "else. Appoint him, will you, and I'll give up "the premier-ship.—How I breakfasted to-day in "the house where Scott lived seven and twenty "years; how I have made solemn pledges to "write about missing children in the *Edinburgh* "*Review*, and will do my best to keep them; how "I have declined to be brought in, free gratis for "nothing and qualified to boot, for a Scotch "county that's going a-begging, lest I should be "thought to have dined on Friday under false "pretences; these, with other marvels, shall be "yours anon. . . . I must leave off sharp, to get "dressed and off upon the seven miles dinner "trip. Kate's affectionate regards. My hearty "loves to Mac and Grim." Grim was another great artist having the same beginning to his name, whose tragic studies had suggested an epithet quite inapplicable to any of his personal qualities.

Allan and Wilkie.

Offer of a seat.

Maclise and Macready.

The narrative of the trip to the Highlands

must have a chapter to itself and its incidents of adventure and comedy. The latter chiefly were due to the guide who accompanied him, a quasi-highlander himself, named a few pages back as Mr. Kindheart, whose real name was Mr. Angus Fletcher, and to whom it hardly needs that I should give other mention than will be supplied by such future notices of him as my friend's letters may contain. He had a wayward kind of talent, which he could never concentrate on a settled pursuit; and though at the time we knew him first he had taken up the profession of a sculptor, he abandoned it soon afterwards. His mother, a woman distinguished by many remarkable qualities, lived now in the English lake-country; and it was no fault of hers that this home was no longer her son's. But what mainly had closed it to him was undoubtedly not less the secret of such liking for him as Dickens had. Fletcher's eccentricities and absurdities, often divided by the thinnest partition from the most foolish extravagance, but occasionally clever, and always the genuine though whimsical outgrowth of the life he led, had a curious sort of charm for Dickens. He enjoyed the oddity and humour; tolerated all the rest; and to none more freely than to Kindheart during the next few years, both in Italy and

EDINBURGH: 1841.

Guide to the Highlands.

Angus Fletcher.

EDINBURGH: 1841. in England, opened his house and hospitality. The close of the poor fellow's life, alas! was in only too sad agreement with all the previous course of it; but this will have mention hereafter. He is waiting now to introduce Dickens to the Highlands.

CHAPTER XVI.

ADVENTURES IN THE HIGHLANDS.

1841.

THE HIGHLANDS: 1841.

C. D. to J. F.

FROM Loch-earn-head Dickens wrote on Monday the 5th of July, having reached it, "wet through," at four that afternoon. "Having had "a great deal to do in a crowded house on Satur-"day night at the theatre, we left Edinburgh "yesterday morning at half past seven, and tra-"velled, with Fletcher for our guide, to a place "called Stewart's-hotel, nine miles further than "Callender. We had neglected to order rooms, "and were obliged to make a sitting-room of our "own bed-chamber; in which my genius for stow-"ing furniture away was of the very greatest ser-"vice. Fletcher slept in a kennel with three panes "of glass in it, which formed part and parcel of "a window; the other three panes whereof be-"longed to a man who slept on the other side of "the partition. He told me this morning that he "had had a nightmare all night, and had screamed

A fright.

THE HIGHLANDS: 1841. C. D. to J. F.

"horribly, he knew. The stranger, as you may "suppose, hired a gig and went off at full gallop "with the first glimpse of daylight.* Being very "tired (for we had not had more than three hours' "sleep on the previous night) we lay till ten this

* Poor good Mr. Fletcher had, among his other peculiarities, a habit of venting any particular emotion in a wildness of cry that went beyond even the descriptive power of his friend, who referred to it frequently in his Broadstairs letters. Here is an instance (20th Sept. 1840) "Mrs. M. being in the "next machine the other day heard him howl like a wolf (as "he does) when he first touched the cold water. I am glad "to have my former story in that respect confirmed. There "is no sound on earth like it. In the infernal regions there "may be, but elsewhere there is no compound addition of "wild beasts that could produce its like for their total. The "description of the wolves in *Robinson Crusoe* is the nearest "thing; but it's feeble—very feeble—in comparison." Of the generally amiable side to all his eccentricities I am tempted to give an illustration from the same letter. "An alarming "report being brought to me the other day that he was "preaching, I betook myself to the spot and found he was "reading Wordsworth to a family on the terrace, outside the "house, in the open air and public way. The whole town "were out. When he had given them a taste of Wordsworth, "he sent home for Mrs. Norton's book, and entertained them "with selections from that. He concluded with an imitation of Mrs. Hemans reading her own poetry, which he "performed with a pocket-handkerchief over his head to "imitate her veil—all this in public, before everybody."

Fletcher's eccentricities.

"morning; and at half past eleven went through "the Trossachs to Loch-katrine, where I walked "from the hotel after tea last night. It is impos- "sible to say what a glorious scene it was. It "rained as it never does rain anywhere but here. "We conveyed Kate up a rocky pass to go and "see the island of the Lady of the Lake, but she "gave in after the first five minutes, and we left "her, very picturesque and uncomfortable, with "Tom" (the servant they had brought with them from Devonshire-terrace) "holding an umbrella "over her head, while we climbed on. When we "came back, she had gone into the carriage. We "were wet through to the skin, and came on in "that state four and twenty miles. Fletcher is "very good natured, and of extraordinary use in "these outlandish parts. His habit of going into "kitchens and bars, disconcerting at Broadstairs, "is here of great service. Not expecting us till "six, they hadn't lighted our fires when we ar- "rived here; and if you had seen him (with whom "the responsibility of the omission rested) running "in and out of the sitting-room and the two bed- "rooms with a great pair of bellows, with which "he distractedly blew each of the fires out in turn, "you would have died of laughing. He had on "his head a great highland cap, on his back a

C. D. to J. F.

The Trossachs.

Island of the Lady of the Lake.

The travellers' guide.

A comical picture.

THE HIGHLANDS: 1841. C. D. to J. F.

"white coat, and cut such a figure as even the "inimitable can't depicter . . .

"The Inns, inside and out, are the queerest "places imaginable. From the road, this one," at Loch-earn-head, "looks like a white wall, with "windows in it by mistake. We have a good "sitting-room though, on the first floor: as large "(but not as lofty) as my study. The bedrooms "are of that size which renders it impossible for "you to move, after you have taken your boots "off, without chipping pieces out of your legs. "There isn't a basin in the Highlands which will "hold my face; not a drawer which will open "after you have put your clothes in it; not a "water-bottle capacious enough to wet your tooth-"brush. The huts are wretched and miserable "beyond all description. The food (for those who "can pay for it) 'not bad,' as M would say: oat-"cake, mutton, hotch potch, trout from the loch, "small beer bottled, marmalade, and whiskey. Of "the last named article I have taken about a pint "to-day. The weather is what they call 'soft'— "which means that the sky is a vast water-spout "that never leaves off emptying itself; and the "liquor has no more effect than water. . . . . . I "am going to work to-morrow, and hope before "leaving here to write you again. The elections

Highland accommodation.

Weather.

Peel's elections.

"have been sad work indeed. That they should "return Sibthorp and reject Bulwer, is, by Heaven, "a national disgrace. ... I don't wonder the devil "flew over Lincoln. The people were far too "addle-headed, even for him. .... I don't bore "you with accounts of Ben this and that, and "Lochs of all sorts of names, but this is a won-"derful region. The way the mists were stalking "about to-day, and the clouds lying down upon "the hills; the deep glens, the high rocks, the "rushing waterfalls, and the roaring rivers down "in deep gulfs below; were all stupendous. This "house is wedged round by great heights that are "lost in the clouds; and the loch, twelve miles "long, stretches out its dreary length before the "windows. In my next, I shall soar to the sublime, "perhaps; in this here present writing I confine "myself to the ridiculous. But I am always," &c. &c.

THE HIGHLANDS: 1841. C. D. to J. F.

Grand scenery.

His next letter bore the date of "Ballechelish, "Friday evening, ninth July, 1841, half-past nine, "P.M." and described what we had often longed to see together, the Pass of Glencoe. . . . "I can't "go to bed without writing to you from here, "though the post will not leave this place until "we have left it, and arrived at another. On look-"ing over the route which Lord Murray made out

From Ballechelish.

THE HIGHLANDS: 1841.

C. D. to J. F.

Changes in route.

"for me, I found he had put down Thursday next "for Abbotsford and Dryburgh-abbey, and a "journey of seventy miles besides! Therefore, "and as I was happily able to steal a march upon "myself at Loch-earn-head, and to finish in two "days what I thought would take me three, we "shall leave here to-morrow morning; and, by "being a day earlier than we intended at all the "places between this and Melrose (which we pro-"pose to reach by Wednesday night), we shall "have a whole day for Scott's house and tomb, "and still be at York on Saturday evening, and "home, God willing, on Sunday. . . . We left "Loch-earn-head last night, and went to a place "called Killin, eight miles from it, where we slept. "I walked some six miles with Fletcher after we

A waterfall.

"got there, to see a waterfall: and truly it was a "magnificent sight, foaming and crashing down "three great steeps of riven rock; leaping over the "first as far off as you could carry your eye, and "rumbling and foaming down into a dizzy pool "below you, with a deafening roar. To-day we "have had a journey of between 50 and 60 miles, "through the bleakest and most desolate part of "Scotland, where the hill-tops are still covered "with great patches of snow, and the road winds "over steep mountain passes, and on the brink of "deep brooks and precipices. The cold all day "has been *intense*, and the rain sometimes most "violent. It has been impossible to keep warm, "by any means; even whiskey failed; the wind "was too piercing even for that. One stage of "ten miles, over a place called the Black-mount, "took us two hours and a half to do; and when "we came to a lone public called the King's-"house, at the entrance to Glencoe—this was "about three o'clock—we were well nigh frozen. "We got a fire directly, and in twenty minutes "they served us up some famous kippered salmon, "broiled; a broiled fowl; hot mutton ham and "poached eggs; pancakes; oatcake; wheaten bread; "butter; bottled porter; hot water, lump sugar, and "whiskey; of which we made a very hearty meal. "All the way, the road had been among moors "and mountains with huge masses of rock, which "fell down God knows where, sprinkling the "ground in every direction, and giving it the "aspect of the burial place of a race of giants. "Now and then we passed a hut or two, with "neither window nor chimney, and the smoke of "the peat fire rolling out at the door. But there "were not six of these dwellings in a dozen "miles; and anything so bleak and wild, and "mighty in its loneliness, as the whole country, it

THE HIGHLANDS: 1841.

C. D. to J. F.

Entrance to Glencoe.

THE HIGHLANDS: 1841.

C. D. to J. F. The pass of Glencoe.

"is impossible to conceive. Glencoe itself is perfectly *terrible*. The pass is an awful place. It "is shut in on each side by enormous rocks from "which great torrents come rushing down in all "directions. In amongst these rocks on one side "of the pass (the left as we came) there are scores "of glens, high up, which form such haunts as "you might imagine yourself wandering in, in the "very height and madness of a fever. They will "live in my dreams for years—I was going to say "as long as I live, and I seriously think so. The "very recollection of them makes me shudder. . . "Well, I will not bore you with my impressions "of these tremendous wilds, but they really are "fearful in their grandeur and amazing solitude. "Wales is a mere toy compared with them."

The further mention of his guide's whimsical ways may stand, for it cannot now be the possible occasion of pain or annoyance, or of anything but very innocent laughter.

Loch Leven.

"We are now in a bare white house on the "banks of Loch-leven, but in a comfortably fur-"nished room on the top of the house—that is, "on the first floor—with the rain pattering against

A July evening.

"the window as though it were December, the "wind howling dismally, a cold damp mist on "everything without, a blazing fire within halfway

"up the chimney, and a most infernal Piper prac- THE HIGHLANDS: 1841. C. D. to J. F.
"tising under the window for a competition of
"pipers which is to come off shortly. . . . The
"store of anecdotes of Fletcher with which we
"shall return, will last a long time. It seems that
"the F's are an extensive clan, and that his father
"was a highlander. Accordingly, wherever he
"goes, he finds out some cotter or small farmer
"who is his cousin. I wish you could see him
"walking into his cousins' curds and cream, and
"into their dairies generally! Yesterday morning
"between eight and nine, I was sitting writing at
"the open window, when the postman came to
"the inn (which at Loch-earn-head is the post of- Postal service at Loch-earn-head.
"fice) for the letters. He is going away, when
"Fletcher, who has been writing somewhere below
"stairs, rushes out, and cries 'Halloa there! Is
"'that the Post?' 'Yes!' somebody answers. 'Call
"'him back!' says Fletcher: 'Just sit down till I've
"'done, *and don't go away till I tell you.'*—Fancy!
"The General Post, with the letters of forty vil-
"lages in a leathern bag! . . . To-morrow at Oban.
"Sunday at Inverary. Monday at Tarbet. Tues- Route homeward.
"day at Glasgow (and that night at Hamilton).
"Wednesday at Melrose. Thursday at Ditto. Fri-
"day I don't know where. Saturday at York.
"Sunday—how glad I shall be to shake hands

THE HIGHLANDS: 1841.

C. D. to J. F.

"with you. My love to Mac. I thought he'd "have written once. Ditto to Macready. I had "a very nice and welcome letter from him, and a "most hearty one from Elliotson. . . . P.S. Half "asleep. So, excuse drowsiness of matter and "composition. I shall be full of joy to meet an-"other letter from you! . . . P.P.S. They speak "Gaelic here, of course, and many of the common "people understand very little English. Since I "wrote this letter, I rang the girl upstairs, and "gave elaborate directions (you know my way) "for a pint of sherry to be made into boiling "negus; mentioning all the ingredients one by "one, and particularly nutmeg. When I had quite "finished, seeing her obviously bewildered, I said, "with great gravity, 'Now you know what you're "'going to order?' 'Oh yes. Sure.' 'What?'—a "pause—'Just'—another pause—'Just plenty of "'*nutbergs!*'"

The maid of the inn.

The impression made upon him by the Pass of Glencoe was not overstated in this letter. It continued with him as he there expresses it; and, as we shall see hereafter, even where he expected to find Nature in her most desolate grandeur on the dreary waste of an American prairie, his imagination went back with a higher satisfaction to Glencoe. But his experience of it is not yet

Effect of Glencoe.

completely told. The sequel was in a letter of two days later date from "Dalmally, Sunday, July "the eleventh, 1841." THE HIGHLANDS: 1841. C. D. to J. F.

"As there was no place of this name in our "route, you will be surprised to see it at the head "of this present writing. But our being here is a "part of such moving accidents by flood and field "as will astonish you. If you should happen to "have your hat on, take it off, that your hair may "stand on end without any interruption. To get "from Ballyhoolish (as I am obliged to spell it "when Fletcher is not in the way; and he is out "at this moment) to Oban, it is necessary to cross "two ferries, one of which is an arm of the sea, "eight or ten miles broad. Into this ferry-boat, "passengers, carriages, horses, and all, get bodily, "and are got across by hook or by crook if the "weather be reasonably fine. Yesterday morning, "however, it blew such a strong gale that the "landlord of the inn, where we had paid for "horses all the way to Oban (thirty miles), honestly "came upstairs just as we were starting, with the "money in his hand, and told us it would be im-"possible to cross. There was nothing to be done "but to come back five and thirty miles, through "Glencoe and Inverouran, to a place called Tyn-"drum, whence a road twelve miles long crosses

At a place not in his route.

An adventure.

THE HIGHLANDS: 1841.

C. D. to J. F.

"to Dalmally, which is sixteen miles from Inver- "ary. Accordingly we turned back, and in a great "storm of wind and rain began to retrace the "dreary road we had come the day before. . . I "was not at all ill pleased to have to come again "through that awful Glencoe. If it had been "tremendous on the previous day, yesterday it was "perfectly horrific. It had rained all night, and "was raining then, as it only does in these parts. "Through the whole glen, which is ten miles long, "torrents were boiling and foaming, and sending "up in every direction spray like the smoke of "great fires. They were rushing down every hill "and mountain side, and tearing like devils across "the path, and down into the depths of the rocks. "Some of the hills looked as if they were full of "silver, and had cracked in a hundred places. "Others as if they were frightened, and had broken "out into a deadly sweat. In others there was no "compromise or division of streams, but one great "torrent came roaring down with a deafening "noise, and a rushing of water that was quite ap- "palling. Such a *spaet*, in short (that's the country "word), has not been known for many years, and "the sights and sounds were beyond description. "The post-boy was not at all at his ease, and the "horses were very much frightened (as well they

Again through Glencoe.

Torrents swollen with rain.

"might be) by the perpetual raging and roaring; "one of them started as we came down a steep "place, and we were within that much (——) of "tumbling over a precipice; just then, too, the "drag broke, and we were obliged to go on as "we best could, without it: getting out every now "and then, and hanging on at the back of the "carriage to prevent its rolling down too fast, and "going Heaven knows where. Well, in this "pleasant state of things we came to King's-house "again, having been four hours doing the sixteen "miles. The rumble where Tom sat was by this "time so full of water, that he was obliged to "borrow a gimlet, and bore holes in the bottom "to let it run out. The horses that were to take "us on, were out upon the hills, somewhere within "ten miles round; and three or four bare-legged "fellows went out to look for 'em, while we sat "by the fire and tried to dry ourselves. At last "we got off again (without the drag and with a "broken spring, no smith living within ten miles), "and went limping on to Inverouran. In the first "three miles we were in a ditch and out again, "and lost a horse's shoe. All this time it never "once left off raining; and was very windy, very "cold, very misty, and most intensely dismal. So

THE HIGHLANDS: 1841.

C. D. to J. F.

Dangerous travelling.

Incidents and accidents.

The Highlands: 1841.

C. D. to J. F.

Broken-down bridge.

"we crossed the Black-mount, and came to a place "we had passed the day before, where a rapid "river runs over a bed of broken rock. Now, this "river, sir, had a bridge last winter, but the bridge "broke down when the thaw came, and has never "since been mended; so travellers cross upon a "little platform, made of rough deal planks stretch-"ing from rock to rock; and carriages and horses "ford the water, at a certain point. As the plat-"form is the reverse of steady (we had proved "this the day before), is very slippery, and affords "anything but a pleasant footing, having only a "trembling little rail on one side, and on the "other nothing between it and the foaming stream, "Kate decided to remain in the carriage, and trust "herself to the wheels rather than to her feet. "Fletcher and I had got out, and it was going "away, when I advised her, as I had done several "times before, to come with us; for I saw that "the water was very high, the current being "greatly swollen by the rain, and that the post-"boy had been eyeing it in a very disconcerted "manner for the last half hour. This decided her "to come out; and Fletcher, she, Tom, and I, "began to cross, while the carriage went about a "quarter of a mile down the bank, in search of a

A fortunate resolve.

"shallow place. The platform shook so much "that we could only come across two at a time, "and then it felt as if it were hung on springs. "As to the wind and rain! . . . well, put into one "gust all the wind and rain you ever saw and "heard, and you'll have some faint notion of it! "When we got safely to the opposite bank, there "came riding up a wild highlander, in a great "plaid, whom we recognized as the landlord of "the inn, and who without taking the least notice "of us, went dashing on,—with the plaid he was "wrapped in, streaming in the wind,—screeching "in Gaelic to the post-boy on the opposite bank, "and making the most frantic gestures you ever "saw, in which he was joined by some other wild "men on foot, who had come across by a short "cut, knee-deep in mire and water. As we began "to see what this meant, we (that is, Fletcher "and I) scrambled on after them, while the boy, "horses, and carriage were plunging in the water, "which left only the horses' heads and the boy's "body visible. By the time we got up to them, "the man on horseback and the men on foot were "perfectly mad with pantomime; for as to any of "their shouts being heard by the boy, the water "made such a great noise that they might as well

THE HIGHLANDS: 1841.

C. D. to J. F.

Post-boy in danger.

THE HIGHLANDS: 1841.

C. D. to J. F.

"have been dumb. It made me quite sick to "think how I should have felt if Kate had been "inside. The carriage went round and round "like a great stone, the boy was as pale as death, "the horses were struggling and plashing and "snorting like sea-animals, and we were all roar-"ing to the driver to throw himself off and let "them and the coach go to the devil, when sud-

The rescue.

"denly it came all right (having got into shallow "water), and, all tumbling and dripping and jog-"ging from side to side, climbed up to the dry "land. I assure you we looked rather queer, as "we wiped our faces and stared at each other in "a little cluster round about it. It seemed that "the man on horseback had been looking at us "through a telescope as we came to the track, and "knowing that the place was very dangerous, and "seeing that we meant to bring the carriage, had "come on at a great gallop to show the driver

Narrow escape.

"the only place where he could cross. By the "time he came up, the man had taken the water "at a wrong place, and in a word was as nearly "drowned (with carriage, horses, luggage, and all) "as ever man was. Was *this* a good adventure?

"We all went on to the inn—the wild man "galloping on first, to get a fire lighted—and there "we dined on eggs and bacon, oat-cake, and "whiskey; and changed and dried ourselves. The "place was a mere knot of little outhouses, and "in one of these there were fifty highlanders *all* "*drunk*. . . . Some were drovers, some pipers, and "some workmen engaged to build a hunting-"lodge for Lord Breadalbane hard by, who had "been driven in by stress of weather. One was "a paper-hanger. He had come out three days "before to paper the inn's best room, a chamber "almost large enough to keep a Newfoundland "dog in; and, from the first half hour after his "arrival to that moment, had been hopelessly "and irreclaimably drunk. They were lying about "in all directions: on forms, on the ground, about "a loft overhead, round the turf-fire wrapped in "plaids, on the tables, and under them. We paid "our bill, thanked our host very heartily, gave "some money to his children, and after an hour's "rest came on again. At ten o'clock at night, "we reached this place, and were overjoyed to "find quite an English inn, with good beds (those "we have slept on, yet, have always been of straw), "and every possible comfort. We breakfasted this "morning at half past ten, and at three go on to "Inverary to dinner. I believe the very rough

THE HIGHLANDS: 1841.

C. D. to J. F.

Highland inn and inmates.

English comfort at Dalmally.

THE HIGHLANDS: 1841.

C. D. to J. F.

"part of the journey is over, and I am really glad "of it. Kate sends all kind of regards. I shall "hope to find a letter from you at Inverary when "the post reaches there, to-morrow. I wrote to "Oban yesterday, desiring the post-office keeper "to send any he might have for us, over to that "place. Love to Mac."

One more letter, brief but overflowing at every word with his generous nature, must close the delightful series written from Scotland. It was dated from Inverary the day following his exciting adventure; promised me another from Melrose (which has unfortunately not been kept with the rest); and enclosed the invitation to a public

C. D. to J. F.

Dinner at Glasgow proposed.

dinner at Glasgow. "I have returned for answer "that I am on my way home, on pressing business connected with my weekly publication, and "can't stop. But I have offered to come down "any day in September or October, and accept "the honour then. Now, I shall come and return "per mail; and if this suits them, enter into a "solemn league and covenant to come with me. "*Do.* You must. I am sure you will . . . Till "my next, and always afterwards, God bless you. "I got your welcome letter this morning, and "have read it a hundred times. What a pleasure "it is. Kate's best regards. I am dying for Sunday, and wouldn't stop now for twenty dinners "of twenty thousand each.

THE HIGHLANDS: 1841.

Impatience for home.

'always your affectionate friend
'D.

"Will Lord John meet the parliament, or resign first?" I agreed to accompany him to Glasgow; but illness intercepted that celebration.

CHAPTER XVII.

AGAIN AT BROADSTAIRS.

1841.

BROADSTAIRS: 1841.

SOON after his return, at the opening of August, he went to Broadstairs; and the direction in which that last question shows his thoughts to have been busy, was that to which he turned his first holiday leisure. He sent me some rhymed squibs as his anonymous contribution to the fight the liberals were then making, against what was believed to be intended by the return to office of the tories; ignorant as we were how much wiser than his party the statesman then at the head of it was, or how greatly what we all most desired would be advanced by the very success that had been most disheartening. There will be no harm now in giving one of these pieces, which will sufficiently show the tone of all of them, and with what a hearty relish they were written. I doubt indeed if he ever enjoyed anything more than the power of thus taking part occasionally, un-

Peel and his party.

BROADSTAIRS: 1841.

C. D. to J. F.

known to outsiders, in the sharp conflict the press was waging at the time. "By Jove how radical "I am getting!" he wrote to me (13th August). "I wax stronger and stronger in the true prin- "ciples every day. I don't know whether it's the "sea, or no, but so it is." He would at times even talk, in moments of sudden indignation at the political outlook, of carrying off himself and his household gods, like Coriolanus, to a world elsewhere! "Thank God there is a Van Diemen's- "land. That's my comfort. Now, I wonder if I "should make a good settler! I wonder, if I went "to a new colony with my head, hands, legs, and "health, I should force myself to the top of the "social milk-pot and live upon the cream! What "do you think? Upon my word I believe I "should."

Thoughts of colonizing.

His political squibs during the tory interregnum comprised some capital subjects for pictures after the manner of Peter Pindar; but that which I select has no touch of personal satire in it, and he would himself, for that reason, have least objected to its revival. Thus ran his new version of "The "Fine Old English Gentleman, to be said or sung "at all conservative dinners."

BROADSTAIRS: 1841.

The fine old English Tory times.

I'll sing you a new ballad, and I'll warrant it first-rate,
Of the days of that old gentleman who had that old estate;
When they spent the public money at a bountiful old rate
On ev'ry mistress, pimp, and scamp, at ev'ry noble gate,
In the fine old English Tory times;
Soon may they come again!

The good old laws were garnished well with gibbets, whips, and chains,
With fine old English penalties, and fine old English pains,
With rebel heads and seas of blood once hot in rebel veins;
For all these things were requisite to guard the rich old gains
Of the fine old English Tory times;
Soon may they come again!

Squib by C. D.

This brave old code, like Argus, had a hundred watchful eyes,
And ev'ry English peasant had his good old English spies,
To tempt his starving discontent with fine old English lies,
Then call the good old Yeomanry to stop his peevish cries,
In the fine old English Tory times;
Soon may they come again!

The good old times for cutting throats that cried out in their need,
The good old times for hunting men who held their fathers' creed,
The good old times when William Pitt, as all good men agreed,
Came down direct from Paradise at more than railroad speed. . . .
Oh the fine old English Tory times;
When will they come again!

BROADSTAIRS: 1841.

The fine old English Tory times.

In those rare days, the press was seldom known to snarl or
bark,
But sweetly sang of men in pow'r, like any tuneful lark;
Grave judges, too, to all their evil deeds were in the dark;
And not a man in twenty score knew how to make his
mark.
Oh the fine old English Tory times;
Soon may they come again! . . . .

But Tolerance, though slow in flight, is strong-wing'd in
the main;
That night must come on these fine days, in course of time
was plain;
The pure old spirit struggled, but its struggles were in vain;
A nation's grip was on it, and it died in choaking pain,
With the fine old English Tory days,
All of the olden time.

Squib by C. D.

The bright old day now dawns again; the cry runs through
the land,
In England there shall be—dear bread! in Ireland—sword
and brand!
And poverty, and ignorance, shall swell the rich and grand,
So, rally round the rulers with the gentle iron hand,
Of the fine old English Tory days;
Hail to the coming time!

Of matters in which he had been specially interested before he quitted London, one or two may properly be named. He had always sympathised, almost as strongly as Archbishop Whately

LONDON: 1841.

Mesmerism.

did, with Doctor Elliotson's mesmeric investigations; and, reinforced as these were in the present year by the displays of a Belgian youth whom another friend, Mr. Chauncy Hare Townshend, brought over to England, the subject, which to the last had an attraction for him, was for the time rather ardently followed up. The improvement

Metropolitan prisons.

during the last few years in the London prisons was another matter of eager and pleased enquiry with him; and he took frequent means of stating what in this respect had been done, since even the date when his *Sketches* were written, by two most efficient public officers at Clerkenwell and Tothill-fields, Mr. Chesterton and Lieutenant Tracey, whom the course of these enquiries turned into private friends. His last letter to me before he quitted town sufficiently explains itself. "Slow "rises worth by poverty deprest" was the thought in his mind at every part of his career, and he never for a moment was unmindful of the duty it imposed upon him. "I subscribed for a couple

Book by a workman.

"of copies" (31st July) "of this little book. I knew "nothing of the man, but he wrote me a very "modest letter of two lines, some weeks ago. I "have been much affected by the little biography "at the beginning, and I thought you would like "to share the emotion it had raised in me. I "wish we were all in Eden again—for the sake "of these toiling creatures." BROADSTAIRS. 1841.

In the middle of August (Monday 16th) I had announcement that he was coming up for special purposes. "I sit down to write to you without an "atom of news to communicate. Yes I have—"something that will surprise you, who are pent "up in dark and dismal Lincoln's-inn-fields. It "is the brightest day you ever saw. The sun is "sparkling on the water so that I can hardly bear "to look at it. The tide is in, and the fishing "boats are dancing like mad. Upon the green-"topped cliffs the corn is cut and piled in shocks; "and thousands of butterflies are fluttering about, "taking the bright little red flags at the mast-heads "for flowers, and panting with delight accordingly. "[Here the Inimitable, unable to resist the bril-"liancy out of doors, breaketh off, rusheth to the "machines, and plungeth into the sea. Returning, "he proceedeth:] Jeffrey is just as he was when "he wrote the letter I sent you. No better, and "no worse. I had a letter from Napier on Satur-"day, urging the children's-labour subject upon "me. But, as I hear from Southwood Smith that "the report cannot be printed until the new parlia-"ment has sat at the least six weeks, it will be "impossible to produce it before the January

C. D. to J. F.

A day in August by the sea.

Edinburgh news.

BROADSTAIRS: 1841.

C. D. to J. F. Another story in prospect.

"number. I shall be in town on Saturday morn-"ing and go straight to you. A letter has come "from little Hall begging that when I *do* come to "town I will dine there, as they wish to talk "about the new story. I have written to say that "I will do so on Saturday, and we will go together; "but I shall be by no means good company. . . . "I have more than half a mind to start a book-"seller of my own. I could; with good capital "too, as you know; and ready to spend it. *G.* "*Varden beware!*"

"Clock" discontents.

Small causes of displeasure had been growing out of the *Clock*, and were almost unavoidably incident to the position in which he found himself respecting it. Its discontinuance had become necessary, the strain upon himself being too great without the help from others which experience had shown to be impracticable; but I thought he had not met the difficulty wisely by undertaking, which already he had done, to begin a new story so early as the following March. On his arrival therefore we decided on another plan, with which we went armed that Saturday afternoon to his publishers; and of which the result will be best told by himself. He had returned to Broadstairs the following morning, and next day (Monday the 23rd of August) he wrote to me in very en-

New adventure.

thusiastic terms of the share I had taken in what he calls "the development on Saturday afternoon; "when I thought Chapman very manly and sensible, Hall morally and physically feeble though "perfectly well intentioned, and both the statement "and reception of the project quite triumphant. "Didn't you think so too?" A fortnight later, Tuesday the 7th of September, the agreement was signed in my chambers, and its terms were to the effect following. The *Clock* was to cease with the close of *Barnaby Rudge*, the respective ownerships continuing as provided; and the new work in twenty numbers, similar to those of *Pickwick* and *Nickleby*, was not to begin until after an interval of twelve months, in November 1842. During its publication he was to receive £200 monthly, to be accounted as part of the expenses; for all which, and all risks incident, the publishers made themselves responsible, under conditions the same as in the *Clock* agreement; except that, out of the profits of each number, they were to have only a fourth, three fourths going to him, and this arrangement was to hold good until the termination of six months from the completed book, when, upon payment to him of a fourth of the value of all existing stock, they were to have half the future interest. During the twelve months' interval be-

BROADSTAIRS: 1841.

C. D. to J. F.

Agreement for it signed.

Terms.

BROAD-STAIRS: 1841.

The book that proved to be *Chuzzlewit.*

fore the book began, he was to be paid £150 each month; but this was to be drawn from his three fourths of the profits, and in no way to interfere with the monthly payments of £200 while the publication was going on.* Such was the "project," excepting only a provision to be mentioned hereafter against the improbable event of the profits being inadequate to the repayment; and my only drawback from the satisfaction of my own share in it, arose from my fear of the use he was likely to make of the leisure it afforded him.

That this fear was not illfounded appeared at the close of the next note I had from him.

C. D. to J. F.

"There's no news" (13th September) "since my "last. We are going to dine with Rogers to-day, "and with Lady Essex, who is also here. Rogers "is much pleased with Lord Ashley, who was of-"fered by Peel a post in the government, but "resolutely refused to take office unless Peel "pledged himself to factory improvement. Peel "'hadn't made up his mind'; and Lord Ashley "was deaf to all other inducements, though they "must have been very tempting. Much do I

Peel and Lord Ashley.

* "M. was quite aghast last night (9th of September) at "the brilliancy of the C. & H. arrangement: which is worth "noting perhaps."

"honour him for it. I am in an exquisitely lazy "state, bathing, walking, reading, lying in the sun, "doing everything but working. This frame of "mind is superinduced by the prospect of rest, "and the promising arrangements which I owe to "you. I am still haunted by visions of America, "night and day. To miss this opportunity would "be a sad thing. Kate cries dismally if I mention "the subject. But, God willing, I think it *must* "be managed somehow!"

BROADSTAIRS: 1841.

Visions of America.

CHAPTER XVIII.

EVE OF THE VISIT TO AMERICA.

1841.

BROADSTAIRS: 1841.

THE notion of America was in his mind, as we have seen, when he first projected the *Clock*, and a very hearty letter from Washington Irving about little Nell and the *Curiosity Shop*, expressing the delight with his writings and the yearnings to himself which had indeed been pouring in upon him for some time from every part of the States, had very strongly revived it. He answered Irving with more than his own warmth: unable to thank him enough for his cordial and generous praise, or to tell him what lasting gratification it had given. "I wish I could find in your welcome "letter," he added, "some hint of an intention to "visit England. I should love to go with you, as "I have gone, God knows how often, into Little-"britain, and East-cheap, and Green-arbour-court, "and Westminster-abbey. . . . It would gladden "my heart to compare notes with you about all

Greetings from America.

Reply to Washington Irving.

"those delightful places and people that I used to "walk about and dream of in the day time, when "a very small and not-over-particularly-taken-care-"of boy." After interchange of these letters the subject was frequently revived; upon his return from Scotland it began to take shape as a thing that somehow or other, at no very distant date, *must be;* and at last, near the end of a letter filled with many unimportant things, the announcement, doubly underlined, came to me.

BROADSTAIRS: 1841.

The decision once taken, he was in his usual fever until its difficulties were disposed of. The objections to separation from the children led at first to the notion of taking them, but this was as quickly abandoned; and what remained to be overcome yielded readily to the kind offices of Macready, the offer of whose home to the little ones during the time of absence, though not accepted to the full extent, gave yet the assurance needed to quiet natural apprehensions. All this, including an arrangement for publication of such notes as might occur to him on the journey, took but a few days; and I was reading in my chambers a letter he had written the previous day from Broadstairs, when a note from him reached me, written that morning in London, to tell me he was on his way to take share of my breakfast.

BROADSTAIRS: 1841.

He had come overland by Canterbury after posting his first letter; had seen Macready the previous night; and had completed some part of the arrangements. This mode of rapid procedure was characteristic of him at all similar times, and will appear in the few following extracts from his letters.

C. D. to J. F.

"Now" (19th September) "to astonish you. "After balancing, considering, and weighing the "matter in every point of view, I HAVE MADE UP "MY MIND (WITH GOD'S LEAVE) TO GO TO AMERICA "—AND TO START AS SOON AFTER CHRISTMAS AS "IT WILL BE SAFE TO GO." Further information was promised immediately; and a request followed, characteristic as any he could have added to his design of travelling so far away, that we should visit once more together the scenes of his boyhood. "On the ninth of October we leave here. "It's a Saturday. If it should be fine dry weather, "or anything like it, will you meet us at Rochester, "and stop there two or three days to see all the "lions in the surrounding country? Think of this. ". . . If you'll arrange to come, I'll have the car-"riage down, and Topping; and, supposing news "from Glasgow don't interfere with us, which I "fervently hope it will not, I will ensure that we "have much enjoyment."

Resolve to go to America.

Wish to revisit scenes of boyhood.

Three days later than that which announced his resolve, the subject was resumed. "I wrote to "Chapman and Hall asking them what they thought "of it, and saying I meant to keep a note-book, "and publish it for half a guinea or thereabouts, "on my return. They instantly sent the warmest "possible reply, and said they had taken it for "granted I would go, and had been speaking of "it only the day before. I have begged them to "make every enquiry about the fares, cabins, berths, "and times of sailing; and I shall make a great "effort to take Kate *and* the children. In that "case I shall try to let the house furnished, for "six months (for I shall remain that time in "America); and if I succeed, the rent will nearly "pay the expenses out, and home. I have heard "of family cabins at £100; and I think one of "these is large enough to hold us all. A single "fare, I think, is forty guineas. I fear I could "not be happy if we had the Atlantic between us; "but leaving them in New York while I ran off a "thousand miles or so, would be quite another "thing. If I can arrange all my plans before "publishing the *Clock* address, I shall state therein "that I am going: which will be no unimportant "consideration, as affording the best possible reason "for a long delay. How I am to get on without

BROADSTAIRS: 1841.

C. D. to J. F.

Proposed book about the States.

Arrangements for the journey.

BROAD-STAIRS: 1841.

C. D. to J. F.

"you for seven or eight months, I cannot, upon "my soul, conceive. I dread to think of breaking "up all our old happy habits, for so long a time. "The advantages of going, however, appear by "steady looking-at so great, that I have come to "persuade myself it is a matter of imperative ne-"cessity. Kate weeps whenever it is spoken of. "Washington Irving has got a nasty low fever. I "heard from him a day or two ago."

LONDON.

C. D. to J. F.

His next letter was the unexpected arrival which came by hand from Devonshire-terrace, when I thought him still by the sea. "This is to "give you notice that I am coming to breakfast "with you this morning on my way to Broad-"stairs. I repeat it, sir,—on my way *to* Broad-"stairs. For, directly I got Macready's note yester-"day I went to Canterbury, and came on by day-"coach for the express purpose of talking with "him; which I did between 11 and 12 last night "in Clarence-terrace. The American preliminaries

Impatience of suspense.

"are necessarily startling, and, to a gentleman of "my temperament, destroy rest, sleep, appetite, "and work, unless definitely arranged.* Macready "has quite decided me in respect of time and so "forth. The instant I have wrung a reluctant

* See Vol. I. p. 153.

"consent from Kate, I shall take our joint pas- BROADSTAIRS: 1841.
"sage in the mail-packet for next January. I never "loved my friends so well as now." We had all discountenanced his first thought of taking the children; and, upon this and other points, the experience of our friend who had himself travelled over the States was very valuable. His next letter, Resolve to leave the children.
two days later from Broadstairs, informed me of the result of the Macready conference. "Only a C. D. to J. F.
"word. Kate is quite reconciled. Anne" (her maid) "goes, and is amazingly cheerful and light "of heart upon it. And I think, at present, that "it's a greater trial to me than anybody. The "4th of January is the day. Macready's note to "Kate was received and acted upon with a per- "fect response. She talks about it quite gaily, Mrs. Dickens reconciled.
"and is satisfied to have nobody in the house but "Fred, of whom, as you know, they are all fond. "He has got his promotion, and they give him "the increased salary from the day on which the "minute was made by Baring. I feel so amiable, "so meek, so fond of people, so full of gratitudes "and reliances, that I am like a sick man. And "I am already counting the days between this "and coming home again."

He was soon, alas! to be what he compared ROCHESTER.
himself to. I met him at Rochester at the end

London: 1841.

of September, as arranged; we passed a day and night there; a day and night in Cobham and its neighbourhood, sleeping at the Leather-bottle; and a day and night at Gravesend. But we were hardly returned when some slight symptoms of bodily trouble took suddenly graver form, and an illness followed involving the necessity of surgical attendance. This, which with mention of the helpful courage displayed by him has before been alluded to,* put off necessarily the Glasgow dinner; and he had scarcely left his bedroom when a trouble arose near home which touched him to the depths of the greatest sorrow of his life, and, in the need of exerting himself for others, what remained of his own illness seemed to pass away.

A grave illness.

Domestic griefs.

His wife's younger brother had died with the same unexpected suddenness that attended her younger sister's death; and the event had followed close upon the decease of Mrs. Hogarth's mother while on a visit to her daughter and Mr. Hogarth. "As no steps had been taken towards the funeral," he wrote (25th October) in reply to my offer of such service as I could render, "I thought it best "at once to bestir myself; and not even you could "have saved my going to the cemetery. It is a

C. D. to J. F.

* See *ante*, p. 50.

"great trial to me to give up Mary's grave; greater "than I can possibly express. I thought of moving her to the catacombs and saying nothing "about it; but then I remembered that the poor "old lady is buried next her at her own desire, "and could not find it in my heart, directly she "is laid in the earth, to take her grandchild away. "The desire to be buried next her is as strong "upon me now, as it was five years ago; and I "*know* (for I don't think there ever was love like "that I bear her) that it will never diminish. I "fear I can do nothing. Do you think I can? "They would move her on Wednesday, if I re-"solved to have it done. I cannot bear the thought "of being excluded from her dust; and yet I feel "that her brothers and sisters, and her mother, "have a better right than I to be placed beside "her. It is but an idea. I neither think nor "hope (God forbid) that our spirits would ever "mingle *there*. I ought to get the better of it, "but it is very hard. I never contemplated this "—and coming so suddenly, and after being ill, "it disturbs me more than it ought. It seems like "losing her a second time . . ." "No," he wrote "the morning after, "I tried that. No, there is no "ground on either side to be had. I must give "it up. I shall drive over there, please God, on

LONDON: 1841.
C. D. to J. F.

The old sorrow.

London: 1841.

"Thursday morning, before they get there; and "look at her coffin."

He suffered more than he let any one perceive, and was obliged again to keep his room for some days. On the second of November he reported himself as progressing and ordered to Richmond, which, after a week or so, he changed to the White-hart at Windsor, where I passed some days with him, Mrs. Dickens, and her younger sister Georgina; but it was not till near the close of that month he could describe himself as thoroughly on his legs again, in the ordinary state on which he was wont to pride himself, bolt upright, staunch at the knees, a deep sleeper, a hearty eater, a good laughter; and nowhere a bit the worse, "'bating a little weak-"ness now and then, and a slight nervousness at "times."

At Windsor.

Convalescent.

Christening of Walter.

We had some days of much enjoyment at the end of the year, when Landor came up from Bath for the christening of his godson; and the "Britannia," which was to take the travellers from us in January, brought over to them in December all sorts of cordialities, anticipations, and stretchings-forth of palms, in token of the welcome awaiting them. On new-year's-eve they dined with me, and I with them on new-year's-day;

when (his house having been taken for the period of his absence by General Sir John Wilson) we sealed up his wine cellar, after opening therein some sparkling Moselle in honour of the ceremony, and drinking it then and there to his happy return. Next morning (it was a Sunday) I accompanied them to Liverpool, Maclise having been suddenly stayed by his mother's death; the intervening day and its occupations have been humorously sketched in his American book; and on the fourth they sailed. I never saw the Britannia after I stepped from her deck back to the small steamer that had taken us to her. "How little I thought" (were the last lines of his first American letter), "the first time you mounted "the shapeless coat, that I should have such a "sad association with its back as when I saw it "by the paddle-box of that small steamer."

LONDON: 1841.

Adieus.

CHAPTER XIX.

FIRST IMPRESSIONS OF AMERICA.

1842.

BANKS OF NEWFOUND-LAND: 1842.

THE first lines of that letter were written as soon as he got sight of earth again, from the banks of Newfoundland, on Monday the seventeenth of January, the fourteenth day from their departure: even then so far from Halifax that they could not expect to make it before Wednesday night, or to reach Boston until Saturday or Sunday. They had not been fortunate in the passage. During the whole voyage, the weather had been unprecedentedly bad, the wind for the most part dead against them, the wet intolerable, the sea horribly disturbed, the days dark, and the nights fearful. On the previous Monday night it had blown a hurricane, beginning at five in the afternoon and raging all night. His description of the storm is published, and the peculiarities of a steamer's behaviour in such circumstances are hit off as if he had been all his life a sailor.

Rough passage.

A steamer in a storm.

Any but so extraordinary an observer would have described a steamer in a storm as he would have described a sailing-ship in a storm. But any description of the latter would be as inapplicable to my friend's account of the other as the ways of a jackass to those of a mad bull. In the letter from which it was taken, however, there were some things addressed to myself alone. "For "two or three hours we gave it up as a lost "thing; and with many thoughts of you, and the "children, and those others who are dearest to "us, waited quietly for the worst. I never ex-"pected to see the day again, and resigned my-"self to God as well as I could. It was a great "comfort to think of the earnest and devoted "friends we had left behind, and to know that "the darlings would not want."

NEWFOUNDLAND: 1842.

C. D. to J. F. Resigned to the worst.

This was not the exaggerated apprehension of a landsman merely. The head engineer, who had been in one or other of the Cunard vessels since they began running, had never seen such stress of weather; and I heard Captain Hewitt himself say afterwards that nothing but a steamer, and one of that strength, could have kept her course and stood it out. A sailing vessel must have beaten off and driven where she could; while through all the fury of that gale they actually

NEWFOUNDLAND: 1842.

Right onward.

made fifty-four miles headlong through the tempest, straight on end, not varying their track in the least.

He stood out against sickness only for the day following that on which they sailed. For the three following days he kept his bed; miserable enough; and had not, until the eighth day of the voyage, six days before the date of his letter, been able to get to work at the dinner table.

Of himself and fellow-travellers.

What he then observed of his fellow-travellers, and had to tell of their life on board, has been set forth in his *Notes* with delightful humour; but in its first freshness I received it in this letter; and some whimsical passages, then suppressed, there will be no harm in printing now.

C. D. to J. F.

"We have 86 passengers; and such a strange "collection of beasts never was got together upon "the sea, since the days of the Ark. I have never "been in the saloon since the first day; the noise, "the smell, and the closeness being quite in-"tolerable. I have only been on deck *once!*— "and then I was surprised and disappointed at

The Atlantic from deck.

"the smallness of the panorama. The sea, run-"ning as it does and has done, is very stupendous, "and viewed from the air or some great height "would be grand no doubt. But seen from the "wet and rolling decks, in this weather and these "circumstances, it only impresses one giddily and "painfully. I was very glad to turn away, and "come below again.

NEWFOUNDLAND: 1842. C. D. to J. F.

"I have established myself, from the first, in "the ladies' cabin—you remember it? I'll describe "its other occupants, and our way of passing the "time, to you.

The ladies' cabin.

"First, for the occupants. Kate, and I, and "Anne—when she is out of bed, which is not "often. A queer little Scotch body, a Mrs. P—,* "whose husband is a silver-smith in New York. "He married her at Glasgow three years ago, "and bolted the day after the wedding; being "(which he had not told her) heavily in debt. "Since then she has been living with her mother; "and she is now going out under the protection "of a male cousin, to give him a year's trial. If "she is not comfortable at the expiration of that "time, she means to go back to Scotland again. "A Mrs. B—, about 20 years old, whose husband "is on board with her. He is a young English-"man domiciled in New York, and by trade (as

* The initials used here are in no case those of the real names, being employed in every case for the express purpose of disguising the names. Generally the remark is applicable to all initials used in the letters printed in the course of this work.

Newfoundland: 1842. C. D. to J. F.

"well as I can make out) a woollen-draper. They "have been married a fortnight. A Mr. and Mrs. "C—, marvellously fond of each other, complete "the catalogue. Mrs. C— I have settled, is a "publican's daughter, and Mr. C— is running "away with her, the till, the time-piece off the "bar mantel-shelf, the mother's gold watch from "the pocket at the head of the bed; and other "miscellaneous property. The women are all "pretty; unusually pretty. I never saw such good "faces together anywhere."

Occupants of ladies' cabin.

Their "way of passing the time" will be found in the *Notes* much as it was written to me; except that there was one point connected with the card-playing which he feared might overtax the credulity of his readers, but which he protested had occurred more than once. "Apropos of "rolling, I have forgotten to mention that in "playing whist we are obliged to put the tricks "in our pockets, to keep them from disappearing "altogether; and that five or six times in the "course of every rubber we are all flung from "our seats, roll out at different doors, and keep "on rolling until we are picked up by stewards. "This has become such a matter of course, that "we go through it with perfect gravity; and "when we are bolstered up on our sofas again,

Card-playing on the Atlantic.

"resume our conversation or our game at the "point where it was interrupted." The news that excited them from day to day, too, of which little more than a hint appears in the *Notes*, is worth giving as originally written.

NEWFOUNDLAND: 1842.

C. D. to J. F.

Ship-news.

"As for news, we have more of that than you "would think for. One man lost fourteen pounds "at vingt-un in the saloon yesterday, or another "got drunk before dinner was over, or another "was blinded with lobster sauce spilt over him "by the steward, or another had a fall on deck "and fainted. The ship's cook was drunk yester-"day morning (having got at some salt-water-"damaged whiskey), and the captain ordered "the boatswain to play upon him with the hose "of the fire engine until he roared for mercy—"which he didn't get; for he was sentenced to "look out, for four hours at a stretch for four "nights running, without a great coat, and to "have his grog stopped. Four dozen plates were "broken at dinner. One steward fell down the "cabin-stairs with a round of beef, and injured "his foot severely. Another steward fell down "after him, and cut his eye open. The baker's "taken ill: so is the pastry-cook. A new man, "sick to death, has been required to fill the place "of the latter officer, and has been dragged out

Cook in disgrace.

NEWFOUNDLAND: 1842. C. D. to J. F. A cook malgré lui.

"of bed and propped up in a little house upon "deck, between two casks, and ordered (the cap-"tain standing over him) to make and roll out "pie-crust; which he protests, with tears in his "eyes, it is death to him in his bilious state to "look at. Twelve dozen of bottled porter has "got loose upon deck, and the bottles are rolling "about distractedly, over-head. Lord Mulgrave "(a handsome fellow, by the bye, to look at, and "nothing but a good 'un to go) laid a wager with "twenty-five other men last night, whose berths, "like his, are in the fore-cabin, which can only "be got at by crossing the deck, that he would "reach his cabin first. Watches were set by the "captain's, and they sallied forth, wrapped up in "coats and storm caps. The sea broke over the "ship so violently, that they were *five and twenty* "*minutes* holding on by the handrail at the star-"board paddle-box, drenched to the skin by every "wave, and not daring to go on or come back, "lest they should be washed overboard. News! "A dozen murders in town wouldn't interest us "half as much."

A wager.

Nevertheless their excitements were not over. At the very end of the voyage came an incident very lightly touched in the *Notes*, but more freely told to me under date of the 21st January. "We

"were running into Halifax-harbour on Wednes- HALIFAX HARBOUR: 1842.
"day night, with little wind and a bright moon; C. D. to J. F.
"had made the light at its outer entrance, and "given the ship in charge to the pilot; were play-"ing our rubber, all in good spirits (for it had "been comparatively smooth for some days, with "tolerably dry decks and other unusual comforts), "when suddenly the ship STRUCK! A rush upon Ship aground.
"deck followed of course. The men (I mean the "crew! think of this) were kicking off their shoes "and throwing off their jackets preparatory to "swimming ashore; the pilot was beside himself; "the passengers dismayed; and everything in the "most intolerable confusion and hurry. Breakers "were roaring ahead; the land within a couple of "hundred yards; and the vessel driving upon the "surf, although her paddles were worked back-"wards, and everything done to stay her course. "It is not the custom of steamers, it seems, to "have an anchor ready. An accident occurred "in getting ours over the side; and for half an "hour we were throwing up rockets, burning blue "lights, and firing signals of distress, all of which Signals of distress.
"remained unanswered, though we were so close "to the shore that we could see the waving "branches of the trees. All this time, as we "veered about, a man was heaving the lead every

HALIFAX HARBOUR: 1842.

C. D. to J. F.

"two minutes; the depths of water constantly de-"creasing; and nobody self-possessed but Hewitt. "They let go the anchor at last, got out a boat, "and sent her ashore with the fourth officer, the "pilot, and four men aboard, to try and find out "where we were. The pilot had no idea; but

Captain Hewitt.

"Hewitt put his little finger upon a certain part "of the chart, and was as confident of the exact "spot (though he had never been there in his "life) as if he had lived there from infancy. The "boat's return about an hour afterwards proved "him to be quite right. We had got into a place "called the Eastern-passage, in a sudden fog and "through the pilot's folly. We had struck upon "a mud-bank, and driven into a perfect little "pond, surrounded by banks and rocks and shoals "of all kinds: the only safe speck in the place. "Eased by this report, and the assurance that the "tide was past the ebb, we turned in at three "o'clock in the morning, to lie there all night."

HALIFAX.

The next day's landing at Halifax, and delivery of the mails, are sketched in the *Notes;* but not his personal part in what followed. "Then,

Speaker of house of assembly.

"sir, comes a breathless man who has been "already into the ship and out again, shouting "my name as he tears along. I stop, arm in arm "with the little doctor whom I have taken ashore

HALIFAX: 1842.

C. D. to J. F.

"for oysters. The breathless man introduces him-"self as The Speaker of the house of assembly; "*will* drag me away to his house; and *will* have "a carriage and his wife sent down for Kate, who "is laid up with a hideously swoln face. Then "he drags me up to the Governor's house (Lord "Falkland is the governor), and then Heaven "knows where; concluding with both houses of "parliament, which happen to meet for the session "that very day, and are opened by a mock speech "from the throne delivered by the governor, with "one of Lord Grey's sons for his aide-de-camp, "and a great host of officers about him. I wish "you could have seen the crowds cheering the "inimitable* in the streets. I wish you could "have seen judges, law-officers, bishops, and law-"makers welcoming the inimitable. I wish you "could have seen the inimitable shown to a great "elbow-chair by the Speaker's throne, and sitting "alone in the middle of the floor of the house of "commons, the observed of all observers, listen-"ing with exemplary gravity to the queerest "speaking possible, and breaking in spite of him-"self into a smile as he thought of this commence-"ment to the Thousand and One stories in re-

Ovation in Halifax.

In the house of assembly.

* This word, applied to him by his old master, Mr. Giles (Vol. I. p. 36), was for a long time the epithet we called him by.

BOSTON: 1842. C. D. to J. F.

"serve for home and Lincoln's-inn fields and Jack "Straw's-castle.—Ah, Forster! when I *do* come "back again!——"

BOSTON.

He resumed his letter at Tremont-house on Saturday the 28th of January, having reached Boston that day week at five in the afternoon; and as his first American experience is very lightly glanced at in the *Notes*, a fuller picture will perhaps be welcome. "As the Cunard boats have a "wharf of their own at the custom-house, and "that a narrow one, we were a long time (an hour "at least) working in. I was standing in full fig "on the paddle-box beside the captain, staring "about me, when suddenly, long before we were "moored to the wharf, a dozen men came leap-"ing on board at the peril of their lives, with "great bundles of newspapers under their arms; "worsted comforters (very much the worse for "wear) round their necks; and so forth. 'Aha!' "says I, 'this is like our London-bridge': believ-"ing of course that these visitors were news-boys.

Incursion of editors.

"But what do you think of their being EDITORS? "And what do you think of their tearing violently "up to me and beginning to shake hands like "madmen? Oh! If you could have seen how I "wrung their wrists! And if you could but know "how I hated one man in very dirty gaiters, and "with very protruding upper teeth, who said to all "comers after him, 'So you've been introduced to "'our friend Dickens—eh?' There was one among "them, though, who really was of use; a Doctor "S, editor of the ——. He ran off here (two "miles at least), and ordered rooms and dinner. "And in course of time Kate, and I, and Lord "Mulgrave (who was going back to his regiment "at Montreal on Monday, and had agreed to live "with us in the meanwhile) sat down in a spa-"cious and handsome room to a very handsome "dinner, 'bating peculiarities of putting on table, "and had forgotten the ship entirely. A Mr. "Alexander, to whom I had written from England "promising to sit for a portrait, was on board "directly we touched the land, and brought us "here in his carriage. Then, after sending a pre-"sent of most beautiful flowers, he left us to our-"selves, and we thanked him for it."

BOSTON: 1842. C. D. to J. F.

At Tremont-house.

What further he had to say of that week's experience, finds its first public utterance here. "How can I tell you," he continues, "what has "happened since that first day? How can I "give you the faintest notion of my reception "here; of the crowds that pour in and out the "whole day; of the people that line the streets "when I go out; of the cheering when I went to

The welcome.

Boston: 1842.

C. D. to J. F.

Proposed dinners and balls.

"the theatre; of the copies of verses, letters of "congratulation, welcomes of all kinds, balls, din- "ners, assemblies without end? There is to be "a public dinner to me here in Boston, next "Tuesday, and great dissatisfaction has been "given to the many by the high price (three "pounds sterling each) of the tickets. There is "to be a ball next Monday week at New York, "and 150 names appear on the list of the com- "mittee. There is to be a dinner in the same "place, in the same week, to which I have had "an invitation with every known name in America "appended to it. But what can I tell you about "any of these things which will give you the "slightest notion of the enthusiastic greeting they "give me, or the cry that runs through the whole

Deputations.

"country! I have had deputations from the Far "West, who have come from more than two thou- "sand miles distance: from the lakes, the rivers, the "back-woods, the log-houses, the cities, factories, "villages, and towns. Authorities from nearly all "the States have written to me. I have heard "from the universities, congress, senate, and bo- "dies, public and private, of every sort and kind. "'It is no nonsense, and no common feeling,'

Dr. Channing to C. D.

"wrote Dr. Channing to me yesterday. 'It is all "'heart. There never was, and never will be, such "'a triumph.' And it is a good thing, is it not, "... . to find those fancies it has given me and "you the greatest satisfaction to think of, at the "core of it all? It makes my heart quieter, and "me a more retiring, sober, tranquil man to watch "the effect of those thoughts in all this noise and "hurry, even than if I sat, pen in hand, to put "them down for the first time. I feel, in the best "aspects of this welcome, something of the pre-"sence and influence of that spirit which directs "my life, and through a heavy sorrow has pointed "upwards with unchanging finger for more than "four years past. And if I know my heart, not "twenty times this praise would move me to an "act of folly." . . . .

BOSTON: 1842. C. D. to J. F.

Effect upon himself.

There were but two days more before the post left for England, and the close of this part of his letter sketched the engagements that awaited him on leaving Boston. "We leave here next Satur-"day. We go to a place called Worcester, about "75 miles off, to the house of the governor of "this place; and stay with him all Sunday. On "Monday we go on by railroad about 50 miles "further to a town called Springfield, where I am "met by a 'reception committee' from Hartford "20 miles further, and carried on by the multi-"tude: I am sure I don't know how, but I shouldn't

Engagements.

BOSTON: 1842.

C. D. to J. F.

Public appearances.

"wonder if they appear with a triumphal car. On "Wednesday I have a public dinner there. On "Friday I shall be obliged to present myself in "public again, at a place called Newhaven, about "30 miles further. On Saturday evening I hope "to be at New York; and there I shall stay ten "days or a fortnight. You will suppose that I "have enough to do. I am sitting for a portrait "and for a bust. I have the correspondence of a "secretary of state, and the engagements of a "fashionable physician. I have a secretary whom "I take on with me. He is a young man of the "name of Q; was strongly recommended to me; "is most modest, obliging, silent, and willing; "and does his work *well*. He boards and lodges "at my expense when we travel; and his salary "is ten dollars per month—about two pounds five "of our English money. There will be dinners "and balls at Washington, Philadelphia, Balti-"more, and I believe everywhere. In Canada, I "have promised to *play* at the theatre with the "officers, for the benefit of a charity. We are al-"ready weary, at times, past all expression; and "I finish this by means of a pious fraud. We "were engaged to a party, and have written to "say we are both desperately ill. . . . . . . 'Well,' "I can fancy you saying, 'but about his impres-

A secretary engaged.

"'sions of Boston and the Americans?'—Of the "latter, I will not say a word until I have seen "more of them, and have gone into the interior. "I will only say, now, that we have never yet "been required to dine at a table d'hôte; that, "thus far, our rooms are as much our own here, "as they would be at the Clarendon; that but for "an odd phrase now and then—such as *Snap of* "*cold weather;* a *tongue-y man* for a talkative fel-"low; *Possible?* as a solitary interrogation; and "*Yes?* for indeed—I should have marked, so far, "no difference whatever between the parties here "and those I have left behind. The women are "very beautiful, but they soon fade; the general "breeding is neither stiff nor forward; the good "nature, universal. If you ask the way to a place "—of some common waterside man, who don't "know you from Adam—he turns and goes with "you. Universal deference is paid to ladies; and "they walk about at all seasons, wholly unpro-"tected. . . . This hotel is a trifle smaller than "Finsbury-square; and is made so infernally hot "(I use the expression advisedly) by means of a "furnace with pipes running through the passages, "that we can hardly bear it. There are no cur-"tains to the beds, or to the bedroom windows. "I am told there never are, hardly, all through

BOSTON: 1842.

C. D. to J. F.

Bostonians.

Phrases.

General characteristics.

Hotels.

Boston: 1842.

C. D. to J. F.

Bedrooms.

"America. The bed-rooms are indeed very bare "of furniture. Ours is nearly as large as your "great room, and has a wardrobe in it of painted "wood not larger (I appeal to K) than an Eng-"lish watch box. I slept in this room for two "nights, quite satisfied with the belief that it was "a shower bath."

The last addition made to this letter, from which many vividest pages of the *Notes* (among them the bright quaint picture of Boston streets) were taken with small alteration, bore date the 29th of January. "I hardly know what to add "to all this long and unconnected history. Dana, "the author of that *Two Years before the Mast*," (a book which I had praised much to him, thinking it like De Foe) "is a very nice fellow indeed; "and in appearance not at all the man you would "expect. He is short, mild-looking, and has a "care-worn face. His father is exactly like George "Cruikshank after a night's jollity—only shorter. "The professors at the Cambridge university, "Longfellow, Felton, Jared Sparks, are noble fel-"lows. So is Kenyon's friend, Ticknor. Bancroft "is a famous man; a straightforward, manly, "earnest heart; and talks much of you, which is "a great comfort. Doctor Channing I will tell "you more of, after I have breakfasted alone with "him next Wednesday. . . . Sumner is of great

Personal notices.

"service to me. . . . The president of the Senate "here presides at my dinner on Tuesday. Lord "Mulgrave lingered with us till last Tuesday (we "had our little captain to dinner on the Monday), "and then went on to Canada. Kate is quite "well, and so is Anne, whose smartness surpasses "belief. They yearn for home, and so do I.

BOSTON: 1842. C. D. to J. F.

"Of course you will not see in the papers any "true account of our voyage, for they keep the "dangers of the passage, when there are any, very "quiet. I observed so many perils peculiar to "steamers that I am still undecided whether we "shall not return by one of the New York liners. "On the night of the storm, I was wondering "within myself where we should be, if the chim-"ney were blown overboard: in which case, it "needs no great observation to discover that the "vessel must be instantly on fire from stem to "stern. When I went on deck next day, I saw "that it was held up by a perfect forest of chains "and ropes, which had been rigged in the night. "Hewitt told me (when we were on shore, not "before) that they had men lashed, hoisted up, "and swinging there, all through the gale, getting "these stays about it. This is not agreeable—"is it?

Perils of steamers.

"I wonder whether you will remember that

A home thought.

BOSTON: 1842. C. D. to J. F.

"next Tuesday is my birthday! This letter will "leave here that morning.

"On looking back through these sheets, I am "astonished to find how little I have told you, "and how much I have, even now, in store which "shall be yours by word of mouth. The American "poor, the American factories, the institutions of "all kinds—I have a book, already. There is no "man in this town, or in this State of New Eng-"land, who has not a blazing fire and a meat "dinner every day of his life. A flaming sword "in the air would not attract so much attention

Beggary.

"as a beggar in the streets. There are no charity "uniforms, no wearisome repetition of the same

Charity.

"dull ugly dress, in that blind school.* All are "attired after their own tastes, and every boy and "girl has his or her individuality as distinct and "unimpaired as you would find it in their own "homes. At the theatres, all the ladies sit in the "fronts of the boxes. The gallery are as quiet "as the dress circle at dear Drury-lane. A man "with seven heads would be no sight at all,

Education.

"compared with one who couldn't read and "write.

"I won't speak (I say 'speak'! I wish I could)

* His descriptions of this school, and of the case of Laura Bridgeman, will be found in the *Notes;* and have therefore been, of course, omitted here.

"about the dear precious children, because I "know how much we shall hear about them when "we receive those letters from home for which "we long so ardently."

BOSTON: 1842. C. D. to J. F

Unmistakeably to be seen, in this earliest of his letters, is the quite fresh and unalloyed impression first received by him at this memorable visit; and it is due, as well to himself as to the great country which welcomed him, that this should be considered independently of any modification it afterwards underwent. Of the fervency and universality of the welcome there could indeed be no doubt, and as little that it sprang from feelings honorable both to giver and receiver. The sources of Dickens's popularity in England were in truth multiplied many-fold in America. The hearty, cordial, and humane side of his genius, had fascinated them quite as much; but there was also something beyond this. The cheerful temper that had given new beauty to the commonest forms of life, the abounding humour which had added largely to all innocent enjoyment, the honorable and in those days rare distinction of America which left no home in the Union inaccessible to such advantages, had made Dickens the object everywhere of grateful admiration, for the most part of personal affection.

How first impressed.

Reasons for the greeting

Why so popular.

BOSTON: 1842.

But even this was not all. I do not say it either to lessen or to increase the value of the tribute, but to express simply what it was; and there cannot be a question that the young English author, whom by his language they claimed equally for their own, was almost universally regarded by the Americans as a kind of embodied protest against what they believed to be worst in the institutions of England, depressing and overshadowing in a social sense, and adverse to purely intellectual influences. In all the papers of every grade in the Union, of which many were sent to me at the time, the feeling of triumph over the mother-country in this particular is everywhere predominant. You worship titles, they said, and military heroes, and millionaires, and we of the New World want to show you, by extending the kind of homage that the Old World reserves for kings and conquerors, to a young man with nothing to distinguish him but his heart and his genius, what it is we think in these parts worthier of honour, than birth, or wealth, a title, or a sword. Well, there was something in this too, apart from a mere crowing over the mother-country. The Americans had honestly more than a common share in the triumphs of a genius, which in more than one sense had made the deserts and wildernesses of life to blossom like the

What was welcomed in C. D.

Old world and New world.

BOSTON: 1842.

rose. They were entitled to select for a welcome, as emphatic as they might please to render it, the writer who pre-eminently in his generation had busied himself to "detect and save," in human creatures, such sparks of virtue as misery or vice had not availed to extinguish; to discover what is beautiful and comely, under what commonly passes for the ungainly and the deformed; to draw happiness and hopefulness from despair itself; and, above all, so to have made known to his own countrymen the wants and sufferings of the poor, the ignorant, and the neglected, that they could be left in absolute neglect no more. "A triumph has been prepared for him," wrote Mr. Ticknor to our dear friend Kenyon, "in "which the whole country will join. He will have "a progress through the States unequalled since "Lafayette's." Daniel Webster told the Americans that Dickens had done more already to ameliorate the condition of the English poor than all the statesmen Great Britain had sent into parliament. His sympathies are such, exclaimed Doctor Channing, as to recommend him in an especial manner to us. He seeks out that class, in order to benefit them, with whom American institutions and laws sympathize most strongly; and it is in the passions, sufferings, and virtues of the mass that he has found his subjects of most thrilling

Ticknor to Kenyon.

Webster as to C. D.

BOSTON: 1842.

Channing as to C. D.

interest. "He shows that life in its rudest form "may wear a tragic grandeur; that amidst follies "and excesses, provoking laughter or scorn, the "moral feelings do not wholly die; and that the "haunts of the blackest crime are sometimes "lighted up by the presence and influence of the "noblest souls. His pictures have a tendency to "awaken sympathy with our race, and to change "the unfeeling indifference which has prevailed "towards the depressed multitude, into a sorrowful "and indignant sensibility to their wrongs and woes."

Subsequent disappointments.

Whatever may be the turn which we are to see the welcome take, by dissatisfaction that arose on both sides, it is well that we should thus understand what in its first manifestations was honorable to both. Dickens had his disappointments, and the Americans had theirs; but what was really genuine in the first enthusiasm remained without grave alloy from either; and the letters, as I proceed to give them, will so naturally explain and illustrate the mis-understanding as to require little further comment. I am happy to be able here to place on record facsimiles of the invitations to the public entertainments in New York which reached him before he quitted Boston. The mere signatures suffice to show how universal the welcome was from that great city of the Union.

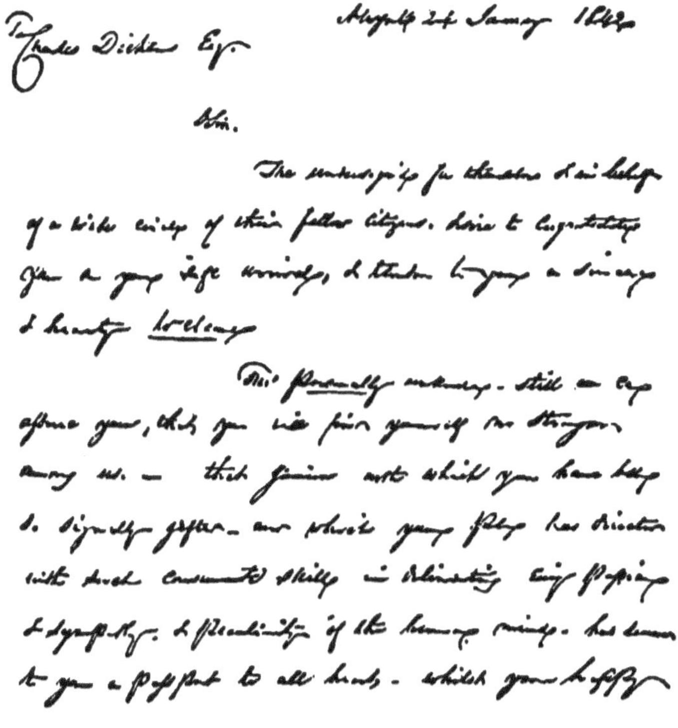
Allegheny 24 January 1842.

To Charles Dickens Esq.

Sir.

The undersigned for themselves & in behalf of a wider circle of their fellow citizens, desire to congratulate you on your safe arrival, & tender to you a sincere & hearty welcome.

Tho' personally unknown — still we can assure you, that you will find yourself no stranger among us. — that genius and art which you have been so signally gifted — and which your pen has directed with such consummate skill in delineating every passion & sympathy & peculiarity of the human mind — has become to you a passport to all hearts — which your happy

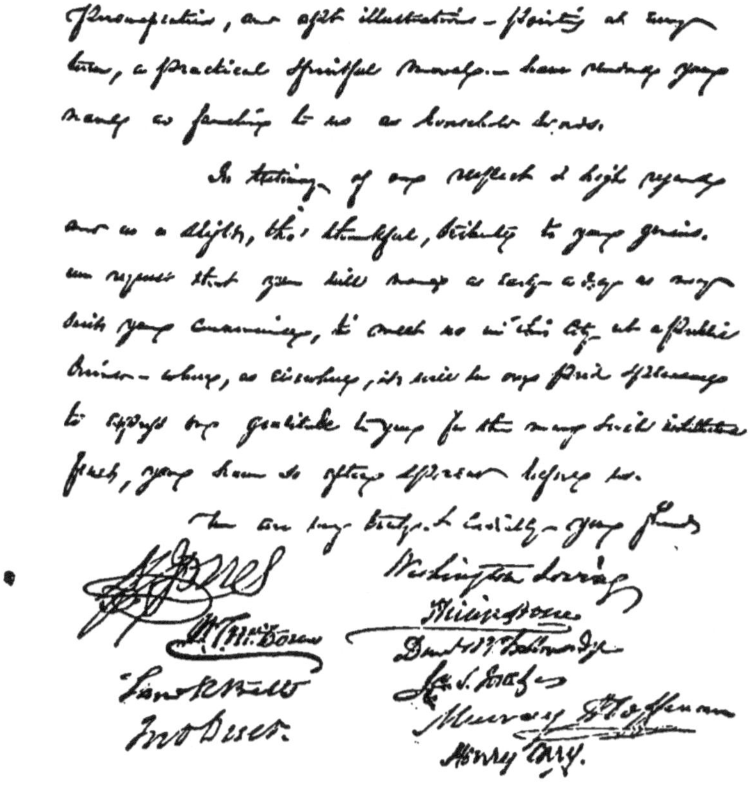

personification, and apt illustration — pointing at every turn, a practical spiritful moral — have rendered your name as familiar to us as household words.

In testimony of our respect & high regard and as a slight, tho' thankful, tribute to your genius, we request that you will name as early a day as may suit your convenience, to meet us in this city at a public dinner — where, as elsewhere, it will be our pride & pleasure to express our gratitude to you for the many social intellectual feasts, you have so often spread before us.

We are very truly & cordially your friends

Washington Irving

Philip Hone

Jno Duer

Henry Cary

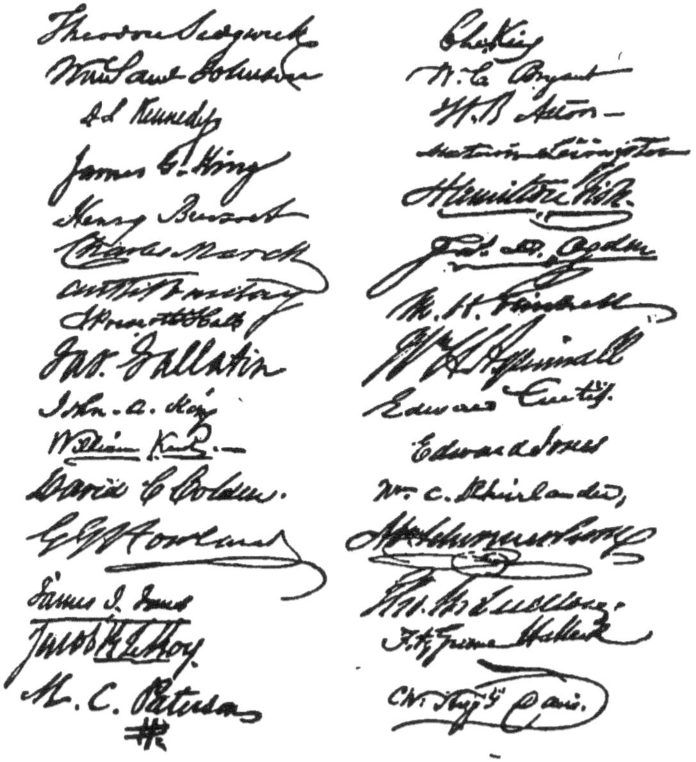

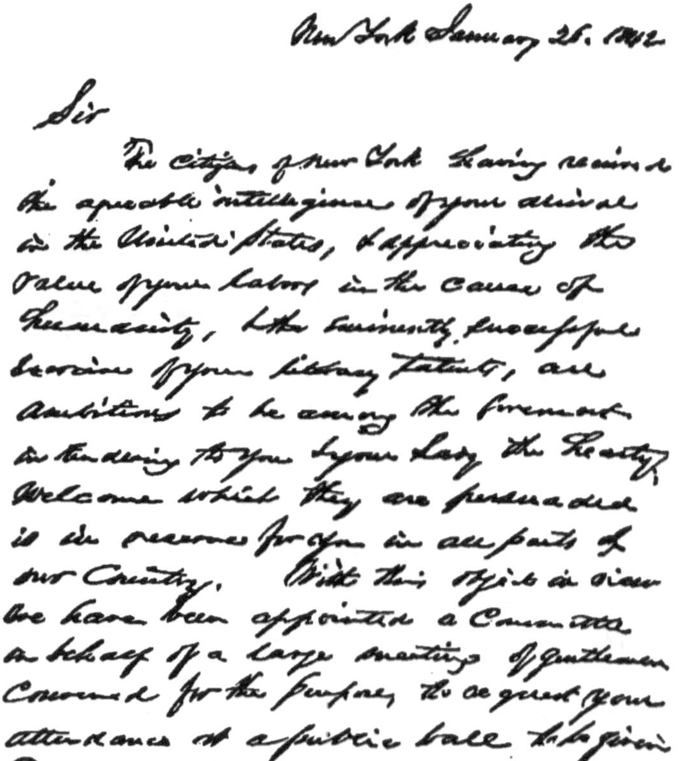

New York January 25. 1842.

Sir

The citizens of New York having received the agreeable intelligence of your arrival in the United States, & appreciating the value of your labors in the cause of humanity, & the eminently successful exercise of your literary talents, are ambitious to be among the foremost in tendering to you & your Lady the hearty welcome which they are persuaded is in reserve for you in all parts of our Country. With this object in view we have been appointed a Committee on behalf of a large meeting of gentlemen convened for the purpose, to request your attendance at a public ball to be given

To Charles Dickens Esq &c

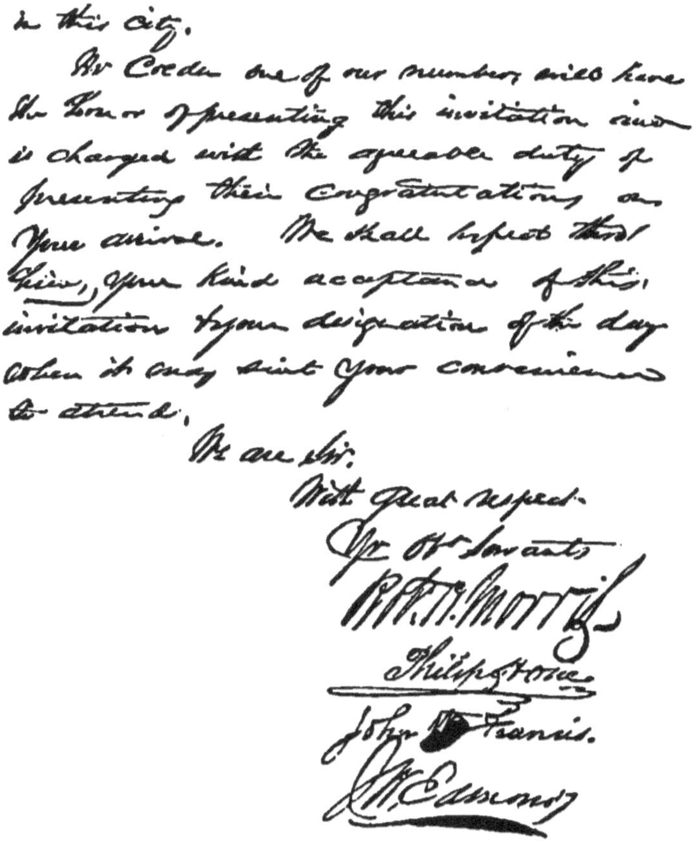

in this city.

Mr Colden one of our members will have the honor of presenting this invitation and is charged with the agreeable duty of presenting their congratulations on your arrival. We shall expect thro' him, your kind acceptance of this invitation & your designation of the day when it may suit your convenience to attend.

We are Sir:
With great respect
Yr Obt Servants
Robt. H. Morris
Philip Hone
John W. Francis
J. W. Edmonds

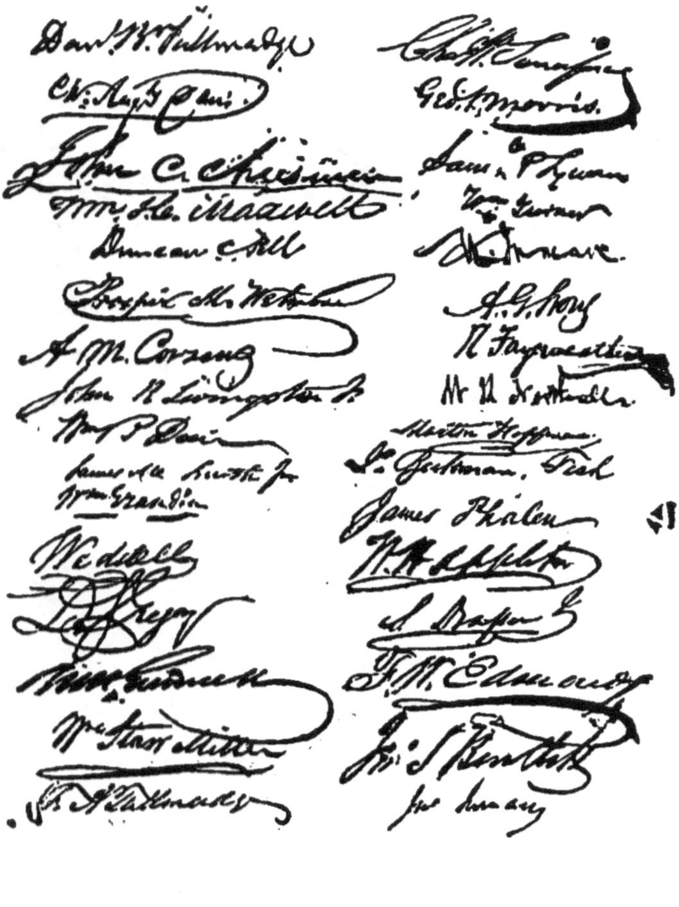

CHAPTER XX.

SECOND IMPRESSIONS OF AMERICA.

1842.

NEW YORK: 1842. Second letter.

HIS second letter, radiant with the same kindly warmth that gave always pre-eminent charm to his genius, was dated from the Carlton-hotel, New York, on the 14th February, but its only allusion of any public interest was to the beginning of his agitation of the question of international copyright. He went to America with no express intention of starting this question in any way; and certainly with no belief that such remark upon it as a person in his position could alone be expected to make, would be resented strongly by any sections of the American people. But he was not long left in doubt on this head. He had spoken upon it twice publicly, "to the "great indignation of some of the editors here, "who are attacking me for so doing, right and "left." On the other hand all the best men had assured him, that, if only at once followed up in

International copyright.

NEW YORK: 1842. England, the blow struck might bring about a change in the law; and, yielding to the pleasant hope that the best men could be a match for the worst, he urged me to enlist on his side what force I could, and in particular, as he had made Scott's claim his war cry, to bring Lockhart into the field. I could not do much, but I did what I could.

Three days later he began another letter; and, as this will be entirely new to the reader, I shall print it as it reached me, with only such omission of matter concerning myself as I think it my duty, however reluctantly, to make throughout these extracts. There was nothing in its personal details, or in those relating to international copyright, available for his *Notes;* from which they were excluded by the two rules he observed in that book, the first to be altogether silent as to the copyright discussion, and the second to abstain from all mention of individuals. But there can be no harm here in violating either rule, for, as Sydney Smith said with his humorous sadness, "We are all dead now."

Third letter. "Carlton-house, New York: Thursday, February Seventeenth, 1842. . . . . . As there is a "sailing-packet from here to England to-morrow "which is warranted (by the owners) to be a "marvellous fast sailer, and as it appears most "probable that she will reach home (I write the "word with a pang) before the Cunard steamer "of next month, I indite this letter. And lest "this letter should reach you before another letter "which I dispatched from here last Monday, let "me say in the first place that I *did* dispatch a "brief epistle to you on that day, together with "a newspaper, and a pamphlet touching the Boz "ball; and that I put in the post-office at Boston "another newspaper for you containing an ac- "count of the dinner, which was just about to "come off, you remember, when I wrote to you "from that city.

NEW YORK: 1842. C. D. to J. F.

"It was a most superb affair; and the speak- "ing *admirable*. Indeed the general talent for "public speaking here, is one of the most striking "of the things that force themselves upon an "Englishman's notice. As every man looks on to "being a member of Congress, every man prepares "himself for it; and the result is quite surprising. "You will observe one odd custom—the drinking "of sentiments. It is quite extinct with us, but "here everybody is expected to be prepared with "an epigram as a matter of course.

The dinner at Boston.

"We left Boston on the fifth, and went away "with the governor of the city to stay till Monday

New York: 1842. C. D. to J. F. At Worcester.

"at his house at Worcester. He married a sister "of Bancroft's, and another sister of Bancroft's "went down with us. The village of Worcester "is one of the prettiest in New England. . . . On "Monday morning at nine o'clock we started again "by railroad and went on to Springfield, where a "deputation of two were waiting, and everything "was in readiness that the utmost attention could "suggest. Owing to the mildness of the weather, "the Connecticut river was 'open,' videlicet not "frozen, and they had a steamboat ready to carry "us on to Hartford; thus saving a land-journey "of only twenty-five miles, but on such roads at "this time of year that it takes nearly twelve "hours to accomplish! The boat was very small, "the river full of floating blocks of ice, and the "depth where we went (to avoid the ice and the "current) not more than a few inches. After two "hours and a half of this queer travelling we got "to Hartford. There, there was quite an English "inn; except in respect of the bed-rooms, which "are always uncomfortable; and the best commit-"tee of management that has yet presented itself. "They kept us more quiet, and were more con-"siderate and thoughtful, even to their own ex-"clusion, than any I have yet had to deal with. "Kate's face being horribly bad, I determined to

From Springfield to Hartford.

Queer travelling.

At Hartford.

"give her a rest here; and accordingly wrote to "get rid of my engagement at Newhaven, on that "plea. We remained in this town until the "eleventh: holding a formal levee every day for "two hours, and receiving on each from two "hundred to three hundred people. At five "o'clock on the afternoon of the eleventh, we set "off (still by railroad) for Newhaven, which we "reached about eight o'clock. The moment we "had had tea, we were forced to open another "levee for the students and professors of the col- "lege (the largest in the States), and the towns- "people. I suppose we shook hands, before going "to bed, with considerably more than five hundred "people; and I stood, as a matter of course, the "whole time . . . .

NEW YORK: 1842.

C. D. to J. F.

Levees at Hartford and Newhaven.

"Now, the deputation of two had come on "with us from Hartford; and at Newhaven there "was another committee; and the immense fatigue "and worry of all this, no words can exaggerate. "We had been in the morning over jails and deaf "and dumb asylums; had stopped on the journey "at a place called Wallingford, where a whole "town had turned out to see me, and to gratify "whose curiosity the train stopped expressly; had "had a day of great excitement and exertion on "the Thursday (this being Friday); and were in-

At Wallingford.

NEW YORK: 1842.

C. D. to J. F.

"expressibly worn out. And when at last we got "to bed and were 'going' to fall asleep, the "choristers of the college turned out in a body, "under the window, and serenaded us! We had "had, by the bye, another serenade at Hartford, "from a Mr. Adams (a nephew of John Quincey "Adams) and a German friend. *They* were most "beautiful singers: and when they began, in the "dead of the night, in a long, musical, echoing "passage outside our chamber door; singing, in "low voices to guitars, about home and absent "friends and other topics that they knew would "interest us; we were more moved than I can tell "you. In the midst of my sentimentality though, "a thought occurred to me which made me laugh "so immoderately that I was obliged to cover my "face with the bedclothes. 'Good Heavens!' I "said to Kate, 'what a monstrously ridiculous and "'commonplace appearance my boots must have, "'outside the door!' I never *was* so impressed "with a sense of the absurdity of boots, in all "my life.

Serenades at Hartford and Newhaven.

Absurdity of boots.

"The Newhaven serenade was not so good; "though there were a great many voices, and a "'reg'lar' band. It hadn't the heart of the other. "Before it was six hours old, we were dressing "with might and main, and making ready for our "departure: it being a drive of twenty minutes to "the steamboat, and the hour of sailing nine "o'clock. After a hasty breakfast we started off; "and after another levee on the deck (actually on "the deck), and 'three times three for Dickens,' "moved towards New York.

NEW YORK: 1842. C. D. to J. F.

"I was delighted to find on board a Mr. "Felton whom I had known at Boston. He is "the Greek professor at Cambridge, and was "going on to the ball and dinner. Like most "men of his class whom I have seen, he is "a most delightful fellow—unaffected, hearty, "genial, jolly; quite an Englishman of the best "sort. We drank all the porter on board, ate all "the cold pork and cheese, and were very merry "indeed. I should have told you, in its proper "place, that both at Hartford and Newhaven a re-"gular bank was subscribed, by these committees, "for *all* my expenses. No bill was to be got at "the bar, and everything was paid for. But as I "would on no account suffer this to be done, "I stoutly and positively refused to budge an inch "until Mr. Q should have received the bills from "the landlord's own hands, and paid them to the "last farthing. Finding it impossible to move me, "they suffered me, most unwillingly, to carry the "point.

Cornelius C. Felton.

New York: 1842.

C. D. to J. F. The Carlton hotel.

"About half past 2, we arrived here. In half "an hour more, we reached this hotel, where a "very splendid suite of rooms was prepared for "us; and where everything is very comfortable, "and no doubt (as at Boston) *enormously* dear. "Just as we sat down to dinner, David Colden "made his appearance; and when he had gone, "and we were taking our wine, Washington Irving "came in alone, with open arms. And here he "stopped, until ten o'clock at night." (Through Lord Jeffrey, with whom he was connected by marriage, and Macready, of whom he was the cordial friend, we already knew Mr. Colden; and his subsequent visits to Europe led to many years' intimate intercourse, greatly enjoyed by us both.) "Having got so far, I shall divide my discourse "into four points. First, the ball. Secondly, some "slight specimens of a certain phase of character "in the Americans. Thirdly, international copy-"right. Fourthly, my life here, and projects to be "carried out while I remain.

Washington Irving.

David Colden.

"Firstly, the ball. It came off last Monday "(vide pamphlet). 'At a quarter past 9, exactly,' "(I quote the printed order of proceeding), we "were waited upon by 'David Colden, Esquire, "'and General George Morris;' habited, the former "in full ball costume, the latter in the full dress "uniform of Heaven knows what regiment of "militia. The general took Kate, Colden gave "his arm to me, and we proceeded downstairs to "a carriage at the door, which took us to the "stage door of the theatre: greatly to the disap-"pointment of an enormous crowd who were be-"setting the main door, and making a most "tremendous hullaballoo. The scene on our en-"trance was very striking. There were three "thousand people present in full dress; from the "roof to the floor, the theatre was decorated mag-"nificently; and the light, glitter, glare, show, "noise, and cheering, baffle my descriptive powers. "We were walked in through the centre of the "centre dress-box, the front whereof was taken "out for the occasion; so to the back of the stage, "where the mayor and other dignitaries received "us; and we were then paraded all round the "enormous ball-room, twice, for the gratification "of the many-headed. That done, we began to "dance—Heaven knows how we did it, for there "was no room. And we continued dancing until, "being no longer able even to stand, we slipped "away quietly, and came back to the hotel. All "the documents connected with this extraordinary "festival (quite unparalleled here) we have pre-"served; so you may suppose that on this head

NEW YORK: 1842.

C. D. to J. F.

The ball.

Description of it.

NEW YORK: 1842. C. D. to J. F.

"alone we shall have enough to show you when "we come home. The bill of fare for supper, "is, in its amount and extent, quite a curiosity.

A phase of character.

"Now, the phase of character in the Ameri- "cans which amuses me most, was put before me "in its most amusing shape by the circumstances "attending this affair. I had noticed it before, "and have since, but I cannot better illustrate it "than by reference to this theme. Of course I "can do nothing but in some shape or other it "gets into the newspapers. All manner of lies "get there, and occasionally a truth so twisted "and distorted that it has as much resemblance "to the real fact as Quilp's leg to Taglioni's. But "with this ball to come off, the newspapers were "if possible unusually loquacious; and in their "accounts of me, and my seeings, sayings, and "doings on the Saturday night and Sunday be- "fore, they describe my manner, mode of speak- "ing, dressing, and so forth. In doing this, they "report that I am a very charming fellow (of "course), and have a very free and easy way with "me; 'which,' say they, 'at first amused a few "'fashionables;' but soon pleased them exceed- "ingly. Another paper, coming after the ball, "dwells upon its splendour and brilliancy; hugs "itself and its readers upon all that Dickens saw;

Newspaper accounts of the ball:

"and winds up by gravely expressing its conviction, that Dickens was never in such society in England as he has seen in New York, and that its high and striking tone cannot fail to make an indelible impression on his mind! For the same reason I am always represented, whenever I appear in public, as being 'very pale;' 'apparently thunderstruck;' and utterly confounded by all I see. . . . You recognize the queer vanity which is at the root of all this? I have plenty of stories in connection with it to amuse you with when I return."

NEW YORK: 1842. C. D. to J. F.

and of the principal guest.

"*Twenty-fourth February.*

"It is unnecessary to say . . . . that this letter "*didn't* come by the sailing packet, and *will* come "by the Cunard boat. After the ball I was laid "up with a very bad sore throat, which confined "me to the house four whole days; and as I was "unable to write, or indeed to do anything but "doze and drink lemonade, I missed the ship. . . "I have still a horrible cold, and so has Kate, "but in other respects we are all right. I proceed "to my third head: the international copyright "question.

"I believe there is no country, on the face of "the earth, where there is less freedom of opinion

Opinion in America.

NEW YORK: 1842.

C. D. to J. F.

"on any subject in reference to which there is a "broad difference of opinion, than in this.— "There!—I write the words with reluctance, dis- "appointment, and sorrow; but I believe it from "the bottom of my soul. I spoke, as you know,

International copyright.

"of international copyright, at Boston; and I spoke "of it again at Hartford. My friends were para- "lysed with wonder at such audacious daring. "The notion that I, a man alone by himself, in "America, should venture to suggest to the Ame- "ricans that there was one point on which they "were neither just to their own countrymen nor "to us, actually struck the boldest dumb! Wash-

American authors.

"ington Irving, Prescott, Hoffman, Bryant, Halleck, "Dana, Washington Allston—every man who writes "in this country is devoted to the question, and "not one of them *dares* to raise his voice and "complain of the atrocious state of the law. It is "nothing that of all men living I am the greatest "loser by it. It is nothing that I have a claim to "speak and be heard. The wonder is that a "breathing man can be found with temerity enough "to suggest to the Americans the possibility of "their having done wrong. I wish you could "have seen the faces that I saw, down both sides "of the table at Hartford, when I began to talk "about Scott. I wish you could have heard how

New York: 1842. — C. D. to J. F.

"I gave it out. My blood so boiled as I thought "of the monstrous injustice that I felt as if I were "twelve feet high when I thrust it down their "throats.

Outcry against the guest of the nation.

"I had no sooner made that second speech "than such an outcry began (for the purpose of "deterring me from doing the like in this city) as "an Englishman can form no notion of. Anony-"mous letters; verbal dissuasions; newspaper at-"tacks making Colt (a murderer who is attract-"ing great attention here) an angel by comparison "with me; assertions that I was no gentleman, "but a mere mercenary scoundrel; coupled with "the most monstrous mis-representations relative "to my design and purpose in visiting the United "States; came pouring in upon me every day. "The dinner committee here (composed of the "first gentlemen in America, remember that) were "so dismayed, that they besought me not to pur-"sue the subject *although they every one agreed* "*with me*. I answered that I would. That nothing "should deter me. . . . That the shame was theirs, "not mine; and that as I would not spare them "when I got home, I would not be silenced here. "Accordingly, when the night came, I asserted "my right, with all the means I could command "to give it dignity, in face, manner, or words;

Asked not to speak on copyright.

Declines to comply.

New York: 1842. | C. D. to J. F.

"and I believe that if you could have seen and "heard me, you would have loved me better for "it than ever you did in your life.

New York Herald.

"The *New York Herald*, which you will re-"ceive with this, is the *Satirist* of America; but "having a great circulation (on account of its "commercial intelligence and early news) it can "afford to secure the best reporters.... My speech "is done, upon the whole, with remarkable ac-"curacy. There are a great many typographical "errors in it; and by the omission of one or two "words, or the substitution of one word for "another, it is often materially weakened. Thus "I did not say that I 'claimed' my right, but that "I 'asserted' it; and I did not say that I had "'some claim,' but that I had 'a most righteous "'claim,' to speak. But altogether it is very cor-"rect."

Speech at dinner.

Washington Irving in the chair.

Washington Irving was chairman of this dinner, and having from the first a dread that he should break down in his speech, the catastrophe came accordingly. Near him sat the Cambridge professor who had come with Dickens by boat from Newhaven, with whom already a warm friendship had been formed that lasted for life, and who has pleasantly sketched what happened. Mr.

Felton saw Irving constantly in the interval of preparation, and could not but despond at his daily iterated foreboding of *I shall certainly break down:* though, besides the real dread, there was a sly humour which heightened its whimsical horror with an irresistible drollery. But the professor plucked up hope a little when the night came, and he saw that Irving had laid under his plate the manuscript of his speech. During dinner, nevertheless, his old foreboding cry was still heard, and "at last the moment arrived; Mr. Irving rose; "and the deafening and long-continued applause "by no means lessened his apprehension. He be-"gan in his pleasant voice; got through two or "three sentences pretty easily, but in the next "hesitated; and, after one or two attempts to go "on, gave it up, with a graceful allusion to the "tournament and the troop of knights all armed "and eager for the fray; and ended with the toast "CHARLES DICKENS, THE GUEST OF THE NATION. "*There!* said he, as he resumed his seat amid "applause as great as had greeted his rising, "*There! I told you I should break down, and I've* "*done it!*" He was in London a few months later, on his way to Spain; and I heard Thomas Moore describe* at Rogers's table the difficulty

NEW YORK: 1842.

Irving's break-down.

* On the 22nd of May, 1842.

NEW YORK: 1842.

At a dinner in London same year.

there had been to overcome his reluctance, because of this break-down, to go to the dinner of the Literary Fund on the occasion of Prince Albert's presiding. "However," said Moore, "I "told him only to attempt a few words, and I "suggested what they should be, and he said "he'd never thought of anything so easy, and he "went and did famously." I knew very well, as I listened, that this had *not* been the result; but as the distinguished American had found himself, on this second occasion, not among orators as in New York, but among men as unable as himself to speak in public, and equally able to do better things,* he was doubtless more reconciled to his own failure. I have been led to this digression by Dickens's silence on his friend's break-down. He had so great a love for Irving that it was painful to speak of him as at any disadvantage,

Laman Blanchard to J. F.

* The dinner was on the 10th of May, and early the following morning I had a letter about it from Mr. Blanchard, containing these words: "Washington Irving couldn't utter "a word for trembling, and Moore was as little as usual. "But, poor Tom Campbell, great Heavens! what a spectacle! "Amid roars of laughter he began a sentence three times "about something that Dugald Stewart or Lord Bacon had "said, and never could get beyond those words. The Prince "was capital, though deucedly frightened. He seems un-"affected and amiable, as well as very clever."

and of the New York dinner he wrote only in its connection with his own copyright speeches. NEW YORK: 1842.

"The effect of all this copyright agitation at "least has been to awaken a great sensation on "both sides of the subject; the respectable news-"papers and reviews taking up the cudgels as "strongly in my favour, as the others have done "against me. Some of the vagabonds take great "credit to themselves (grant us patience!) for hav-"ing made me popular by publishing my books "in newspapers: as if there were no England, no "Scotland, no Germany, no place but America in "the whole world. A splendid satire upon this "kind of trash has just occurred. A man came "here yesterday, and demanded, not besought "but demanded, pecuniary assistance; and fairly "bullied Mr. Q for money. When I came home, "I dictated a letter to this effect—that such ap-"plications reached me in vast numbers every day; "that if I were a man of fortune, I could not "render assistance to all who sought it; and that, "depending on my own exertion for all the help "I could give, I regretted to say I could afford "him none. Upon this, my gentleman sits down "and writes me that he is an itinerant bookseller;

Results of copyright speeches.

C. D. to J. F.

A demand for help.

NEW YORK: 1842. C. D. to J. F. A bookseller in distress.

"that he is the first man who sold my books in "New York; that he is distressed in the city where "I am revelling in luxury; that he thinks it rather "strange that the man who wrote *Nickleby* should "be utterly destitute of feeling; and that he would "have me 'take care I don't repent it.' What do "you think of *that?*—as Mac would say. I thought "it such a good commentary, that I dispatched "the letter to the editor of the only English news-"paper here, and told him he might print it if he "liked.

A suggestion.

"I will tell you what *I* should like, my dear "friend, always supposing that your judgment con-"curs with mine; and that you would take the "trouble to get such a document. I should like "to have a short letter addressed to me, by the "principal English authors who signed the inter-"national copyright petition, expressive of their "sense that I have done my duty to the cause. I "am sure I deserve it, but I don't wish it on that "ground. It is because its publication in the best "journals here would unquestionably do great "good. As the gauntlet is down, let us go on.

Henry Clay's opinion.

"Clay has already sent a gentleman to me ex-"press from Washington (where I shall be on the "6th or 7th of next month) to declare his strong "interest in the matter, his cordial approval of "the 'manly' course I have held in reference to it, "and his desire to stir in it if possible. I have "lighted up such a blaze that a meeting of the "foremost people on the other side (very respect-"fully and properly conducted in reference to me, "personally, I am bound to say) was held in this "town 'tother night. And it would be a thousand "pities if we did not strike as hard as we can, "now that the iron is so hot.

NEW YORK: 1842.
C. D. to J. F.

"I have come at last, and it is time I did, to "my life here, and intentions for the future. I "can do nothing that I want to do, go nowhere "where I want to go, and see nothing that I want "to see. If I turn into the street, I am followed "by a multitude. If I stay at home, the house "becomes, with callers, like a fair. If I visit a "public institution, with only one friend, the "directors come down incontinently, waylay me "in the yard, and address me in a long speech. "I go to a party in the evening, and am so in-"closed and hemmed about by people, stand "where I will, that I am exhausted for want of "air. I dine out, and have to talk about every-"thing, to everybody. I go to church for quiet, "and there is a violent rush to the neighbourhood "of the pew I sit in, and the clergyman preaches "*at* me. I take my seat in a railroad car, and

Life in New York.

Distresses of popularity.

NEW YORK: 1842. — C. D. to J. F.

"the very conductor won't leave me alone. I get "out at a station, and can't drink a glass of water, "without having a hundred people looking down my "throat when I open my mouth to swallow. Conceive "what all this is! Then by every post, letters on "letters arrive, all about nothing, and all demand-"ing an immediate answer. This man is offended "because I won't live in his house; and that man "is thoroughly disgusted because I won't go out "more than four times in one evening. I have "no rest or peace, and am in a perpetual worry.

Intentions for the future.

"Under these febrile circumstances, which this "climate especially favors, I have come to the re-"solution that I will not (so far as my will has "anything to do with the matter) accept any more "public entertainments or public recognitions of "any kind, during my stay in the United States; "and in pursuance of this determination I have

Refusal of invitations.

"refused invitations from Philadelphia, Baltimore, "Washington, Virginia, Albany, and Providence. "Heaven knows whether this will be effectual, but "I shall soon see, for on Monday morning the "28th we leave for Philadelphia. There, I shall "only stay three days. Thence we go to Balti-"more, and *there* I shall only stay three days. "Thence to Washington, where we may stay per-"haps ten days; perhaps not so long. Thence to

"Virginia, where we may halt for one day; and "thence to Charleston, where we may pass a week "perhaps; and where we shall very likely remain "until your March letters reach us, through David "Colden. I had a design of going from Charleston "to Columbia in South Carolina, and there en-"gaging a carriage, a baggage-tender and negro "boy to guard the same, and a saddle-horse for "myself—with which caravan I intended going "'right away,' as they say here, into the west, "through the wilds of Kentucky and Tennessee, "across the Alleghany-mountains, and so on until "we should strike the lakes and could get to "Canada. But it has been represented to me "that this is a track only known to travelling mer-"chants; that the roads are bad, the country a "tremendous waste, the inns log-houses, and the "journey one that would play the very devil with "Kate. I am staggered, but not deterred. If I "find it possible to be done in the time, I mean "to do it; being quite satisfied that without some "such dash, I can never be a free agent, or see "anything worth the telling.

NEW YORK: 1842. C. D. to J. F. Going south: and west.

"We mean to return home in a packet-ship—"not a steamer. Her name is the George Wash-"ington, and she will sail from here, for Liverpool, "on the seventh of June. At that season of the

As to return.

New York: 1842. C. D. to J. F.

"year, they are seldom more than three weeks "making the voyage; and I never will trust myself "upon the wide ocean, if it please Heaven, in a "steamer again. When I tell you all that I ob-"served on board that Britannia, I shall astonish "you. Meanwhile, consider two of their dangers.

Dangers incident to steamers.

"First, that if the funnel were blown overboard, "the vessel must instantly be on fire, from stem "to stern: to comprehend which consequence, you "have only to understand that the funnel is more "than 40 feet high, and that at night you see the "solid fire two or three feet above its top. Imagine "this swept down by a strong wind, and picture "to yourself the amount of flame on deck; and "that a strong wind is likely to sweep it down "you soon learn, from the precautions taken to "keep it up in a storm, when it is the first thing

Two named.

"thought of. Secondly, each of these boats con-"sumes between London and Halifax 700 tons of "coals; and it is pretty clear, from this enormous "difference of weight in a ship of only 1200 tons "burden in all, that she must either be too heavy "when she comes out of port, or too light when "she goes in. The daily difference in her rolling, "as she burns the coals out, is something ab-"solutely fearful. Add to all this, that by day "and night she is full of fire and people, that she "has no boats, and that the struggling of that "enormous machinery in a heavy sea seems as "though it would rend her into fragments—and "you may have a pretty con-siderable damned "good sort of a feeble notion that it don't fit no-"how; and that it a'nt calculated to make you "smart, overmuch; and that you don't feel 'special "bright; and by no means first rate; and not at "all tonguey (or disposed for conversation); and "that however rowdy you may be by natur', it "does use you up com-plete, and that's a fact; "and makes you quake considerable, and disposed "toe damn the ĕngīne!—All of which phrases, I "beg to add, are pure Americanisms of the first "water.

NEW YORK: 1842. C. D. to J. F.

Pure Americanisms.

"When we reach Baltimore, we are in the "regions of slavery. It exists there, in its least "shocking and most mitigated form; but there it "is. They whisper, here (they dare only whisper, "you know, and that below their breaths), that on "that place, and all through the South, there is "a dull gloomy cloud on which the very word "seems written. I shall be able to say, one of "these days, that I accepted no public mark of "respect in any place where slavery was;—and "that's something.

Slavery.

"The ladies of America are decidedly and

NEW YORK: 1842. C. D. to J. F. Ladies of America.

"unquestionably beautiful. Their complexions are "not so good as those of Englishwomen; their "beauty does not last so long; and their figures "are very inferior. But they are most beautiful. "I still reserve my opinion of the national char-"acter—just whispering that I tremble for a radical "coming here, unless he is a radical on principle, "by reason and reflection, and from the sense of "right. I fear that if he were anything else, he "would return home a tory. . . . . . I say no more "on that head for two months from this time, "save that I do fear that the heaviest blow ever "dealt at liberty will be dealt by this country, in "the failure of its example to the earth. The "scenes that are passing in Congress now, all "tending to the separation of the States, fill one "with such a deep disgust that I dislike the very "name of Washington (meaning the place, not the "man), and am repelled by the mere thought of "approaching it.

Party conflicts.

"Twenty-seventh February. Sunday.

A Cunard steamer missing.

"There begins to be great consternation here, "in reference to the Cunard packet which (we "suppose) left Liverpool on the fourth. She has "not yet arrived. We scarcely know what to do "with ourselves in our extreme anxiety to get let-

"ters from home. I have really had serious "thoughts of going back to Boston, alone, to be "nearer news. We have determined to remain "here until Tuesday afternoon, if she should not "arrive before, and to send Mr. Q and the lug- "gage on to Philadelphia to-morrow morning. "God grant she may not have gone down: but "every ship that comes in brings intelligence of "a terrible gale (which indeed was felt ashore "here) on the night of the fourteenth; and the "sea-captains swear (not without some prejudice "of course) that no steamer could have lived "through it, supposing her to have been in its "full fury. As there is no steam packet to go to "England, supposing the Caledonia not to arrive, "we are obliged to send our letters by the Garrick "ship, which sails early to-morrow morning. Con- "sequently I must huddle this up, and dispatch it "to the post-office with all speed. I have so much "to say that I could fill quires of paper, which "renders this sudden pull-up the more provoking.

NEW YORK: 1842. C. D. to J. F.

Misgivings.

Non-arrival of Caledonia.

"I have in my portmanteau a petition for an "international copyright law, signed by all the "best American writers with Washington Irving "at their head. They have requested me to hand "it to Clay for presentation, and to back it with "any remarks I may think proper to offer. So

Petition for Congress.

NEW YORK: 1842. — C. D. to J. F.

"'Hoo-roar for the principle, as the money-lender "'said, ven he vouldn't renoo the bill.'

"God bless you. . . . . . You know what I "would say about home and the darlings. A "hundred times God bless you. . . . . . Fears are "entertained for Lord Ashburton also. Nothing "has been heard of him."

A brief letter, sent me next day by the minister's bag, was in effect a postscript to the foregoing; and expressed still more strongly the doubts and apprehensions his voyage out had impressed him with, and which, though he afterwards saw reason greatly to modify his misgivings, were not so strange at that time as they appear to us now.

No hope of the Caledonia.

"Carlton-house, New York, February twenty-"eighth, 1842 . . . . The Caledonia, I grieve and "regret to say, has not arrived. If she left Eng-"land to her time, she has been four and twenty "days at sea. There is no news of her; and on "the nights of the fourteenth and eighteenth it "blew a terrible gale, which almost justifies the "worst suspicions. For myself, I have hardly any "hope of her; having seen enough, in our passage "out, to convince me that steaming across the "ocean in heavy weather is as yet an experiment "of the utmost hazard. NEW YORK: 1842. C. D. to J. F.

"As it was supposed that there would be no "steamer whatever for England this month (since "in ordinary course the Caledonia would have "returned with the mails on the 2nd of March), "I hastily got the letters ready yesterday and sent "them by the Garrick; which may perhaps be "three weeks out, but is not very likely to be "longer. But belonging to the Cunard company "is a boat called the Unicorn, which in the "summer time plies up the St. Lawrence, and "brings passengers from Canada to join the "British and North American steamers at Halifax. "In the winter she lies at the last-mentioned "place; from which news has come this morning "that they have sent her on to Boston for the "mails; and, rather than interrupt the communica-"tion, mean to dispatch her to England in lieu "of the poor Caledonia. This in itself, by the 'way, is a daring deed; for she was originally "built to run between Liverpool and Glasgow, "and is no more designed for the Atlantic than "a Calais packet-boat; though she once crossed "it, in the summer season. Substitute for the Caledonia.

"You may judge, therefore, what the owners "think of the probability of the Caledonia's ar-

New York: 1842.

C. D. to J. F.

"rival. How slight an alteration in our plans "would have made us passengers on board of "her!

"It would be difficult to tell you, my dear "fellow, what an impression this has made upon "our minds, or with what intense anxiety and "suspense we have been waiting for your letters "from home. We were to have gone South to-"day, but linger here until to-morrow afternoon "(having sent the secretary and luggage forward) "for one more chance of news. Love to dear "Macready, and to dear Mac, and every one we "care for. It's useless to speak of the dear chil-"dren. It seems now as though we should never "hear of them. . . . . .

Of distinguished Americans.

"P.S. Washington Irving is *a great* fellow. "We have laughed most heartily together. He is "just the man he ought to be. So is Doctor "Channing, with whom I have had an interesting "correspondence since I saw him last at Boston. "Halleck is a merry little man. Bryant a sad "one, and very reserved. Washington Allston "the painter (who wrote *Monaldi*) is a fine "specimen of a glorious old genius. Longfellow, "whose volume of poems I have got for you, is "a frank accomplished man as well as a fine "writer, and will be in town 'next fall.' Tell

NEW YORK: 1842. C. D. to J. F. Hotel bills.

"Macready that I suspect prices here must have "rather altered since his time. I paid our fort-"night's bill here, last night. We have dined out "every day (except when I was laid up with a "sore throat), and only had in all four bottles of "wine. The bill was 70*l*. English ! ! !

"You will see, by my other letter, how we "have been fêted and feasted; and how there is "war to the knife about the international copy-"right; and how I *will* speak about it, and de-"cline to be put down . . . .

Thoughts of the children.

"Oh for news from home! I think of your "letters so full of heart and friendship, with per-"haps a little scrawl of Charley's or Mamey's, lying "at the bottom of the deep sea; and am as full "of sorrow as if they had once been living crea-"tures.—Well! they *may* come, yet."

Disaster to the Caledonia.

They did reach him, but not by the Caledonia. His fears as to that vessel were but too well founded. On the very day when she was due in Boston (the 18th of February) it was learnt in London that she had undergone misadventure; that, her decks having been swept and her rudder torn away, though happily no lives were lost,

New York: 1842. — Acadia takes her place. she had returned disabled to Cork; and that the Acadia, having received her passengers and mails, was to sail with them from Liverpool next day.

International copyright. Of the main subject of that letter written on the day preceding; of the quite unpremeditated impulse, out of which sprang his advocacy of claims which he felt to be represented in his person; of the injustice done by his entertainers to their guest in ascribing such advocacy to selfishness; and of the graver wrong done by them to their own highest interests, nay, even to their commonest and most vulgar interests, in continuing to reject those claims; I will add nothing now to what all those years ago I laboured very hard to lay before many readers. It will be enough if I here print, from the authors' letters I sent out to him by the next following mail in compliance with his wish, this which follows from a very dear friend of his and mine. I fortunately had it transcribed before I posted it to him; Mr. Carlyle having in some haste written from "Templand, 26 March, 1842," and taken no copy.

Letter to Dickens from Carlyle. "We learn by the newspapers that you every-"where in America stir up the question of inter-"national copyright, and thereby awaken huge "dissonance where all else were triumphant unison "for you. I am asked my opinion of the matter, "and requested to write it down in words.

NEW YORK: 1842.

Carlyle to C. D.

"Several years ago, if memory err not, I was "one of many English writers, who, under the "auspices of Miss Martineau, did already sign a "petition to congress praying for an international "copyright between the two Nations,—which pro- "perly are not two Nations, but one; *indivisible* "by parliament, congress, or any kind of human "law or diplomacy, being already *united* by "Heaven's Act of Parliament, and the everlasting "law of Nature and Fact. To that opinion I still "adhere, and am like to continue adhering.

"In discussion of the matter before any con- "gress or parliament, manifold considerations and "argumentations will necessarily arise; which to "me are not interesting, nor essential for helping "me to a decision. They respect the time and "manner in which the thing should be; not at all "whether the thing should be or not. In an "ancient book, reverenced I should hope on both "sides of the Ocean, it was thousands of years "ago written down in the most decisive and ex- "plicit manner, 'Thou *shalt not* steal.' That thou "belongest to a different 'Nation,' and canst steal "without being certainly hanged for it, gives thee "no permission to steal! Thou shalt *not* in any-

Argument against stealing.

NEW YORK: 1842.

Carlyle to C. D.

"wise steal at all! So it is written down, for "Nations and for Men, in the Law-Book of the "Maker of this Universe. Nay, poor Jeremy Bent-"ham and others step in here, and will demon-"strate that it is actually our true convenience and "expediency not to steal; which I for my share, "on the great scale and on the small, and in all "conceivable scales and shapes, do also firmly "believe it to be. For example, if Nations ab-"stained from stealing, what need were there of "fighting,—with its butcherings and burnings, de-"cidedly the most expensive thing in this world? "How much more two Nations, which, as I said, "are but one Nation; knit in a thousand ways by "Nature and Practical Intercourse; indivisible "brother elements of the same great SAXONDOM, "to which in all honorable ways be long life!

Rob Roy's plan;

"When Mr. Robert Roy M'Gregor lived in the "district of Menteith on the Highland border two "centuries ago, he for his part found it more "convenient to supply himself with beef by stealing "it alive from the adjacent glens, than by buying "it killed in the Stirling butchers'-market. It was "Mr. Roy's plan of supplying himself with beef

not the best.

"in those days, this of stealing it. In many a "little 'Congress' in the district of Menteith, there "was debating, doubt it not, and much specious "argumentation this way and that, before they "could ascertain that, really and truly, buying "was the best way to get your beef; which how- "ever in the long run they did with one assent "find it indisputably to be: and accordingly they "hold by it to this day."

NEW YORK: 1842.

C. D.'s admiration of Carlyle.

This brave letter was an important service rendered at a critical time, and Dickens was very grateful for it. But, as time went on, he had other and higher causes for gratitude to its writer. Admiration of Carlyle increased in him with his years; and there was no one whom in later life he honoured so much, or had a more profound regard for.

CHAPTER XXI.

PHILADELPHIA, WASHINGTON, AND THE SOUTH.

1842.

PHILADELPHIA: 1842.

DICKENS's next letter was begun in the "United-states-hotel, Philadelphia," and bore date "Sunday, sixth March, 1842." It treated of much dealt with afterwards at greater length in the *Notes*, but the freshness and vivacity of the first impressions in it have surprised me. I do not however print any passage here which has not its own interest independently of anything contained in that book. The rule will be continued, as in the portions of letters already given, of not transcribing anything before printed, or anything having even but a near resemblance to descriptions that appear in the *Notes*.

C. D. to J. F.

". . . . . As this is likely to be the "only quiet day I shall have for a long time, I "devote it to writing to you. We have heard no-"thing from you* yet, and only have for our con-

* At the top of the sheet, above the address and date,

"solation the reflection that the Columbia* is "now on her way out. No news had been heard "of the Caledonia yesterday afternoon, when we "left New York. We *were* to have quitted that "place last Tuesday, but have been detained "there all the week by Kate having so bad a "sore throat that she was obliged to keep her "bed. We left yesterday afternoon at five o'clock, "and arrived here at eleven last night. Let me "say, by the way, that this is a very trying "climate.

PHILADELPHIA: 1842.

C. D. to J. F.

"I have often asked Americans in London "which were the better railroads—ours or theirs? "They have taken time for reflection, and gener-"ally replied on mature consideration that they "rather thought we excelled; in respect of the "punctuality with which we arrived at our stations, "and the smoothness of our travelling. I wish "you could see what an American railroad is, in "some parts where I now have seen them. I "won't say I wish you could feel what it is, be-"cause that would be an unchristian and savage "aspiration. It is never inclosed, or warded off.

Promise as to railroads.

are the words "Read on. We *have* your precious letters, "but you'll think, at first, we have not. C. D."

* The ship next in rotation to the Caledonia from Liverpool.

PHILADELPHIA: 1842. C. D. to J. F.

"You walk down the main street of a large town: "and, slap-dash, headlong, pell-mell, down the "middle of the street; with pigs burrowing, and "boys flying kites and playing marbles, and men "smoking, and women talking, and children "crawling, close to the very rails; there comes "tearing along a mad locomotive with its train of "cars, scattering a red-hot shower of sparks (from "its *wood* fire) in all directions; screeching, hiss-"ing, yelling, and panting; and nobody one atom "more concerned than if it were a hundred miles "away. You cross a turnpike-road; and there is "no gate, no policeman, no signal—nothing to "keep the wayfarer or quiet traveller out of the "way, but a wooden arch on which is written in "great letters 'Look out for the locomotive.' And "if any man, woman, or child, don't look out, "why it's his or her fault, and there's an end "of it.

Experience of them.

"The cars are like very shabby omnibuses—"only larger; holding sixty or seventy people. "The seats, instead of being placed long ways, "are put cross-wise, back to front. Each holds "two. There is a long row of these on each side "of the caravan, and a narrow passage up the "centre. The windows are usually all closed, "and there is very often, in addition, a hot,

Railway cars.

"close, most intolerable charcoal stove in a red-"hot glow. The heat and closeness are quite in-"supportable. But this is the characteristic of all "American houses, of all the public institutions, "chapels, theatres, and prisons. From the con-"stant use of the hard anthracite coal in these "beastly furnaces, a perfectly new class of diseases "is springing up in the country. Their effect "upon an Englishman is briefly told. He is al-"ways very sick and very faint; and has an in-"tolerable headache, morning, noon, and night.

PHILADELPHIA: 1842.

C. D. to J. F. Charcoal stoves.

"In the ladies' car, there is no smoking of "tobacco allowed. All gentlemen who have ladies "with them, sit in this car; and it is usually very "full. Before it, is the gentlemen's car; which is "something narrower. As I had a window close "to me yesterday which commanded this gen-"tlemen's car, I looked at it pretty often, perforce. "The flashes of saliva flew so perpetually and "incessantly out of the windows all the way, that "it looked as though they were ripping open "feather-beds inside, and letting the wind dispose "of the feathers.* But this spitting is universal. "In the courts of law, the judge has his spittoon "on the bench, the counsel have theirs, the wit-

Ladies' cars.

* This comparison is employed in another descriptive passage to be found in the *Notes* (Tauchn. Ed. p. 117).

12*

PHILADELPHIA: 1842. C. D. to J. F.

"ness has his, the prisoner his, and the crier his. "The jury are accommodated at the rate of three "men to a spittoon (or spit-box as they call it "here); and the spectators in the gallery are "provided for, as so many men who in the course "of nature expectorate without cessation. There "are spit-boxes in every steamboat, bar-room, "public dining-room, house of office, and place "of general resort, no matter what it be. In the "hospitals, the students are requested, by placard, "to use the boxes provided for them, and not to "spit upon the stairs. I have twice seen gen-"tlemen, at evening parties in New York, turn "aside when they were not engaged in conversa-"tion, and spit upon the drawing-room carpet. "And in every bar-room and hotel passage the "stone floor looks as if it were paved with open "oysters—from the quantity of this kind of deposit "which tesselates it all over . . .

Spittoons.

Contrasts in Massachusetts and New York.

"The institutions at Boston, and at Hartford, "are most admirable. It would be very difficult "indeed to improve upon them. But this is not "so at New York; where there is an ill-managed "lunatic asylum, a bad jail, a dismal workhouse, "and a perfectly intolerable place of police-impri-"sonment. A man is found drunk in the streets, "and is thrown into a cell below the surface of "the earth; profoundly dark; so full of noisome "vapours that when you enter it with a candle "you see a ring about the light, like that which "surrounds the moon in wet and cloudy weather; "and so offensive and disgusting in its filthy "odours, that you *cannot bear* its stench. He is "shut up, within an iron door, in a series of "vaulted passages where no one stays; has no "drop of water, or ray of light, or visitor, or help "of any kind; and there he remains until the "magistrate's arrival. If he die (as one man did "not long ago) he is half eaten by the rats in an "hour's time (as this man was). I expressed, on "seeing these places the other night, the disgust "I felt, and which it would be impossible to re-"press. 'Well; I don't know,' said the night con-"stable—that's a national answer by the bye— "'Well; I don't know. I've had six and twenty "'young women locked up here together, and "'beautiful ones too, and that's a fact.' The cell "was certainly no larger than the wine-cellar in "Devonshire-terrace; at least three feet lower; "and stunk like a common sewer. There was "one woman in it, then. The magistrate begins "his examinations at five o'clock in the morning; "the watch is set at seven at night; if the pri-"soners have been given in charge by an officer,

Police-cells in New York.

"And that's a fact!"

PHILADELPHIA: 1842. C. D. to J. F.

"they are not taken out before nine or ten; and "in the interval they remain in these places, "where they could no more be heard to cry for "help, in case of a fit or swoon among them, "than a man's voice could be heard after he was "coffined up in his grave.

Prisons.

"There is a prison in this same city, and "indeed in the same building, where prisoners "for grave offences await their trial, and to which "they are sent back when under remand. It "sometimes happens that a man or woman will "remain here for twelve months, waiting the result "of motions for new trial, and in arrest of judg-"ment, and what not. I went into it the other "day: without any notice or preparation, other-"wise I find it difficult to catch them in their "work-a-day aspect. I stood in a long, high, "narrow building, consisting of four galleries one "above the other, with a bridge across each, on "which sat a turnkey, sleeping or reading as the "case might be. From the roof, a couple of "windsails dangled and drooped, limp and use-"less; the skylight being fast closed, and they "only designed for summer use. In the centre "of the building was the eternal stove; and along "both sides of every gallery was a long row of "iron doors—looking like furnace doors, being

House of detention in New York.

PHILADELPHIA: 1842. C. D. to J. F.

"very small, but black and cold as if the fires "within had gone out.

"A man with keys appears, to show us round. "A good-looking fellow, and, in his way, civil "and obliging." (I omit a dialogue of which the substance has been printed,* and give only that which appears for the first time here.)

"'Suppose a man's here for twelve months. "'Do you mean to say he never comes out at "'that little iron door.'

"'He *may* walk some, perhaps—not much.'

"'Will you show me a few of them?'

"'Ah! All, if you like.'

A prisoner.

"'He threw open a door, and I looked in. An "old man was sitting on his bed, reading. The "light came in through a small chink, very high "up in the wall. Across the room ran a thick "iron pipe to carry off filth; this was bored for "the reception of something like a big funnel in "shape; and over the funnel was a watercock. "This was his washing apparatus and water-closet. "It was not savoury, but not very offensive. He "looked up at me; gave himself an odd, dogged "kind of shake; and fixed his eyes on his book "again. I came out, and the door was shut and

* *Notes*, Tauchn. Ed. pp. 99. 100.

PHILADELPHIA: 1842. C. D. to J. F.

"locked. He had been there a month, and would "have to wait another month for his trial. 'Has "'he ever walked out now, for instance?' "'No.' . . .

"'In England, if a man is under sentence of "'death even, he has a yard to walk in at certain "'times.'

"'Possible?'

Women prisoners.

" . . . Making me this answer with a coolness "which is perfectly untranslateable and inexpres- "sible, and which is quite peculiar to the soil, he "took me to the women's side; telling me, upon "the way, all about this man, who, it seems, mur- "dered his wife, and will certainly be hanged. "The women's doors have a small square aper- "ture in them; I looked through one, and saw a "pretty boy about ten or twelve years old, who "seemed lonely and miserable enough—as well "he might. 'What's *he* been doing?' says I. 'No- "'thing' says my friend. 'Nothing!' says I. 'No,' "says he. 'He's here for safe keeping. He saw "'his father kill his mother, and is detained to "'give evidence against him—that was his father, "'you saw just now.' 'But that's rather hard treat- "'ment for a witness, isn't it?'—'Well! I don't "'know. It a'nt a very rowdy life, and *that's* a "'fact.' So my friend, who was an excellent fel-

Boy prisoner

"low in his way, and very obliging, and a hand-"some young man to boot, took me off to show "me some more curiosities; and I was very much "obliged to him, for the place was so hot, and I "so giddy, that I could scarcely stand. . . .

PHILADELPHIA: 1842.

C. D. to J. F.

"When a man is hanged in New York, he is "walked out of one of these cells, without any "condemned sermon or other religious formalities, "straight into the narrow jail yard, which may be "about the width of Cranbourn-alley. There, a "gibbet is erected, which is of curious construc-"tion; for the culprit stands on the earth with the "rope about his neck, which passes through a "pulley in the top of the 'Tree' (see *Newgate* "*Calendar* passim), and is attached to a weight "something heavier than the man. This weight "being suddenly let go, drags the rope down with "it, and sends the criminal flying up fourteen "feet into the air; while the judge, and jury, and "five and twenty citizens (whose presence is re-"quired by the law), stand by, that they may "afterwards certify to the fact. This yard is a "very dismal place; and when I looked at it, I "thought the practice infinitely superior to ours: "much more solemn, and far less degrading and "indecent.

Capital punishment in New York: better than ours then was.

"There is another prison near New York

Philadelphia: 1842.

C. D. to J. F.

"which is a house of correction. The convicts "labour in stone-quarries near at hand, but the "jail has no covered yards or shops, so that "when the weather is wet (as it was when I was "there) each man is shut up in his own little cell, "all the live-long day. These cells, in all the "correction-houses I have seen, are on one uni-"form plan—thus:

A correction-house:

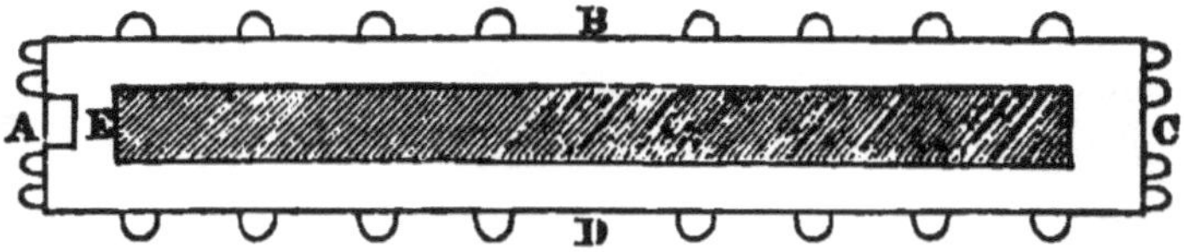

"A, B, C, and D, are the walls of the building with "windows in them, high up in the wall. The "shaded place in the centre represents four tiers "of cells, one above the other, with doors of "grated iron, and a light grated gallery to each "tier. Four tiers front to B, and four to D, so "that by this means you may be said, in walking "round, to see eight tiers in all. The interme-"diate blank space you walk in, looking up at "these galleries; so that, coming in at the door "E, and going either to the right or left till you "come back to the door again, you see all the "cells under one roof and in one high room. "Imagine them in number 400, and in every one "a man locked up; this one with his hands

with four hundred single cells.

"through the bars of his grate; this one in bed "(in the middle of the day, remember), and this "one flung down in a heap upon the ground with "his head against the bars like a wild beast. "Make the rain pour down in torrents outside. "Put the everlasting stove in the midst; hot, suf-"focating, and vaporous, as a witch's cauldron. "Add a smell like that of a thousand old mil-"dewed umbrellas wet through, and a thousand "dirty clothes-bags musty, moist, and fusty, and "you will have some idea—a very feeble one, my "dear friend, on my word—of this place yester-"day week. You know of course that we adopted "our improvements in prison-discipline from the "American pattern; but I am confident that the "writers who have the most lustily lauded the "American prisons, have never seen Chesterton's "domain or Tracey's.* There is no more com-"parison between these two prisons of ours, and "any I have seen here YET, than there is between "the keepers here, and those two gentlemen. "Putting out of sight the difficulty we have in "England of finding *useful* labour for the pri-"soners (which of course arises from our being "an older country, and having vast numbers of

PHILADELPHIA: 1842. C. D. to J. F.

Comparison with English prisons.

* See *ante*, p. 98.

PHILADELPHIA: 1842.

C. D. to J. F.

"artizans unemployed), our system is more complete, more impressive, and more satisfactory in every respect. It is very possible that I have not come to the best, not having yet seen Mount Auburn. I will tell you when I have. And also when I have come to those inns, mentioned—vaguely rather—by Miss Martineau, where they undercharge literary people for the love the landlords bear them. My experience, so far, has been of establishments where (perhaps for the same reason) they very monstrously and violently overcharge a man whose position forbids remonstrance.

Inns and landlords.

"Washington, Sunday, March the Thirteenth, 1842.

WASHINGTON: 1842.

"In allusion to the last sentence, my dear friend, I must tell you a slight experience I had in Philadelphia. My rooms had been ordered for a week, but, in consequence of Kate's illness, only Mr. Q and the luggage had gone on. Mr. Q always lives at the table d'hôte, so that while we were in New York our rooms were empty. The landlord not only charged me half the full rent for the time during which the rooms were reserved for us (which was quite right), but charged me also *for board for myself and Kate and Anne, at the rate of nine dollars*

Hotel extortion.

"*per day* for the same period, when we were ac- "tually living, at the same expense, in New "York !!! I *did* remonstrate upon this head; but "was coolly told it was the custom (which I have "since been assured is a lie), and had nothing for "it but to pay the amount. What else could I "do? I was going away by the steamboat at five "o'clock in the morning; and the landlord knew "perfectly well that my disputing an item of his "bill would draw down upon me the sacred wrath "of the newspapers, which would one and all de- "mand in capitals if THIS was the gratitude of "the man whom America had received as she "had never received any other man but La "Fayette?

WASHINGTON: 1842. C. D. to J. F.

Philadelphia Penitentiary.

"I went last Tuesday to the Eastern Peniten- "tiary near Philadelphia, which is the only prison "in the States, or I believe in the world, on the "principle of hopeless, strict, and unrelaxed soli- "tary confinement, during the whole term of the "sentence. It is wonderfully kept, but a most "dreadful, fearful place. The inspectors, imme- "diately on my arrival in Philadelphia, invited "me to pass the day in the jail, and to dine with "them when I had finished my inspection, that "they might hear my opinion of the system. Ac- "cordingly I passed the whole day in going from

The solitary system.

WASHINGTON: 1842. C. D. to J. F.

"cell to cell, and conversing with the prisoners. "Every facility was given me, and no constraint "whatever imposed upon any man's free speech. "If I were to write you a letter of twenty sheets, "I could not tell you this one day's work; so I "will reserve it until that happy time when we "shall sit round the table at Jack Straw's—you, "and I, and Mac—and go over my diary. I never "shall be able to dismiss from my mind, the im-"pressions of that day. Making notes of them, "as I have done, is an absurdity, for they are "written, beyond all power of erasure, in my

Solitary prisoners.

"brain. I saw men who had been there, five "years, six years, eleven years, two years, two "months, two days; some whose term was nearly "over, and some whose term had only just begun. "Women too, under the same variety of circum-"stances. Every prisoner who comes into the "jail, comes at night; is put into a bath, and

How received and kept.

"dressed in the prison garb; and then a black "hood is drawn over his face and head, and he "is led to the cell from which he never stirs "again until his whole period of confinement has "expired. I looked at some of them with the "same awe as I should have looked at men who "had been buried alive, and dug up again.

"We dined in the jail: and I told them after

WASHINGTON: 1842.

C. D. to J. F. Talk with the inspectors.

"dinner how much the sight had affected me, "and what an awful punishment it was. I dwelt "upon this; for, although the inspectors are ex-"tremely kind and benevolent men, I question "whether they are sufficiently acquainted with the "human mind to know what it is they are doing. "Indeed, I am sure they do not know. I bore "testimony, as every one who sees it must, to the "admirable government of the institution (Stan-"field is the keeper: grown a little younger, that's "all); but added that nothing could justify such a "punishment, but its working a reformation in the "prisoners. That for short terms—say two years "for the maximum—I conceived, especially after "what they had told me of its good effects in "certain cases, it might perhaps be highly bene-"ficial; but that, carried to so great an extent, I "thought it cruel and unjustifiable; and further, "that their sentences for small offences were very "rigorous, not to say savage. All this, they took "like men who were really anxious to have one's "free opinion and to do right. And we were "very much pleased with each other, and parted "in the friendliest way.

"They sent me back to Philadelphia in a car-"riage they had sent for me in the morning; and "then I had to dress in a hurry, and follow Kate

WASHINGTON: 1842. C. D. to J. F. Bookseller Cary.

"to Cary's the bookseller's where there was a party. "He married a sister of Leslie's. There are three "Miss Leslies here, very accomplished; and one "of them has copied all her brother's principal "pictures. These copies hang about the room. "We got away from this as soon as we could; "and next morning had to turn out at five. In "the morning I had received and shaken hands

A levee.

"with five hundred people, so you may suppose "that I was pretty well tired. Indeed I am obliged "to be very careful of myself; to avoid smoking "and drinking; to get to bed soon; and to be "particular in respect of what I eat. . . . You "cannot think how bilious and trying the climate "is. One day it is hot summer, without a breath

Changes of temperature.

"of air; the next, twenty degrees below freezing, "with a wind blowing that cuts your skin like "steel. These changes have occurred here several "times since last Wednesday night.

"I have altered my route, and don't mean to "go to Charleston. The country, all the way "from here, is nothing but a dismal swamp; there "is a bad night of sea-coasting in the journey;

Henry Clay.

"the equinoctial gales are blowing hard; and Clay "(a most *charming* fellow, by the bye), whom I "have consulted, strongly dissuades me. The "weather is intensely hot there; the spring fever "is coming on; and there is very little to see, "after all. We therefore go next Wednesday night "to Richmond, which we shall reach on Thurs-"day. There, we shall stop three days; my object "being to see some tobacco plantations. Then "we shall go by James river back to Baltimore, "which we have already passed through, and "where we shall stay two days. Then we shall "go West at once, straight through the most "gigantic part of this continent: across the Al-"leghany-mountains, and over a prairie.

WASHINGTON: 1842.

C. D. to J. F.

Proposed journeyings.

"STILL AT WASHINGTON, Fifteeenth March, "1842. . . . It is impossible, my dear friend, to "tell you what we felt, when Mr. Q (who is a "fearfully sentimental genius, but heartily in-"terested in all that concerns us) came to where "we were dining last Sunday, and sent in a note "to the effect that the Caledonia* had arrived! "Being really assured of her safety, we felt as if "the distance between us and home were dimi-"nished by at least one half. There was great "joy everywhere here, for she had been quite "despaired of, but *our* joy was beyond all telling. "This news came on by express. Last night your "letters reached us. I was dining with a club

Arrival of Acadia with Caledonia mails.

* This was the Acadia with the Caledonia mails.

WASHINGTON: 1842.

C. D. to J. F.

"(for I can't avoid a dinner of that sort, now and "then), and Kate sent me a note about nine "o'clock to say they were here. But she didn't "open them—which I consider heroic—until I "came home. That was about half past ten; and "we read them until nearly two in the morning.

Letters from England.

"I won't say a word about your letters; ex-"cept that Kate and I have come to a conclusion "which makes me tremble in my shoes, for we "decide that humorous narrative is your forte, "and not statesmen of the commonwealth. I "won't say a word about your news; for how "could I in that case, while you want to hear "what we are doing, resist the temptation of ex-"pending pages on those darling children.........

Congress and Senate.

"I have the privilege of appearing on the floor "of both houses here, and go to them every day. "They are very handsome and commodious. There "is a great deal of bad speaking, but there are a "great many very remarkable men, in the legis-"lature: such as John Quincey Adams, Clay, "Preston, Calhoun, and others: with whom I need "scarcely add I have been placed in the friend-"liest relations. Adams is a fine old fellow—

Quincey Adams.

"seventy-six years old, but with most surprising "vigour, memory, readiness, and pluck. Clay is "perfectly enchanting; an irresistible man. There

WASHINGTON: 1842. C. D. to J. F. Leading American statesmen.

"are some very noble specimens, too, out of the "West. Splendid men to look at, hard to deceive, "prompt to act, lions in energy, Crichtons in "varied accomplishments, Indians in quickness of "eye and gesture, Americans in affectionate and "generous impulse. It would be difficult to ex-"aggerate the nobility of some of these glorious "fellows.

Preston.

"When Clay retires, as he does this month, "Preston will become the leader of the whig party. "He so solemnly assures me that the international "copyright shall and will be passed, that I almost "begin to hope; and I shall be entitled to say, if "it be, that I have brought it about. You have "no idea how universal the discussion of its "merits and demerits has become; or how eager "for the change I have made a portion of the "people.

International copyright.

"You remember what —— was, in England. "If you *could* but see him here! If you could "only have seen him when he called on us the "other day—feigning abstraction in the dreadful "pressure of affairs of state; rubbing his forehead "as one who was a-weary of the world; and ex-"hibiting a sublime caricature of Lord Burleigh. "He is the only thoroughly unreal man I have "seen, on this side the ocean. Heaven help the

13*

WASHINGTON: 1842.

C. D. to J. F.

President Tyler.

"President! All parties are against him, and he "appears truly wretched. We go to a levee at "his house to-night. He has invited me to dinner "on Friday, but I am obliged to decline; for we "leave, per steamboat, to-morrow night.

Concerning the American people.

"I said I wouldn't write anything more con-"cerning the American people, for two months. "Second thoughts are best. I shall not change, "and may as well speak out—to *you*. They are "friendly, earnest, hospitable, kind, frank, very "often accomplished, far less prejudiced than you "would suppose, warm-hearted, fervent, and en-"thusiastic. They are chivalrous in their universal "politeness to women, courteous, obliging, dis-"interested; and, when they conceive a perfect "affection for a man (as I may venture to say of "myself), entirely devoted to him. I have received "thousands of people of all ranks and grades, "and have never once been asked an offensive or "unpolite question—except by Englishmen, who, "when they have been 'located' here for some "years, are worse than the devil in his blackest "painting. The State is a parent to its people; "has a parental care and watch over all poor "children, women labouring of child, sick persons, "and captives. The common men render you as-"sistance in the streets, and would revolt from

Englishmen "located" in America.

"the offer of a piece of money. The desire to "oblige is universal; and I have never once travelled in a public conveyance, without making "some generous acquaintance whom I have been "sorry to part from, and who has in many cases "come on miles, to see us again. But I don't "like the country. I would not live here, on any "consideration. It goes against the grain with "me. It would with you. I think it impossible, "utterly impossible, for any Englishman to live "here, and be happy. I have a confidence that I "must be right, because I have everything, God "knows, to lead me to the opposite conclusion: "and yet I cannot resist coming to this one. As "to the causes, they are too many to enter upon "here. . . . . .

WASHINGTON: 1842.

O. D. to J. F.

"Surgit amari aliquid."

"One of two petitions for an international "copyright which I brought here from American "authors, with Irving at their head, has been pre-"sented to the house of representatives. Clay "retains the other for presentation to the senate "after I have left Washington. The presented "one has been referred to a committee; the "Speaker has nominated as its chairman Mr. "Kennedy, member for Baltimore, who is himself "an author and notoriously favourable to such a "law; and I am going to assist him in his report.

The copyright petition.

WASHINGTON: 1842.

C. D. to J. F. RICHMOND. Washington Irving:

"RICHMOND, IN VIRGINIA. Thursday Night, March 17.

"Irving was with me at Washington yesterday, "and *wept heartily* at parting. He is a fine fellow, "when you know him well; and you would relish "him, my dear friend, of all things. We have "laughed together at some absurdities we have "encountered in company, quite in my vociferous "Devonshire-terrace style. The 'Merrikin' govern-"ment have treated him, he says, most liberally "and handsomely in every respect. He thinks of "sailing for Liverpool on the 7th of April; passing "a short time in London; and then going to "Paris. Perhaps you may meet him. If you do, "he will know that you are my dearest friend, "and will open his whole heart to you at once. "His secretary of legation, Mr. Coggleswell, is a "man of very remarkable information, a great "traveller, a good talker, and a scholar."

appointed Minister to Spain.

"I am going to sketch you our trip here from "Washington, as it involves nine miles of a 'Vir-"'ginny Road.' That done, I must be brief, good "brother. . . .

The reader of the *American Notes* will remember the admirable and most humorous description of the night steamer on the Potomac, and of the black driver over the Virginia-road. Both were in this letter; which, after three days, he resumed "At Washington again, Monday, March the twenty-"first.

"We had intended to go to Baltimore from "Richmond, by a place called Norfolk: but one "of the boats being under repair, I found we "should probably be detained at this Norfolk two "days. Therefore we came back here yesterday, "by the road we had travelled before; lay here "last night; and go on to Baltimore this after-"noon, at four o'clock. It is a journey of only "two hours and a half. Richmond is a prettily "situated town; but, like other towns in slave "districts (as the planters themselves admit), has "an aspect of decay and gloom which to an un-"accustomed eye is *most* distressing. In the black "car (for they don't let them sit with the whites), "on the railroad as we went there, were a mother "and family, whom the steamer was conveying "away, to sell; retaining the man (the husband "and father I mean) on his plantation. The chil-"dren cried the whole way. Yesterday, on board "the boat, a slave owner and two constables were "our fellow-passengers. They were coming here "in search of two negroes who had run away on "the previous day. On the bridge at Richmond "there is a notice against fast driving over it, as

Richmond.

Incidents of slave-life.

WASHINGTON: 1842. C. D. to J. F.

"it is rotten and crazy: penalty—for whites, five "dollars; for slaves, fifteen stripes. My heart is "lightened as if a great load had been taken "from it, when I think that we are turning our "backs on this accursed and detested system. I "really don't think I could have borne it any "longer. It is all very well to say 'be silent on "'the subject.' They won't let you be silent. They "*will* ask you what you think of it; and *will* ex- "patiate on slavery as if it were one of the "greatest blessings of mankind. 'It's not,' said "a hard, bad-looking fellow to me the other day, "'it's not the interest of a man to use his slaves "'ill. It's damned nonsense that you hear in "'England.'—I told him quietly that it was not a "man's interest to get drunk, or to steal, or to "game, or to indulge in any other vice, but he "*did* indulge in it for all that. That cruelty, and "the abuse of irresponsible power, were two of "the bad passions of human nature, with the "gratification of which, considerations of interest "or of ruin had nothing whatever to do; and "that, while every candid man must admit that "even a slave might be happy enough with a "good master, all human beings knew that bad "masters, cruel masters, and masters who dis- "graced the form they bore, were matters of ex-

Impossible to be silent on slavery.

Discussion with a slave-holder.

"perience and history, whose existence was as "undisputed as that of slaves themselves. He "was a little taken aback by this, and asked me "if I believed in the bible. Yes, I said, but if "any man could prove to me that it sanctioned "slavery, I would place no further credence in it. "'Well then,' he said, 'by God, sir, the niggers "'must be kept down, and the whites have put "'down the coloured people wherever they have "'found them.' 'That's the whole question,' said "I. 'Yes, and by God,' says he, 'the British had "'better not stand out on that point when Lord "'Ashburton comes over, for I never felt so war- "'like as I do now,—and that's a fact.' I was "obliged to accept a public supper in this Rich- "mond, and I saw plainly enough, there, that the "hatred which these Southern States bear to us "as a nation has been fanned up and revived "again by this Creole business, and can scarcely "be exaggerated.

WASHINGTON: 1842. O. D. to J. F.

Feeling of South to England.

. . . .

. . . . "We were desperately tired at Rich- "mond, as we went to a great many places, and "received a very great number of visitors. We "appoint usually two hours in every day for this "latter purpose, and have our room so full at that "period that it is difficult to move or breathe. "Before we left Richmond, a gentleman told me,

Levees at Richmond.

WASHINGTON: 1842. O. D. to J. F.

"when I really was so exhausted that I could "hardly stand, that 'three people of great fashion' "were much offended by having been told, when "they called last evening, that I was tired and not "visible, then, but would be 'at home' from twelve "to two next day! Another gentleman (no doubt "of great fashion also) sent a letter to me two "hours after I had gone to bed, preparatory to "rising at four next morning, with instructions to "the slave who brought it to knock me up and "wait for an answer!

One more banquet accepted.

"I am going to break my resolution of ac-"cepting no more public entertainments, in favour "of the originators of the printed document over-"leaf. They live upon the confines of the Indian "territory, some two thousand miles or more "west of New York! Think of my dining there! "And yet, please God, the festival will come off "—I should say about the 12th or 15th of next "month." . . . .

The printed document was a series of resolutions, moved at a public meeting attended by all the principal citizens, judges, professors, and doctors, of St. Louis, urgently inviting, to that city of the Far West, the distinguished writer then the guest of America, eulogizing his genius, and tendering to him their warmest hospitalities. He was at Baltimore when he closed his letter. BALTIMORE: 1842.

BALTIMORE, *Tuesday, March 22nd.*

"I have a great diffidence in running counter "to any impression formed by a man of Maclise's "genius, on a subject he has fully considered." (Referring apparently to some remark by myself on the picture of the Play-scene in *Hamlet*, exhibited this year.) "But I quite agree with you, "about the King in *Hamlet*. Talking of Hamlet, "I constantly carry in my great-coat pocket the "*Shakespeare* you bought for me in Liverpool. "What an unspeakable source of delight that "book is to me!

C. D. to J. F.

My gift of Shakespeare.

"Your Ontario letter, I found here to-night: "sent on by the vigilant and faithful Colden, who "makes every thing having reference to us, or "our affairs, a labour of the heartiest love. We "devoured its contents, greedily. Good Heaven, "my dear fellow, how I miss you! and how I count "the time 'twixt this and coming home again. "Shall I ever forget the day of our parting at "Liverpool! when even —— became jolly and "radiant in his sympathy with our separation! "Never, never shall I forget that time. Ah! how "seriously I thought then, and how seriously I

Letters from home.

Baltimore: 1842. — C. D. to J. F.

"have thought many, many times since, of the "terrible folly of ever quarrelling with a true "friend, on good for nothing trifles! Every little "hasty word that has ever passed between us, "rose up before me like a reproachful ghost. "At this great distance, I seem to look back upon "any miserable small interruption of our affec-"tionate intercourse, though only for the instant "it has never outlived, with a sort of pity for my-"self as if I were another creature.

Self-reproach of a noble nature.

"I have bought another accordion. The steward "lent me one, on the passage out, and I regaled "the ladies' cabin with my performances. You "can't think with what feeling I play *Home Sweet* "*Home* every night, or how pleasantly sad it makes "us. . . . . And so God bless you. . . . . I leave "space for a short postscript before sealing this, "but it will probably contain nothing. The dear, "dear children! what a happiness it is to know "that they are in such hands.

"P.S. Twenty-third March, 1842. Nothing "new. And all well. I have not heard that the "Columbia is in, but she is hourly expected. "Washington Irving has come on for another "leave-taking,* and dines with me to-day. We

* At his second visit to America, when in Washington

"start for the West, at half after eight to-morrow "morning. I send you a newspaper, the most "respectable in the States, with a very just copy-"right article." BALTIMORE: 1842. C. D. to J. F.

in February 1868, Dickens, replying to a letter in which Irving was named, thus describes the last meeting and leave-taking to which he alludes above. "Your reference to my "dear friend, Washington Irving, renews the vivid impres-"sions reawakened in my mind at Baltimore but the other "day. I saw his fine face for the last time in that city. He "came there from New York to pass a day or two with me "before I went westward; and they were made among the "most memorable of my life by his delightful fancy and "genial humor. Some unknown admirer of his books and "mine sent to the hotel a most enormous mint-julep, wreathed "with flowers. We sat, one on either side of it, with great "solemnity (it filled a respectably-sized round table), but the "solemnity was of very short duration. It was quite an en-"chanted julep, and carried us among innumerable people "and places that we both knew. The julep held out far "into the night, and my memory never saw him afterwards "otherwise than as bending over it, with his straw, with an "attempted air of gravity (after some anecdote involving "some wonderfully droll and delicate observation of character), "and then, as his eye caught mine, melting into that capti-"vating laugh of his, which was the brightest and best I "have ever heard." Washington Irving's leave-taking.

CHAPTER XXII.

CANAL BOAT JOURNEYS: BOUND FAR WEST.

1842.

AMERICA: 1842.

Character in the letters.

IT would not be possible that a more vivid or exact impression, than that which is derivable from these letters, could be given of either the genius or the character of the writer. The whole man is here in the supreme hour of his life, and in all the enjoyment of its highest sensations. Inexpressibly sad to me has been the task of going over them, but the surprise has equalled the sadness. I had forgotten what was in them. That they contained, in their first vividness, all the most prominent descriptions of his published book, I knew. But the reproduction of any part of these was not permissible here; and believing that the substance of them had been thus almost wholly embodied in the *American Notes*, when they were lent to assist in its composition, I turned to them with very small expectation of finding anything available for present use. Yet the difficulty has been, not to find but to reject; and the rejection when most unavoidable has not been most easy. Even where the subjects recur that are in the printed volume, there is a freshness of first impressions in the letters that renders it no small trial to act strictly on the rule adhered to in these extracts from them. In the *Notes* there is of course very much, masterly in observation and description, of which there is elsewhere no trace; but the passages amplified from the letters have not been improved, and the manly force and directness of some of their views and reflections, conveyed by touches of a picturesque completeness that no elaboration could give, have here and there not been strengthened by rhetorical additions in the printed work. There is also a charm in the letters which the plan adopted in the book necessarily excluded from it. It will always of course have value as a deliberate expression of the results gathered from the American experiences, but the *personal narrative* of this famous visit to America is in the letters alone. In what way his experiences arose, the desire at the outset to see nothing that was not favourable, the slowness with which adverse impressions were formed, and the eager recognition of every truthful and noble quality that arose and remained

The *Notes* less satisfactory.

A charm in letters excluded from *Notes*.

Personal narrative in them.

AMERICA: 1842: above the fault-finding, are discoverable only in the letters.

Already it is manifest from them that the before-named disappointments, as well of the guest in his entertainers as of the entertainers in their guest, had their beginning in the copyright differences; but it is not less plain that the social dissatisfactions on his side were of even earlier date, and with the country itself had certainly nothing to do. It was objected to him, I well remember, that in making such unfavourable remarks as his published book did on many points, he was assailing the democratic institutions that had formed the character of the nation: but the answer is obvious, that, democratic institutions being universal in America, they were as fairly entitled to share in the good as in the bad; and in what he praised, of which there is here abundant testimony, he must be held to have exalted those institutions as much, as in what he blamed he could be held to depreciate them. He never sets himself up in judgment on the entire people. As we see, from the way the letters show us that the opinions he afterwards published were formed, he does not draw conclusions while his observation is only half-concluded; and he refrains throughout from the example too strongly set him,

The copyright differences.

Social dissatisfactions.

Fairness of judgment.

even in the very terms of his welcome by the writers of America,* of flinging one nation in the other's face. He leaves each upon its own ground. His great business in his publication, as in the first impressions recorded here, is to exhibit social influences at work as he saw them himself; and it would surely have been of all bad compliments the worst, when resolving, in the tone and with the purpose of a friend, to make public what he had observed in America, if he had supposed that such a country would take truth amiss.

AMERICA: 1842.

The real compliment to America.

There is however one thing to be especially remembered, as well in reading the letters as in judging of the book which was founded on them. It is a point to which I believe Mr. Emerson directed the attention of his countrymen. Everything of an objectionable kind, whether the author would have it so or not, stands out more prominently and distinctly than matter of the opposite description. The social sin is a more tangible thing than the social virtue. Pertinaciously to insist upon the charities and graces of life, is to outrage their quiet and unobtrusive character; but we incur the danger of extending the vulgarities and indecencies, if we seem to countenance by omitting to expose them. And if this is only

A fact to be remembered.

* See *ante*, p. 134-5.

AMERICA: 1842.

kept in view in reading what is here given, the proportion of censure will be found not to overbalance the just admiration and unexaggerated praise.

Literary merits of the letters.

Apart from such considerations, it is to be also said, the letters, from which I am now printing exactly as they were written, have claims, as mere literature, of an unusual kind. Unrivalled quickness of observation, the rare faculty of seizing out of a multitude of things the thing only that is essential, the irresistible play of humour, such pathos as only humourists of this high order possess, and the unwearied unforced vivacity of ever fresh, buoyant, bounding animal spirits, never found more natural, variously easy, or picturesque

How written.

expression. Written amid such distraction, fatigue, and weariness as they describe, amid the jarring noises of hotels and streets, aboard steamers, on canal boats, and in log huts, there is not an erasure in them. Not external objects only, but feelings, reflections, and thoughts, are photographed into visible forms with the same unexampled ease. They borrow no help from the matters of which they treat. They would have given, to the subjects described, old acquaintance and engrossing interest if they had been about a people in the moon. Of the personal character at the same time self-pourtrayed, others, whose emotions it less vividly awakens, will judge more calmly and clearly than myself. Yet to myself only can it be known how small were the services of friendship that sufficed to rouse all the sensibilities of this beautiful and noble nature. Throughout our life-long intercourse it was the same. His keenness of discrimination failed him never excepting here, when it was lost in the limitless extent of his appreciation of all kindly things; and never did he receive what was meant for a benefit that he was not eager to return it a hundred-fold. No man more truly generous ever lived.

AMERICA: 1842.

Personal character pourtrayed.

His next letter was begun from "on board "the canal boat. Going to Pittsburgh. Monday, "March twenty-eighth, 1842;" and the difficulties of rejection, to which reference has just been made, have been nowhere felt by me so much. Several of the descriptive master-pieces of the book are in it, with such touches of original freshness as might fairly have justified a reproduction of them in their first form. Among these are the Harrisburgh coach on its way through the Susquehanah valley; the railroad across the mountain; the brown-forester of the Mississippi, the interrogative man in pepper-and-salt, and the affecting scene of the emigrants put ashore as the

On board for Pittsburgh.

Choicest passages of *Notes*.

CANAL BOAT FOR PITTSBURGH: 1842.

steamer passes up the Ohio. But all that I may here give, bearing any resemblance to what is given in the *Notes*, are, the opening sketch of the small creature on the top of the queer stage coach, to which the printed version fails to do adequate justice; and an experience to which the interest belongs of having suggested the settlement of Eden in *Martin Chuzzlewit*. . . . . "We

C. D. to J. F.

"left Baltimore last Thursday the twenty-fourth "at half-past eight in the morning, by railroad; "and got to a place called York, about twelve. "There we dined, and took a stage-coach for "Harrisburgh; twenty-five miles further. This "stage-coach was like nothing so much as the "body of one of the swings you see at a fair—set "upon four wheels and roofed and covered at "the sides with painted canvas. There were "twelve *inside!* I, thank my stars, was on "the box. The luggage was on the roof; among

Queer stage-coach.

"it, a good-sized dining table, and a big rocking-"chair. We also took up an intoxicated gentle-"man, who sat for ten miles between me and the "coachman; and another intoxicated gentleman "who got up behind, but in the course of a mile "or two fell off without hurting himself, and was "seen in the distant perspective reeling back to "the grog-shop where we had found him. There "were four horses to this land-ark, of course; but "we did not perform the journey until after half-"past six o'clock that night. . . . The first half of "the journey was tame enough, but the second "lay through the valley of the Susquehanah (I "think I spell it right, but I haven't that Ame-"rican Geography at hand) which is very beau-"tiful. . . . . CANAL BOAT FOR PITTSBURGH: 1842.

"I think I formerly made a casual remark to "you touching the precocity of the youth of this "country. When we changed horses on this "journey I got down to stretch my legs, refresh "myself with a glass of whiskey and water, and "shake the wet off my great coat—for it was "raining very heavily, and continued to do so, "all night. Mounting to my seat again, I ob-"served something lying on the roof of the coach, "which I took to be a rather large fiddle in a "brown bag. In the course of ten miles or so, "however, I discovered that it had a pair of dirty "shoes at one end, and a glazed cap at the other; "and further observation demonstrated it to be a "small boy, in a snuff-coloured coat, with his "arms quite pinioned to his sides by deep for-"cing into his pockets. He was, I presume, a re-"lative or friend of the coachman's, as he lay a-"top of the luggage, with his face towards the Something on the roof:

CANAL BOAT FOR PITTSBURGH: 1842. C. D. to J. F.

"rain; and, except when a change of position "brought his shoes in contact with my hat, he "appeared to be asleep. Sir, when we stopped "to water the horses, about two miles from Har-"risburgh, this thing slowly upreared itself to the "height of three foot eight, and fixing its eyes on "me with a mingled expression of complacency, "patronage, national independence, and sympathy "for all outer barbarians and foreigners, said, in "shrill piping accents, 'Well now, stranger, I "'guess you find this, a'most like an English "'a'ternoon,—hey?' It is unnecessary to add that "I thirsted for his blood. . . .

reveals itself.

At Harrisburgh.

"We had all next morning in Harrisburgh, as "the canal-boat was not to start until three o'clock "in the afternoon. The officials called upon me "before I had finished breakfast; and as the town "is the seat of the Pennsylvanian legislature, I "went up to the capitol. I was very much inter-"ested in looking over a number of treaties made "with the poor Indians, their signatures being "rough drawings of the creatures or weapons they "are called after; and the extraordinary drawing "of these emblems, showing the queer, unused, "shaky manner in which each man has held the "pen, struck me very much.

Treaties with Indians.

"You know my small respect for our house

"of commons. These local legislatures are too "insufferably apish of mighty legislation, to be "seen without bile, for which reason, and because "a great crowd of senators and ladies had as- "sembled in both houses to behold the inimit- "able, and had already begun to pour in upon "him even in the secretary's private room, I went "back to the hotel, with all speed. The members "of both branches of the legislature followed me "there, however, so we had to hold the usual "levee before our half-past one o'clock dinner. "We received a great number of them. Pretty "nearly every man spat upon the carpet, as usual; "and one blew his nose with his fingers—also on "the carpet, which was a very neat one, the room "given up to us being the private parlor of the "landlord's wife. This has become so common "since, however, that it scarcely seems worth "mentioning. Please to observe that the gentle- "man in question was a member of the senate, "which answers (as they very often tell me) to "our house of lords.

CANAL BOAT FOR PITTSBURGH: 1842.

C. D. to J. F.

Local legislatures.

A levee.

"The innkeeper was the most attentive, civil, "and obliging person I ever saw in my life. On "being asked for his bill, he said there was no "bill: the honor and pleasure &c. being more

A model innkeeper.

Canal Boat for Pittsburgh: 1842.

C. D. to J. F.

"than sufficient.* I did not permit this, of course; "and begged Mr. Q to explain to him, that, "travelling four strong, I could not hear of it on "any account.

The canal boat.

"And now I come to the Canal Boat. Bless "your heart and soul, my dear fellow,—if you "could only see us on board the canal boat! Let "me think, for a moment, at what time of the "day or night I should best like you to see us.

In the morning.

"In the morning? Between five and six in the "morning, shall I say? Well! you *would* like to "see me, standing on the deck, fishing the dirty "water out of the canal with a tin ladle chained "to the boat by a long chain; pouring the same "into a tin-basin (also chained up in like man-"ner); and scrubbing my face with the jack "towel. At night, shall I say? I don't know that "you *would* like to look into the cabin at night, "only to see me lying on a temporary shelf "exactly the width of this sheet of paper when "it's open (*I measured it this morning*),** with one

At night.

"man above me, and another below; and, in all, "eight and twenty in a low cabin, which you

* Miss Martineau was perhaps partly right then? *Ante*, p. 188.

** 16 inches exactly.

"can't stand upright in with your hat on. I don't "think you would like to look in at breakfast "time either, for then these shelves have only "just been taken down and put away, and the "atmosphere of the place is, as you may sup- "pose, by no means fresh; though there *are* upon "the table tea and coffee, and bread and butter, "and salmon, and shad, and liver, and steak, and "potatoes, and pickles, and ham, and pudding, "and sausages; and three and thirty people sitting "round it, eating and drinking; and savoury "bottles of gin, and whiskey, and brandy, and "rum, in the bar hard by; and seven and twenty "out of the eight and twenty men, in foul linen, "with yellow streams from half-chewed tobacco "trickling down their chins. Perhaps the best "time for you to take a peep would be the pre- "sent: eleven o'clock in the forenoon: when the "barber is at his shaving, and the gentlemen are "lounging about the stove waiting for their turns, "and not more than seventeen are spitting in con- "cert, and two or three are walking overhead "(lying down on the luggage every time the man "at the helm calls 'Bridge!'), and I am writing "this in the ladies'-cabin, which is a part of the "gentlemen's, and only screened off by a red "curtain. Indeed it exactly resembles the dwarf's

CANAL BOAT FOR PITTSBURGH: 1842.

C. D. to J. F.

At breakfast.

After breakfast.

The ladies' cabin.

CANAL BOAT FOR PITTSBURGH: 1842.

C. D. to J. F.

"private apartment in a caravan at a fair; and "the gentlemen, generally, represent the spectators "at a penny-a-head. The place is just as clean "and just as large as that caravan you and I "were in at Greenwich-fair last past. Outside, it "is exactly like any canal-boat you have seen "near the Regent's-park, or elsewhere.

"You never can conceive what the hawking "and spitting is, the whole night through. Last "night was the worst. *Upon my honor and word* "I was obliged, this morning, to lay my fur-coat "on the deck, and wipe the half dried flakes of

Disagreeable.

"spittle from it with my handkerchief: and the "only surprise seemed to be, that I should con-"sider it necessary to do so. When I turned in "last night, I put it on a stool beside me, and "there it lay, under a cross fire from five men—"three opposite; one above; and one below. I

Making the best of it.

"make no complaints, and shew no disgust. I "am looked upon as highly facetious at night, "for I crack jokes with everybody near me until "we fall asleep. I am considered very hardy in "the morning, for I run up, bare-necked, and "plunge my head into the half-frozen water, by

Hardy habits.

"half past five o'clock. I am respected for my "activity, inasmuch as I jump from the boat to "the towing-path, and walk five or six miles be-

"fore breakfast; keeping up with the horses all "the time. In a word, they are quite astonished "to find a sedentary Englishman roughing it so "well, and taking so much exercise; and ques- "tion me very much on that head. The greater "part of the men will sit and shiver round the "stove all day, rather than put one foot before "the other. As to having a window open, that's "not to be thought of.

CANAL BOAT FOR PITTSBURGH: 1842.

C. D. to J. F.

"We expect to reach Pittsburgh to-night, be- "tween eight and nine o'clock; and there we "ardently hope to find your March letters awaiting "us. We have had, with the exception of Friday "afternoon, exquisite weather, but cold. Clear "starlight and moonlight nights. The canal has "run, for the most part, by the side of the Susque- "hanah and Iwanata rivers; and has been carried "through tremendous obstacles. Yesterday, we "crossed the mountain. This is done *by railroad.* " . . . You dine at an inn upon the mountain; "and, including the half hour allowed for the "meal, are rather more than five hours performing "this strange part of the journey. The people "north and 'down east' have terrible legends of "its danger; but they appear to be exceedingly "careful, and don't go to work at all wildly. "There are some queer precipices close to the

By rail across a mountain.

CANAL BOAT FOR PITTSBURGH: 1842.

C. D. to J. F.

"rails, certainly; but every precaution is taken, I "am inclined to think, that such difficulties, and "such a vast work, will admit of.

Mountain scenery.

"The scenery, before you reach the mountains, "and when you are on them, and after you have "left them, is very grand and fine; and the canal "winds its way through some deep, sullen gorges, "which, seen by moonlight, are very impressive: "though immeasurably inferior to Glencoe, to "whose terrors I have not seen the smallest *ap-* "*proach.* We have passed, both in the mountains "and elsewhere, a great number of new settle- "ments, and detached log-houses. Their utterly "forlorn and miserable appearance baffles all de- "scription. I have not seen six cabins out of six "hundred, where the windows have been whole. Old "hats, old clothes, old boards, old fragments of "blanket and paper, are stuffed into the broken "glass; and their air is misery and desolation. It "pains the eye to see the stumps of great trees thickly "strewn in every field of wheat; and never to lose "the eternal swamp and dull morass, with hun- "dreds of rotten trunks, of elm and pine and "sycamore and logwood, steeped in its unwhole- "some water; where the frogs so croak at night "that after dark there is an incessant sound as if "millions of phantom teams, with bells, were

New settlers.

Original of *Chuzzlewit* settlement.

"travelling through the upper air, at an enormous "distance off. It is quite an oppressive circum- "stance, too, to *come* upon great tracks, where "settlers have been burning down the trees; and "where their wounded bodies lie about, like those "of murdered creatures; while here and there "some charred and blackened giant rears two bare "arms aloft, and seems to curse his enemies. The "prettiest sight I have seen was yesterday, when "we—on the heights of the mountain, and in a "keen wind—looked down into a valley full of "light and softness: catching glimpses of scattered "cabins; children running to the doors; dogs "bursting out to bark; pigs scampering home, like "so many prodigal sons; families sitting out in "their gardens; cows gazing upward, with a stupid "indifference; men in their shirt-sleeves, looking "on at their unfinished houses, and planning work "for to-morrow;--and the train riding on, high "above them, like a storm. But I know this is "beautiful—very—very beautiful!

CANAL BOAT FOR PITTSBURGH: 1842.

C. D. to J. F.

View from heights of a mountain.

" . . I wonder whether you and Mac mean to "go to Greenwich-fair! Perhaps you dine at the "Crown-and-sceptre to-day, for it's Easter-Monday "—who knows! I wish you drank punch, dear "Forster. It's a shabby thing, not to be able to "picture you with that cool green glass . . .

"I told you of the many uses of the word

Useful word.

CANAL BOAT FOR PITTSBURGH: 1842. — C. D. to J. F.

"'fix.' I ask Mr. Q on board a steamboat if "breakfast be nearly ready, and he tells me yes "he should think so, for when he was last below "the steward was 'fixing the tables'—in other "words, laying the cloth. When we have been "writing, and I beg him (do you remember anything "of my love of order, at this distance of time?) "to collect our papers, he answers that he'll 'fix "''em presently.' So when a man's dressing he's "'fixing' himself, and when you put yourself under "a doctor he 'fixes' you in no time. T'other "night, before we came on board here, when I "had ordered a bottle of mulled claret, and waited "some time for it, it was put on table with an "apology from the landlord (a lieutenant-colonel) "that 'he feared it wasn't fixed properly.' And "here, on Saturday morning, a Western man, hand- "ing the potatoes to Mr. Q at breakfast, enquired

Fixings.

"if he wouldn't take some of 'these fixings' with "his meat. I remained as grave as a judge. I "catch them looking at me sometimes, and feel "that they think I don't take any notice. Politics

Party in America.

"are very high here; dreadfully strong; handbills, "denunciations, invectives, threats, and quarrels. "The question is, who shall be the next President. "The election comes off in *three years and a half* "from this time."

He resumed his letter, "on board the steam

"boat from Pittsburgh to Cincinnati, April the "first, 1842. A very tremulous steam boat, which "makes my hand shake. This morning, my dear "friend, this very morning, which, passing by with-"out bringing news from England, would have "seen us on our way to St. Louis (viâ Cincinnati "and Louisville) with sad hearts and dejected "countenances, and the prospect of remaining for "at least three weeks longer without any intel-"ligence of those so inexpressibly dear to us—this "very morning, bright and lucky morning that it "was, a great packet was brought to our bed-room "door, from HOME. How I have read and re-"read your affectionate, hearty, interesting, funny, "serious, delightful, and thoroughly Forsterian "Columbia letter, I will not attempt to tell you; "or how glad I am that you liked my first; or "how afraid I am that my second was not written "in such good spirits as it should have been; or "how glad I am again to think that my third "*was;* or how I hope you will find some amuse-"ment from my fourth: this present missive. All "this, and more affectionate and earnest words "than the post office would convey at any price, "though they have no sharp edges to hurt the "stamping-clerk—you will understand, I know, "without expression, or attempt at expression. So

STEAM BOAT TO CINCINNATI: 1842.

C. D. to J. F.

News from home.

Steam Boat to Cincinnati: 1842.

C. D. to J. F.

"having got over the first agitation of so much "pleasure; and having walked the deck; and being "now in the cabin, where one party are playing "at chess, and another party are asleep, and an-"other are talking round the stove, and all are "spitting; and a persevering bore of a horrible "New Englander with a droning voice like a gi-"gantic bee *will* sit down beside me, though I am "writing, and talk incessantly, in my very ear, to "Kate;—here goes again.

At Pittsburgh.

"Let me see. I should tell you, first, that we "got to Pittsburgh between eight and nine o'clock "of the evening of the day on which I left off at "the top of this sheet; and were there received "by a little man (a very little man) whom I knew "years ago in London. He rejoiceth in the name "of D G; and, when I knew him, was in partner-"ship with his father on the stock-exchange, and "lived handsomely at Dalston. They failed in "business soon afterwards, and then this little "man began to turn to account what had pre-"viously been his amusement and accomplish-"ment, by painting little subjects for the fancy "shops. So I lost sight of him, nearly ten years "ago; and here he turned up t'other day, as a "portrait painter in Pittsburgh! He had pre-"viously written me a letter which moved me a

Meets an early acquaintance.

"Smallness of the world."

"good deal, by a kind of quiet independence "and contentment it breathed, and still a painful "sense of being alone, so very far from home. I "received it in Philadelphia, and answered it. "He dined with us every day of our stay in Pitts-"burgh (they were only three), and was truly "gratified and delighted to find me unchanged—"more so than I can tell you. I am very glad "to-night to think how much happiness we have "fortunately been able to give him.

STEAM BOAT TO CINCINNATI: 1842.

C. D. to J. F.

"Pittsburgh is like Birmingham—at least its "townsfolks say so; and I didn't contradict them. "It is, in one respect. There is a great deal of "smoke in it. I quite offended a man at our "yesterday's levee, who supposed I was 'now "'quite at home,' by telling him that the notion "of London being so dark a place was a popular "mistake. We had very queer customers at our "receptions, I do assure you. Not least among "them, a gentleman with his inexpressibles im-"perfectly buttoned and his waistband resting on "his thighs, who stood behind the half-opened "door, and could by no temptation or induce-"ment be prevailed upon to come out. There "was also another gentleman, with one eye and one "fixed gooseberry, who stood in a corner, motion-"less like an eight-day clock, and glared upon

Of Pittsburgh.

Queer customers at the levees.

STEAM BOAT TO CINCINNATI: 1842. — C. D. to J. F.

"me, as I courteously received the Pittsburgians. "There were also two red-headed brothers—boys "—young dragons rather—who hovered about "Kate, and wouldn't go. A great crowd they "were, for three days; and a very queer one."

"STILL IN THE SAME BOAT. *April the Second*, 1842.

Our anniversary.

"Many, many, happy returns of the day. It's "only eight o'clock in the morning now, but we "mean to drink your health after dinner, in a "bumper; and scores of Richmond dinners to us! "We have some wine (a present sent on board "by our Pittsburgh landlord) in our own cabin; "and we shall tap it to good purpose, I assure "you; wishing you all manner and kinds of hap-"piness, and a long life to ourselves that we may "be partakers of it. We have wondered a hun-"dred times already, whether you and Mac will "dine anywhere together, in honour of the day. "I say yes, but Kate says no. She predicts that "you'll ask Mac, and he won't go. I have not "yet heard from him.

The Cincinnati steamer.

"We have a better cabin here, than we had "on board the Britannia; the berths being much "wider, and the den having two doors: one open-"ing on the ladies' cabin, and one upon a little "gallery in the stern of the boat. We expect to "be at Cincinnati some time on Monday morn-"ing, and we carry about fifty passengers. The "cabin for meals goes right through the boat, "from the prow to the stern, and is very long; "only a small portion of it being divided off, by "a partition of wood and ground-glass, for the "ladies. We breakfast at half after seven, dine "at one, and sup at six. Nobody will sit down "to any one of these meals, though the dishes "are smoking on the board, until the ladies have "appeared, and taken their chairs. It was the "same in the canal boat.

STEAM BOAT TO CINCINNATI: 1842.

C. D. to J. F.

Deference to ladies.

"The washing department is a little more "civilized than it was on the canal, but bad is "the best. Indeed the Americans when they are "travelling, as Miss Martineau seems disposed to "admit, are exceedingly negligent: not to say "dirty. To the best of my making out, the ladies, "under most circumstances, are content with "smearing their hands and faces in a very small "quantity of water. So are the men; who "superadd to that mode of ablution, a hasty use "of the common brush and comb. It is quite "a practice, too, to wear but one cotton shirt a "week, and three or four fine linen *fronts*. Anne "reports that this is Mr. Q's course of proceeding: "and my portrait-painting friend told me that it

Frugality in water and linen.

Steam Boat to Cincinnati: 1842. — C. D. to J. F.

"was the case with pretty nearly all his sitters; "so that when he bought a piece of cloth not "long ago, and instructed the sempstress to make "it *all* into shirts, not fronts, she thought him "deranged.

"My friend the New Englander, of whom I "wrote last night, is perhaps the most intolerable "bore on this vast continent. He drones, and "snuffles, and writes poems, and talks small phi-"losophy and metaphysics, and never *will* be "quiet, under any circumstances. He is going "to a great temperance convention at Cincinnati; "along with a doctor of whom I saw something "at Pittsburgh. The doctor, in addition to being "everything that the New Englander is, is a "phrenologist besides. I dodge them about the "boat. Whenever I appear on deck, I see them "bearing down upon me—and fly. The New "Englander was very anxious last night that he "and I should 'form a magnetic chain,' and "magnetize the doctor, for the benefit of all in-"credulous passengers; but I declined, on the "plea of tremendous occupation in the way of "letter-writing.

Magnetic experiments.

"And speaking of magnetism, let me tell you "that the other night at Pittsburgh, there being "present only Mr. Q and the portrait-painter,

"Kate sat down, laughing, for me to try my "hand upon her. I had been holding forth upon "the subject rather luminously, and asserting that "I thought I could exercise the influence, but had "never tried. In six minutes, I magnetized her "into hysterics, and then into the magnetic sleep. "I tried again next night, and she fell into the "slumber in little more than two minutes. . . . I "can wake her with perfect ease; but I confess "(not being prepared for anything so sudden and "complete), I was on the first occasion rather "alarmed. . . . The Western parts being some-"times hazardous, I have fitted out the whole of "my little company with LIFE PRESERVERS, which "I inflate with great solemnity when we get "aboard any boat, and keep, as Mrs. Cluppins "did her umbrella in the court of common pleas, "ready for use upon a moment's notice." . . .

STEAM BOAT TO CINCINNATI: 1842.

C. D. to J. F.

Life preservers.

He resumed his letter, on "Sunday, April the "third," with allusion to a general who had called upon him in Washington with two literary ladies, and had written to him next day for an immediate interview, as "the two LL's" were ambitious of the honour of a personal introduction. "Besides the doctor and the dread New Eng-"lander, we have on board that valiant general "who wrote to me about the 'two LL's.' He is

STEAM BOAT TO CINCINNATI: 1842. C. D. to J. F.

"an old, old man with a weazen face, and the "remains of a pigeon-breast in his military sur-"tout. He is acutely gentlemanly and officer-"like. The breast has so subsided, and the face "has become so strongly marked, that he seems "like a pigeon-pie, to show only the feet of the "bird outside, and to keep the rest to himself.

Bores.

"He is perhaps *the* most horrible bore in this "country. And I am quite serious when I say "that I do not believe there are, on the whole "earth besides, so many intensified bores as in "these United States. No man can form an "adequate idea of the real meaning of the word, "without coming here. There are no particular "characters on board, with these three exceptions. "Indeed I seldom see the passengers but at meal-"times, as I read and write in our own little state "room. . . . I have smuggled two chairs into our "crib; and write this on a book upon my knee. "Everything is in the neatest order, of course;

Habits of neatness.

"and my shaving tackle, dressing case, brushes, "books, and papers, are arranged with as much "precision as if we were going to remain here a "month. Thank God we are not.

The Ohio.

"The average width of the river rather ex-"ceeds that of the Thames at Greenwich. In "parts it is much broader; and then there is

"usually a green island, covered with trees, divid- STEAM BOAT TO CINCINNATI: 1842. C. D. to J. F.
"ing it into two streams. Occasionally we stop "for a few minutes at a small town, or village (I "ought to say city, everything is a city here); but "the banks are for the most part deep solitudes, "overgrown with trees, which, in these western "latitudes, are already in leaf, and very green ....

"All this I see, as I write, from the little door "into the stern-gallery which I mentioned just "now. It don't happen six times in a day that "any other passenger comes near it; and, as the "weather is amply warm enough to admit of our "sitting with it open, here we remain from morn-"ing until night: reading, writing, talking. What "our theme of conversation is, I need not tell "you. No beauty or variety makes us weary less Wearying for home. "for home. We count the days, and say, 'When "'May comes, and we can say—*next month*—the "'time will seem almost gone.' We are never "tired of imagining what you are all about. I al-"low of no calculation for the difference of clocks, "but insist on a corresponding minute in London. "It is much the shortest way, and best. . . . "Yesterday, we drank your health and many 2nd April. "happy returns—in wine, after dinner; in a small "milk-pot jug of gin-punch, at night. And when "I made a temporary table, to hold the little

STEAM BOAT TO CINCINNATI: 1842.

C. D. to J. F.

"candle-stick, of one of my dressing-case trays; "cunningly inserted under the mattress of my "berth with a weight a-top of it to keep it in its "place, so that it made a perfectly exquisite "bracket; we agreed, that, please God, this should "be a joke at the Star-and-garter on the second "of April eighteen hundred and forty-three. If "your blank *can* be surpassed . . . believe me "ours transcends it. My heart gets, sometimes, "SORE for home.

Another solitary prison.

"At Pittsburgh I saw another solitary confine- "ment prison: Pittsburgh being also in Pennsyl- "vania. A horrible thought occurred to me when "I was recalling all I had seen, that night. *What "if ghosts be one of the terrors of these jails?* I "have pondered on it often, since then. The "utter solitude by day and night; the many hours "of darkness; the silence of death; the mind for "ever brooding on melancholy themes, and having "no relief; sometimes an evil conscience very "busy; imagine a prisoner covering up his head "in the bedclothes and looking out from time to "time, with a ghastly dread of some inexplicable "silent figure that always sits upon his bed, or "stands (if a thing can be said to stand, that "never walks as men do) in the same corner of "his cell. The more I think of it, the more cer-

New terror to solitude.

CINCINNATI: 1842. C. D. to J. F.

"tain I feel that not a few of these men (during "a portion of their imprisonment at least) are "nightly visited by spectres. I did ask one man "in this last jail, if he dreamed much. He gave "me a most extraordinary look, and said—under "his breath—in a whisper—'No.' . . .

"CINCINNATI. *Fourth April*, 1842.

"We arrived here this morning: about three "o'clock, I believe, but I was fast asleep in my "berth. I turned out soon after six, dressed, and "breakfasted on board. About half after eight, "we came ashore and drove to the hotel, to which "we had written on from Pittsburgh ordering "rooms; and which is within a stone's throw of "the boat wharf. Before I had issued an official "notification that we were 'not at home,' two "Judges called, on the part of the inhabitants, to "know when we would receive the townspeople. "We appointed to-morrow morning, from half-"past eleven to one; arranged to go out, with "these two gentlemen, to see the town, *at* one; 'and were fixed for an evening party to-morrow "night at the house of one of them. On Wednes-"day morning we go on by the mail-boat to Louis-"ville, a trip of fourteen hours; and from that "place proceed in the next good boat to St. Louis,

Two Judges in attendance.

Cincinnati: 1842. — C. D. to J. F. Change of route.

"which is a voyage of four days. Finding from "my judicial friends (well-informed and most "agreeable gentlemen) this morning, that the "prairie travel to Chicago is a very fatiguing one, "and that the lakes are stormy, sea-sicky, and not "over-safe at this season, I wrote by our captain "to St. Louis (for the boat that brought us here "goes on there) to the effect that I should not "take the lake route, but should come back here; "and should visit the prairies, which are within "thirty miles of St. Louis, immediately on my ar-"rival there. . . . .

Description of the city.

"I have walked to the window, since I turned "this page, to see what aspect the town wears. "We are in a wide street: paved in the carriage "way with small white stones, and in the footway "with small red tiles. The houses are for the "most part one story high; some are of wood; "others of a clean white brick. Nearly all have "green blinds outside every window. The prin-"cipal shops over the way, are, according to the "inscriptions over them, a Large Bread Bakery; "a Book Bindery; a Dry Goods Store; and a Car-"riage Repository; the last named establishment "looking very like an exceedingly small retail "coal-shed. On the pavement under our window, "a black man is chopping wood; and another "black man is talking (confidentially) to a pig. "The public table, at this hotel and at the hotel "opposite, has just now finished dinner. The "diners are collected on the pavement, on both "sides of the way, picking their teeth, and talking. "The day being warm, some of them have brought "chairs into the street. Some are on three chairs; "some on two; and some, in defiance of all known "laws of gravity, are sitting quite comfortably on "one: with three of the chair's legs, and their own "two, high up in the air. The loungers, under-"neath our window, are talking of a great Tem-"perance convention which comes off here to-"morrow. Others, about me. Others, about Eng-"land. Sir Robert Peel is popular here, with "everybody. . . ."

CINCINNATI: 1842.

C. D. to J. F.

On the pavement.

CHAPTER XXIII.

THE FAR WEST: TO NIAGARA FALLS.

1842.

THE next letter described his experiences in the Far West, his stay in St. Louis, his visit to a Prairie, the return to Cincinnati, and, after a stage-coach ride from that city to Columbus, the travel thence to Sandusky, and so, by Lake Erie, to the Falls of Niagara. All these subjects appear in the *Notes*, but nothing printed there is repeated in the extracts now to be given. Of the closing passages of his journey, when he turned from Columbus in the direction of home, the story, here for the first time told, is in his most characteristic vein; the account that will be found of the Prairie will probably be preferred to what is given in the *Notes;* the Cincinnati sketches are very pleasant; and even such a description as that of the Niagara Falls, of which so much is made in the book, has here an independent novelty and freshness. The first vividness is in his

Descriptions in letters and in *Notes*.

letter. The naturalness of associating no image or sense but of repose, with a grandeur so mighty and resistless, is best presented suddenly; and, in a few words, we have the material as well as moral beauty of a scene unrivalled in its kind upon the earth. The instant impression we find to be worth more than the eloquent recollection.

BACK TO CINCINNATI: 1842.

The captain of the boat that had dropped them at Cincinnati and gone to St. Louis, had stayed in the latter place until they were able to join and return with him; this letter bears date accordingly, "On board the Messenger again. "Going from St. Louis back to Cincinnati. Fri-"day, fifteenth April, 1842;" and its first paragraph is an outline of the movements which it afterwards describes in detail. "We remained in "Cincinnati one whole day after the date of my "last, and left on Wednesday morning the 6th. "We reached Louisville soon after midnight on "the same night; and slept there. Next day at "one o'clock we put ourselves on board another "steamer, and travelled on until last Sunday even-"ing the tenth; when we reached St. Louis at "about nine o'clock. The next day we devoted "to seeing the city. Next day, Tuesday the twelfth, "I started off with a party of men (we were four-"teen in all) to see a prairie; returned to St. Louis

C. D. to J. F.

Outline of westward travel.

BACK TO CINCINNATI: 1842. C. D. to J. F.

"about noon on the thirteenth; attended a soirée "and ball—not a dinner—given in my honor that "night; and yesterday afternoon at four o'clock "we turned our faces homewards. Thank Heaven!

An Arabian-night city.

"Cincinnati is only fifty years old, but is a "very beautiful city: I think the prettiest place I "have seen here, except Boston. It has risen out "of the forest like an Arabian-night city; is well "laid out; ornamented in the suburbs with pretty "villas; and above all, for this is a very rare "feature in America, has smooth turf-plots and "well kept gardens. There happened to be a

Temperance festival.

"great temperance festival; and the procession "mustered under, and passed, our windows early "in the morning. I suppose they were twenty "thousand strong, at least. Some of the banners "were quaint and odd enough. The ship-car-"penters, for instance, displayed on one side of "their flag, the good Ship Temperance in full "sail; on the other, the Steamer Alcohol blowing "up sky-high. The Irishmen had a portrait of "Father Mathew, you may be sure. And Wash-"ington's broad lower jaw (by the bye, Washing-"ton had not a pleasant face) figured in all parts "of the ranks. In a kind of square at one out-"skirt of the city, they divided into bodies, and

Dry speaking

"were addressed by different speakers. Drier

BACK TO CINCINNATI: 1842. C. D. to J. F.

"speaking I never heard. I own that I felt quite "uncomfortable to think they could take the taste "of it out of their mouths with nothing better "than water.

A party at Judge Walker's.

"In the evening we went to a party at Judge "Walker's, and were introduced to at least one "hundred and fifty first-rate bores, separately and "singly. I was required to sit down by the greater "part of them, and talk!* In the night we were

The party from another view.

* A young lady's account of this party, written next morning, and quoted in one of the American memoirs of Dickens, enables us to contemplate his suffering from the point of view of those who inflicted it. "I went last even-"ing to a party at Judge Walker's, given to the hero of the "day. . . . When we reached the house Mr. Dickens had "left the crowded rooms, and was in the hall with his wife, "about taking his departure when we entered the door. "We were introduced to him in our wrapping; and in the "flurry and embarrassment of the meeting, one of the party "dropped a parcel, containing shoes, gloves, &c. Mr. "Dickens, stooping, gathered them up and restored them "with a laughing remark, and we bounded upstairs to get "our things off. Hastening down again, we found him with "Mrs. Dickens seated upon a sofa, surrounded by a group "of ladies; Judge Walker having requested him to delay his "departure for a few moments, for the gratification of some "tardy friends who had just arrived, ourselves among the "number. Declining to re-enter the rooms where he had "already taken leave of the guests, he had seated himself in

BACK TO CINCINNATI: 1842.

C. D. to J. F.

"serenaded (as we usually are in every place we "come to), and very well serenaded, I assure you.

"the hall. He is young and handsome, has a mellow, beau-"tiful eye, fine brow, and abundant hair. His mouth is "large, and his smile so bright it seemed to shed light and "happiness all about him. His manner is easy, negligent, "but not elegant. His dress was foppish; in fact, he was "overdressed, yet his garments were worn so easily they ap-"peared to be a necessary part of him. (!) He had a dark "coat, with lighter pantaloons; a black waistcoat, embroidered "with colored flowers; and about his neck, covering his "white shirt-front, was a black neckcloth, also embroidered "in colors, in which were placed two large diamond pins "connected by a chain. A gold watch-chain, and a large "red rose in his button-hole, completed his toilet. He ap-"peared a little weary, but answered the remarks made to "him—for he originated none—in an agreeable manner. Mr. "Beard's portrait of Fagin was so placed in the room that "we could see it from where we stood surrounding him. "One of the ladies asked him if it was his idea of the Jew. "He replied, 'Very nearly.' Another, laughingly, requested "that he would give her the rose he wore, as a memento. "He shook his head and said: 'That will not do; he could "'not give it to one; the others would be jealous.' A half "dozen then insisted on having it, whereupon he proposed "to divide the leaves among them. In taking the rose from "his coat, either by design or accident, the leaves loosened "and fell upon the floor, and amid considerable laughter the "ladies stooped and gathered them. He remained some "twenty minutes, perhaps, in the hall, and then took his "leave. I must confess to considerable disappointment in

Young lady's description of C. D.

"But we were very much knocked up. I really "think my face has acquired a fixed expression "of sadness from the constant and unmitigated "boring I endure. The LL's have carried away "all my cheerfulness. There is a line in my chin "(on the right side of the under-lip), indelibly "fixed there by the New-Englander I told you of "in my last. I have the print of a crow's foot on "the outside of my left eye, which I attribute to "the literary characters of small towns. A dimple "has vanished from my cheek, which I felt myself "robbed of at the time by a wise legislator. But "on the other hand I am really indebted for a "good broad grin to P. . E. ., literary critic of "Philadelphia, and sole proprietor of the English "language in its grammatical and idiomatical "purity; to P. . E. ., with the shiny straight hair "and turned-down shirt collar, who taketh all of "us English men of letters to task in print, "roundly and uncompromisingly, but told me, at "the same time, that I had 'awakened a new era' "in his mind. . . .

BACK TO CINCINNATI: 1842.

C. D. to J. F.

Mournful results of boredom.

"The last 200 miles of the voyage from Cin-

"the personal of my idol. I felt that his throne was shaken, "although it never could be destroyed." This appalling picture supplements and very sufficiently explains the mournful passage in the text.

From Cincinnati to St. Louis: 1842.

C. D. to J. F.

"cinnati to St. Louis are upon the Mississippi, "for you come down the Ohio to its mouth. It "is well for society that this Mississippi, the re-"nowned father of waters, had no children who "take after him. It is the beastliest river in the "world." . . . (His description is in the *Notes*.)

Down the Mississippi.

"Conceive the pleasure of rushing down this "stream by night (as we did last night) at the "rate of fifteen miles an hour; striking against "floating blocks of timber every instant; and "dreading some infernal blow at every bump. "The helmsman in these boats is in a little glass-"house upon the roof. In the Mississippi, another "man stands in the very head of the vessel, listen-

Listening and watching.

"ing and watching intently; listening, because "they can tell in dark nights by the noise when "any great obstruction is at hand. This man "holds the rope of a large bell which hangs close "to the wheel-house, and whenever he pulls it, "the engine is to stop directly, and not to stir "until he rings again. Last night, this bell rang "at least once in every five minutes; and at each "alarm there was a concussion which nearly flung "one out of bed. . . . While I have been writing "this account, we have shot out of that hideous "river, thanks be to God; never to see it again, "I hope, but in a nightmare. We are now on the "smooth Ohio, and the change is like the transition from pain to perfect ease. ST. LOUIS: 1842. C. D. to J. F.

"We had a very crowded levee in St. Louis. "Of course the paper had an account of it. If I "were to drop a letter in the street, it would be "in the newspaper next day, and nobody would "think its publication an outrage. The editor "objected to my hair, as not curling sufficiently. "He admitted an eye; but objected again to "dress, as being somewhat foppish, 'and indeed "'perhaps rather flash.'—'But such,' he benevolently adds, 'are the differences between American and English taste—rendered more ap"'parent, perhaps, by all the other gentlemen "'present being dressed in black.' Oh, that you "could have seen the other gentlemen! . . . . A levee at St. Louis.

"A St. Louis lady complimented Kate upon "her voice and manner of speaking: assuring her "that she should never have suspected her of "being Scotch, or even English. She was so "obliging as to add that she would have taken "her for an American, anywhere: which she (Kate) "was no doubt aware was a very great compli"ment, as the Americans were admitted on all "hands to have greatly refined upon the English "language! I need not tell you that out of Boston "and New York a nasal drawl is universal, but I Compliments.

ST. LOUIS: 1842. C. D. to J. F. Peculiarities of speech.

"may as well hint that the prevailing grammar is "also more than doubtful; that the oddest vul-"garisms are received idioms; that all the women "who have been bred in slave-states speak more "or less like negroes, from having been constantly "in their childhood with black nurses; and that "the most fashionable and aristocratic (these are "two words in great use), instead of asking you "in what place you were born, enquire where "you 'hail from?'!!

"Lord Ashburton arrived at Annapolis t' other "day, after a voyage of forty odd days in heavy "weather. Straightway the newspapers state, on "the authority of a correspondent who 'rowed "'round the ship' (I leave you to fancy her con-"dition), that America need fear no superiority "from England, in respect of her wooden walls. "The same correspondent is 'quite pleased' with "the frank manner of the English officers; and "patronizes them as being, for John Bulls, quite "refined. My face, like Haji Baba's, turns upside "down, and my liver is changed to water, when I "come upon such things, and think who writes "and who read them. . . .

Lord Ashburton's arrival.

"They won't let me alone about slavery. A "certain Judge in St. Louis went so far yester-"day, that I fell upon him (to the indescribable

ST. LOUIS: 1842.

O. D. to J. F.

Talk with a judge on slavery.

"horror of the man who brought him) and told "him a piece of my mind. I said that I was very "averse to speaking on the subject here, and al- "ways forbore, if possible: but when he pitied "our national ignorance of the truths of slavery, "I must remind him that we went upon indisput- "able records, obtained after many years of care- "ful investigation, and at all sorts of self-sacrifice; "and that I believed we were much more compe- "tent to judge of its atrocity and horror, than he "who had been brought up in the midst of it. "I told him that I could sympathise with men "who admitted it to be a dreadful evil, but "frankly confessed their inability to devise a "means of getting rid of it: but that men who "spoke of it as a blessing, as a matter of course, "as a state of things to be desired, were out of "the pale of reason; and that for them to speak "of ignorance or prejudice was an absurdity too "ridiculous to be combated. . .

"It is not six years ago, since a slave in this "very same St. Louis, being arrested (I forget for "what), and knowing he had no chance of a fair "trial, be his offence what it might, drew his "bowie knife and ripped the constable across the "body. A scuffle ensuing, the desperate negro "stabbed two others with the same weapon. The

St. Louis: 1842.

C. D. to J. F.

"mob who gathered round (among whom were "men of mark, wealth, and influence in the place) "overpowered him by numbers; carried him away "to a piece of open ground beyond the city; *and*

A negro burnt alive.

"*burned him alive.* This, I say, was done within "six years in broad day; in a city with its courts, "lawyers, tipstaffs, judges, jails, and hangman; "and not a hair on the head of one of those men "has been hurt to this day. And it is, believe "me, it is the miserable, wretched independence "in small things; the paltry republicanism which "recoils from honest service to an honest man, "but does not shrink from every trick, artifice, "and knavery in business; that makes these slaves "necessary, and will render them so, until the in-"dignation of other countries sets them free.

Feeling of slaves themselves.

"They say the slaves are fond of their mas-"ters. Look at this pretty vignette* (part of the "stock-in-trade of a newspaper), and judge how "you would feel, when men, looking in your face, "told you such tales with the newspaper lying on "the table. In all the slave districts, advertise-

* "Runaway Negro in Jail" was the heading of the advertisement enclosed, which had a woodcut of master and slave in its corner, and announced that Wilford Garner, sheriff and jailer of Chicot County, Arkansas, requested owner to come and prove property—or——

"ments for runaways are as much matters of "course as the announcement of the play for the "evening with us. The poor creatures themselves "fairly worship English people: they would do "anything for them. They are perfectly acquainted "with all that takes place in reference to emanci-"pation; and *of course* their attachment to us "grows out of their deep devotion to their owners. "I cut this illustration out of a newspaper which "had a leader in reference to *the abominable and* "*hellish doctrine of Abolition—repugnant alike to* "*every law of God and Nature.* 'I know some-"'thing' said a Dr. Bartlett (a very accomplished "man), late a fellow-passenger of ours: 'I know "'something of their fondness for their masters. "'I live in Kentucky; and I can assert upon my "'honour, that, in my neighbourhood, it is as "'common for a runaway slave, retaken, to draw "'his bowie knife and rip his owner's bowels "'open, as it is for you to see a drunken fight in "'London.'"

ST. LOUIS: 1842. C. D. to J. F.

Dr. Bartlett.

"SAME BOAT, *Saturday, Sixteenth April*, 1842.

"Let me tell you, my dear Forster, before I "forget it, a pretty little scene we had on board "the boat between Louisville and St. Louis, as "we were going to the latter place. It is not

Pretty little scene.

St. Louis: 1842. C. D. to J. F.

"much to tell, but it was very pleasant and inter-"esting to witness."

What follows has been printed in the *Notes*, and ought not, by the rule I have laid down, to be given here. But, beautiful as the printed description is, it has not profited by the alteration of some touches and the omission of others in the first fresh version of it, which, for that reason, I here preserve—one of the most charming soul-felt pictures of character and emotion that ever warmed the heart in fact or fiction. It was, I think, Jeffrey's favorite passage in all the writings of Dickens: and certainly, if anyone would learn the secret of their popularity, it is to be read in the observation and description of this little incident.

A little mother:

"There was a little woman on board, with a "little baby; and both little woman and little child "were cheerful, good-looking, bright-eyed, and "fair to see. The little woman had been passing "a long time with a sick mother in New York, "and had left her home in St. Louis in that con-"dition in which ladies who truly love their lords "desire to be. The baby had been born in her "mother's house, and she had not seen her hus-"band (to whom she was now returning) for twelve "months: having left him a month or two after

returning to her husband.

ST. LOUIS: 1842. C. D. to J. F.

"their marriage. Well, to be sure, there never was "a little woman so full of hope, and tenderness, "and love, and anxiety, as this little woman was: "and there she was, all the livelong day, wonder-"ing whether 'he' would be at the wharf; and "whether 'he' had got her letter; and whether, if "she sent the baby on shore by somebody else, "*'he' would know it, meeting it in the street:* which, "seeing that he had never set eyes upon it in his "life, was not very likely in the abstract, but was "probable enough to the young mother. She "was such an artless little creature; and was in "such a sunny, beaming, hopeful state; and let "out all this matter, clinging close about her heart, "so freely; that all the other lady passengers "entered into the spirit of it as much as she: and "the captain (who heard all about it from his "wife) was wondrous sly, I promise you: enquiring, "every time we met at table, whether she expected "anybody to meet her at St. Louis, and supposing "she wouldn't want to go ashore the night we "reached it, and cutting many other dry jokes "which convulsed all his hearers, but especially "the ladies. There was one little, weazen, dried-"apple old woman among them, who took occa-"sion to doubt the constancy of husbands under "such circumstances of bereavement; and there

The ladies and the captain.

ST. LOUIS: 1842.

C. D. to J. F.

The little mother and her baby.

St. Louis in sight.

"was another lady (with a lap dog), old enough "to moralize on the lightness of human affections, "and yet not so old that she could help nursing "the baby now and then, or laughing with the "rest when the little woman called it by its father's "name, and asked it all manner of fantastic ques-"tions concerning him, in the joy of her heart. "It was something of a blow to the little woman, "that when we were within twenty miles of our "destination, it became clearly necessary to put "the baby to bed; but she got over that with the "same good humour, tied a little handkerchief "over her little head, and came out into the gal-"lery with the rest. Then, such an oracle as she "became in reference to the localities! and such "facetiousness as was displayed by the married "ladies! and such sympathy as was shown by the "single ones! and such peals of laughter as the "little woman herself (who would just as soon "have cried) greeted every jest with! At last, "there were the lights of St. Louis—and here was "the wharf—and those were the steps—and the "little woman, covering her face with her hands, "and laughing, or seeming to laugh, more than "ever, ran into her own cabin, and shut herself up "tight. I have no doubt, that, in the charming "inconsistency of such excitement, she stopped "her ears lest she should hear 'him' asking for "her; but I didn't see her do it. Then a great "crowd of people rushed on board, though the "boat was not yet made fast, and was staggering "about among the other boats to find a landing- "place; and everybody looked for the husband, "and nobody saw him; when all of a sudden, "right in the midst of them—God knows how she "ever got there—there was the little woman "hugging with both arms round the neck of a "fine, good-looking, sturdy fellow! And in a "moment afterwards, there she was again, dragging "him through the small door of her small cabin, "to look at the baby as he lay asleep!—What a "good thing it is to know that so many of us "would have been quite downhearted and sorry "if that husband had failed to come."

ST. LOUIS: 1842. — C. D. to J. F.

The meeting.

He then resumes: but in what follows nothing is repeated that will be found in his printed description of the jaunt to the looking-glass prairie.

Trip to a prairie.

"But about the Prairie—it is not, I must con- "fess, so good in its way as this; but I'll tell you "all about that too, and leave you to judge for "yourself. Tuesday the 12th was the day fixed; "and we were to start at five in the morning— "sharp. I turned out at four; shaved and dressed; "got some bread and milk; and throwing up the

St. Louis: 1842. O. D. to J. F.

"window, looked down into the street. Deuce a "coach was there, nor did anybody seem to be "stirring in the house. I waited until half-past "five; but no preparations being visible even then, "I left Mr. Q to look out, and lay down upon "the bed again. There I slept until nearly seven, "when I was called. . . . Exclusive of Mr. Q and "myself, there were twelve of my committee in "the party: all lawyers except one. He was an "intelligent, mild, well-informed gentleman of my "own age—the unitarian minister of the place. "With him, and two other companions, I got in- "to the first coach. . . .

A good inn.

"We halted at so good an inn at Lebanon "that we resolved to return there at night, if pos- "sible. One would scarcely find a better village "alehouse of a homely kind in England. During "our halt I walked into the village, and met a "*dwelling-house* coming down-hill at a good round "trot, drawn by some twenty oxen! We resumed "our journey as soon as possible, and got upon "the looking-glass prairie at sunset. We halted "near a solitary log-house for the sake of its water; "unpacked the baskets; formed an encampment "with the carriages; and dined.

On the prairie at sunset.

"Now, a prairie is undoubtedly worth seeing "—but more, that one may say one has seen it, "than for any sublimity it possesses in itself. "Like most things, great or small, in this country, you hear of it with considerable exaggerations. Basil Hall was really quite right in depreciating the general character of the scenery. "The widely-famed Far West is not to be compared with even the tamest portions of Scotland "or Wales. You stand upon the prairie, and see "the unbroken horizon all round you. You are "on a great plain, which is like a sea without "water. I am exceedingly fond of wild and lonely scenery, and believe that I have the faculty "of being as much impressed by it as any man "living. But the prairie fell, by far, short of my "preconceived idea. I felt no such emotions as "I do in crossing Salisbury plain. The excessive "flatness of the scene makes it dreary, but tame. "Grandeur is certainly not its characteristic. I "retired from the rest of the party, to understand "my own feelings the better; and looked all "round, again and again. It was fine. It was "worth the ride. The sun was going down, very "red and bright; and the prospect looked like "that ruddy sketch of Catlin's, which attracted "our attention (you remember?); except that there "was not so much ground as he represents, between the spectator and the horizon. But to

ST. LOUIS: 1842. — C. D. to J. F.

General character of scenery.

The prairie described.

ST. LOUIS: 1842. C. D. to J. F. Disappointment.

"say (as the fashion is, here) that the sight is a "landmark in one's existence, and awakens a new "set of sensations, is sheer gammon. I would "say to every man who can't see a prairie—go "to Salisbury plain, Marlborough downs, or any "of the broad, high, open lands near the sea. "Many of them are fully as impressive; and Salis-"bury plain is *decidedly* more so.

Enjoyment.

"We had brought roast fowls, buffalo's tongue, "ham, bread, cheese, butter, biscuits, sherry, "champagne, lemons and sugar for punch, and "abundance of ice. It was a delicious meal: and "as they were most anxious that I should be "pleased, I warmed myself into a state of surpass-"ing jollity; proposed toasts from the coach-box "(which was the chair); ate and drank with the "best; and made, I believe, an excellent com-"panion to a very friendly companionable party. "In an hour or so, we packed up, and drove "back to the inn at Lebanon. While supper was "preparing, I took a pleasant walk with my uni-"tarian friend; and when it was over (we drank "nothing with it but tea and coffee) we went to "bed. The clergyman and I had an exquisitely "clean little chamber of our own: and the rest of "the party were quartered overhead. . . . .

"We got back to St. Louis soon after twelve

"at noon; and I rested during the remainder of "the day. The soirée came off at night, in a very "good ball-room at our inn—the Planter's-house. "The whole of the guests were introduced to us, "singly. We were glad enough, you may believe, "to come away at midnight; and were very tired. "Yesterday, I wore a blouse. To-day, a fur-coat. "Trying changes!

ST. LOUIS: 1842. — C. D. to J. F. Soirée at the Planter's-house.

"IN THE SAME BOAT.
"*Sunday, Sixteenth April*, 1842.

"The inns in these outlandish corners of the "world, would astonish you by their goodness. "The Planter's-house is as large as the Middle-"sex-hospital and built very much on our hospital "plan, with long wards abundantly ventilated, "and plain whitewashed walls. They had a fa-"mous notion of sending up at breakfast-time "large glasses of new milk with blocks of ice in "them as clear as crystal. Our table was abun-"dantly supplied indeed at every meal. One day "when Kate and I were dining alone together, in "our own room, we counted sixteen dishes on "the table at the same time.

Planters' inns. Good fare.

"The society is pretty rough, and intolerably "conceited. All the inhabitants are young. *I* "*didn't see one grey head in St. Louis*. There is "an island close by, called bloody island. It is

No grey heads in St. Louis.

ST. LOUIS: 1842. — C. D. to J. F.

"the duelling ground of St. Louis; and is so "called from the last fatal duel which was fought "there. It was a pistol duel, breast to breast, "and both parties fell dead at the same time. "One of our prairie party (a young man) had acted "as second there, in several encounters. The last "occasion was a duel with rifles, at forty paces; "and coming home he told us how he had bought "his man a coat of green linen to fight in, wool-"len being usually fatal to rifle wounds. Prairie "is variously called (on the refinement principle "I suppose) Para*a*rer; par*e*arer; and paro*a*rer. I "am afraid, my dear fellow, you will have had "great difficulty in reading all the foregoing text. "I have written it, very laboriously, on my knee; "and the engine throbs and starts as if the boat "were possessed with a devil.

Duelling.

"SANDUSKY.
"*Sunday, Twenty-fourth April*, 1842.

From Louisville to Cincinnati.

"We went ashore at Louisville this night week, "where I left off, two lines above; and slept at "the hotel, in which we had put up before. The "Messenger being abominably slow, we got our "luggage out next morning, and started on again "at eleven o'clock in the Benjamin Franklin mail "boat: a splendid vessel with a cabin more than "two hundred feet long, and little state-rooms "affording proportionate conveniences. She got "in at Cincinnati by one o'clock next morning, "when we landed in the dark and went back to "our old hotel. As we made our way on foot "over the broken pavement, Anne measured her "length upon the ground, but didn't hurt herself. "I say nothing of Kate's troubles—but you recol-"lect her propensity? She falls into, or out of, "every coach or boat we enter; scrapes the skin "off her legs; brings great sores and swellings on "her feet; chips large fragments out of her ankle-"bones; and makes herself blue with bruises. She "really has, however, since we got over the first "trial of being among circumstances so new and "so fatiguing, made a *most admirable* traveller in "every respect. She has never screamed or ex-"pressed alarm under circumstances that would "have fully justified her in doing so, even in my "eyes; has never given way to despondency or "fatigue, though we have now been travelling in-"cessantly, through a very rough country, for "more than a month, and have been at times, as "you may readily suppose, most thoroughly tired; "has always accommodated herself, well and "cheerfully, to everything; and has pleased me "very much, and proved herself perfectly game.

SANDUSKY: 1842. C. D. to J. F.

Mrs. Dickens as a traveller.

SANDUSKY: 1842.

C. D. to J. F. From Cincinnati to Columbus.

"We remained at Cincinnati, all Tuesday the "nineteenth, and all that night. At eight o'clock "on Wednesday morning the twentieth, we left in "the mail stage for Columbus: Anne, Kate, and "Mr. Q inside; I on the box. The distance is a "hundred and twenty miles; the road macadam-"ized; and for an American road, very good. We "were three and twenty hours performing the "journey. We travelled all night; reached Co-"lumbus at seven in the morning; breakfasted; "and went to bed until dinner time. At night "we held a levee for half an hour, and the people "poured in as they always do: each gentleman "with a lady on each arm, exactly like the Chorus "to God Save the Queen. I wish you could see "them, that you might know what a splendid "comparison this is. They wear their clothes, "precisely as the chorus people do; and stand—"supposing Kate and me to be in the centre of "the stage, with our backs to the footlights—just "as the company would, on the first night of the "season. They shake hands exactly after the "manner of the guests at a ball at the Adelphi or "the Haymarket; receive any facetiousness on my "part, as if there were a stage direction 'all laugh;' "and have rather more difficulty in 'getting off' "than the last gentlemen, in white pantaloons,

A levee at Columbus.

What a levee is like.

SANDUSKY: 1842.

C. D. to J. F.

From Columbus to Sandusky.

"polished boots, and berlins, usually display, "under the most trying circumstances.

"Next morning, that is to say on Friday the "22nd at seven o'clock exactly, we resumed our "journey. The stage from Columbus to this place "only running thrice a week, and not on that day, "I bargained for an 'exclusive extra' with four "horses, for which I paid forty dollars, or eight "pounds English: the horses changing, as they "would if it were the regular stage. To ensure "our getting on properly, the proprietors sent an "agent on the box; and, with no other company "but him and a hamper full of eatables and "drinkables, we went upon our way. It is im-"possible to convey an adequate idea to you of "the kind of road over which we travelled. I can "only say that it was, at the best, but a track "through the wild forest, and among the swamps, "bogs, and morasses of the withered bush. A "great portion of it was what is called a 'corduroy "'road:' which is made by throwing round logs "or whole trees into a swamp, and leaving them "to settle there. Good Heaven! if you only felt "one of the least of the jolts with which the "coach falls from log to log! It is like nothing "but going up a steep flight of stairs in an "omnibus. Now the coach flung us in a heap on

A corduroy road.

17*

SANDUSKY: 1842.

C. D. to J. F.

"its floor, and now crushed our heads against its "roof. Now one side of it was deep in the mire, "and we were holding on to the other. Now it "was lying on the horses' tails, and now again "upon its back. But it never, never, was in any "position, attitude, or kind of motion, to which "we are accustomed in coaches; or made the "smallest approach to our experience of the pro-"ceedings of any sort of vehicle that goes on "wheels. Still, the day was beautiful, the air de-"licious, and we were *alone:* with no tobacco "spittle, or eternal prosy conversation about dol-"lars and politics (the only two subjects they ever "converse about, or can converse upon) to bore "us. We really enjoyed it; made a joke of the "being knocked about; and were quite merry. At "two o'clock we stopped in the wood to open "our hamper and dine; and we drank to our "darlings and all friends at home. Then we "started again and went on until ten o'clock at "night: when we reached a place called Lower "Sandusky, sixty-two miles from our starting point. "The last three hours of the journey were not "very pleasant, for it lightened—awfully: every "flash very vivid, very blue, and very long: and, "the wood being so dense that the branches on "*either* side of the track rattled and broke *against*

The travellers alone.

A thunder storm.

"the coach, it was rather a dangerous neighbour-"hood for a thunder storm.

A log-house inn.

"The inn at which we halted was a rough "log-house. The people were all abed, and we "had to knock them up. We had the queerest "sleeping room, with two doors, one opposite the "other; both opening directly on the wild black "country, and neither having any lock or bolt. "The effect of these opposite doors was, that one "was always blowing the other open: an ingenuity "in the art of building, which I don't remember "to have met with before. You should have seen "me, in my shirt, blockading them with portman-"teaus, and desperately endeavouring to make "the room tidy! But the blockading was really "needful, for in my dressing case I have about "250*l.* in gold; and for the amount of the middle "figure in that scarce metal, there are not a few "men in the West who would murder their fathers. "Apropos of this golden store, consider at your "leisure the strange state of things in this country. "It has no money; really *no money*. The bank "paper won't pass; the newspapers are full of ad-"vertisements from tradesmen who sell by barter; "and American gold is not to be had, or pur-"chased. I bought sovereigns, English sovereigns, "at first: but as I could get none of them at Cin-

Making tidy.

A monetary crisis.

Sandusky: 1842. C. D. to J. F.

"cinnati, to this day, I have had to purchase "French gold; 20-franc pieces; with which I am "travelling as if I were in Paris!

"But let's go back to Lower Sandusky. Mr. Q "went to bed up in the roof of the log-house "somewhere, but was so beset by bugs that he "got up after an hour and *lay in the coach* ...... "where he was obliged to wait till breakfast time.

Breakfast at the inn.

"We breakfasted, driver and all, in the one com- "mon room. It was papered with newspapers, "and was as rough a place as need be. At half "past seven we started again, and we reached "Sandusky at six o'clock yesterday afternoon. It "is on Lake Erie, twenty-four hours' journey by "steam boat from Buffalo. We found no boat "here, nor has there been one, since. We are "waiting, with every thing packed up, ready to "start on the shortest notice; and are anxiously "looking out for smoke in the distance.

"There was an old gentleman in the Log inn "at Lower Sandusky who treats with the Indians "on the part of the American government, and "has just concluded a treaty with the Wyandot "Indians at that place to remove next year to "some land provided for them west of the Mis- "sissippi: a little way beyond St. Louis. He de- "scribed his negotiation to me, and their reluc-

"tance to go, exceedingly well. They are a fine "people, but degraded and broken down. If you "could see any of their men and women on a "race-course in England, you would not know "them from gipsies.

SANDUSKY: 1842.

C. D. to J. F.

Indians.

"We are in a small house here, but a very "comfortable one, and the people are exceedingly "obliging. Their demeanour in these country "parts is invariably morose, sullen, clownish, and "repulsive. I should think there is not, on the "face of the earth, a people so entirely destitute "of humour, vivacity, or the capacity of enjoy-"ment. It is most remarkable. I am quite serious "when I say that I have not heard a hearty laugh "these six weeks, except my own; nor have I seen "a merry face on any shoulders but a black man's. "Lounging listlessly about; idling in bar-rooms; "smoking; spitting; and lolling on the pavement "in rocking-chairs, outside the shop doors; are "the only recreations. I don't think the national "shrewdness extends beyond the Yankees; that "is, the Eastern men. The rest are heavy, dull, "and ignorant. Our landlord here is from the "East. He is a handsome, obliging, civil fellow. "He comes into the room with his hat on; spits "in the fire place as he talks; sits down on the "sofa with his hat on; pulls out his newspaper,

American people not given to humour.

The only recreations.

A landlord.

NIAGARA FALLS: 1842.

C. D. to J. F.

"and reads; but to all this I am accustomed. He "is anxious to please—and that is enough.

"We are wishing very much for a boat; for "we hope to find our letters at Buffalo. It is half "past one; and as there is no boat in sight, we "are fain (sorely against our wills) to order an "early dinner.

"*Tuesday, April Twenty-sixth*, 1842.
"NIAGARA FALLS!!! (UPON THE ENGLISH* SIDE).

From Sandusky to Buffalo.

"I don't know at what length I might have "written you from Sandusky, my beloved friend, "if a steamer had not come in sight just as I "finished the last unintelligible sheet (oh! the ink "in these parts!): whereupon I was obliged to "pack up bag and baggage, to swallow a hasty "apology for a dinner, and to hurry my train on "board with all the speed I might. She was a "fine steamship, four hundred tons burden, name "the Constitution, had very few passengers on "board, and had bountiful and handsome accom-"modation. It's all very fine talking about Lake "Erie, but it won't do for persons who are liable "to sea-sickness. We were all sick. It's almost "as bad in that respect as the Atlantic. The

On Lake Erie.

* Ten dashes underneath the word.

"waves are very short, and horribly constant. We "reached Buffalo at six this morning; went ashore "to breakfast; sent to the post-office forthwith; "and received—oh! who or what can say with "how much pleasure and what unspeakable de-"light!—our English letters!

"We lay all Sunday night, at a town (and a "beautiful town too) called Cleveland; on Lake "Erie. The people poured on board, in crowds, "by six on Monday morning, to see me; and a "party of 'gentlemen' actually planted themselves "before our little cabin, and stared in at the door "and windows *while I was washing, and Kate lay* "*in bed.* I was so incensed at this, and at a cer-"tain newspaper published in that town which I "had accidentally seen in Sandusky (advocating "war with England to the death, saying that Bri-"tain must be 'whipped again,' and promising "all true Americans that within two years they "should sing Yankee-doodle in Hyde-park and "Hail Columbia in the courts of Westminster), "that when the mayor came on board to present "himself to me, according to custom, I refused to "see him, and bade Mr. Q tell him why and "wherefore. His honor took it very coolly, and "retired to the top of the wharf, with a big stick "and a whittling knife, with which he worked so

Gazed at.

Rude reception of a mayor: his consolation.

NIAGARA FALLS: 1842. C. D. to J. F.

"lustily (staring at the closed door of our cabin "all the time) that long before the boat left, the "big stick was no bigger than a cribbage peg!

From Buffalo to Niagara.

"I never in my life was in such a state of ex-"citement as coming from Buffalo here, this "morning. You come by railroad; and are nigh "two hours upon the way. I looked out for the "spray, and listened for the roar, as far beyond "the bounds of possibility, as though, landing in "Liverpool, I were to listen for the music of your "pleasant voice in Lincoln's-inn-fields. At last, "when the train stopped, I saw two great white "clouds rising up from the depths of the earth— "nothing more. They rose up slowly, gently,

Nearing the Falls.

"majestically, into the air. I dragged Kate down "a deep and slippery path leading to the ferry "boat; bullied Anne for not coming fast enough; "perspired at every pore; and felt, it is impossible "to say how, as the sound grew louder and louder "in my ears, and yet nothing could be seen for "the mist.

"There were two English officers with us (ah! "what *gentlemen*, what noblemen of nature they "seemed), and they hurried off with me; leaving "Kate and Anne on a crag of ice; and clambered "after me over the rocks at the foot of the small

Nearer still.

"Fall, while the ferryman was getting the boat

"ready. I was not disappointed—but I could "make out nothing. In an instant, I was blinded "by the spray, and wet to the skin. I saw the "water tearing madly down from some immense "height, but could get no idea of shape, or situa-"tion, or anything but vague immensity. But "when we were seated in the boat, and crossing "at the very foot of the cataract—then I began "to feel what it was. Directly I had changed my "clothes at the inn I went out again, taking Kate "with me; and hurried to the Horse-shoe-fall. I "went down alone, into the very basin. It would "be hard for a man to stand nearer God than he "does there. There was a bright rainbow at my "feet; and from that I looked up to—great Heaven! "to *what* a fall of bright green water! The broad, "deep, mighty stream seems to die in the act of "falling; and, from its unfathomable grave arises "that tremendous ghost of spray and mist which "is never laid, and has been haunting this place "with the same dread solemnity—perhaps from "the creation of the world.

NIAGARA FALLS: 1842.

C. D. to J. F.

Horse-shoe-fall.

A fancy.

"We purpose remaining here a week. In my "next, I will try to give you some idea of my im-"pressions, and to tell you how they change with "every day. At present it is impossible. I can "only say that the first effect of this tremendous

Effect upon him of Niagara.

NIAGARA FALLS: 1842. C. D. to J. F.

"spectacle on me, was peace of mind—tran-"quillity—great thoughts of eternal rest and hap-"piness—nothing of terror. I can shudder at the "recollection of Glencoe (dear friend, with Heaven's "leave we must see Glencoe together), but when-"ever I think of Niagara, I shall think of its "beauty.

"If you could hear the roar that is in my ears "as I write this. Both Falls are under our windows. "From our sitting-room and bed-room we look "down straight upon them. There is not a soul "in the house but ourselves. What would I give "if you and Mac were here, to share the sensa-"tions of this time! I was going to add, what "would I give if the dear girl whose ashes lie in "Kensal-green, had lived to come so far along "with us—but she has been here many times, I "doubt not, since her sweet face faded from my "earthly sight.

The old recollection.

"One word on the precious letters before I "close. You are right, my dear fellow, about the "papers; and you are right (I grieve to say) about "the people. *Am I right?* quoth the conjuror. "*Yes!* from gallery, pit, and boxes. I *did* let out "those things, at first, against my will, but when

"I come to tell you all—well; only wait—only "wait—till the end of July. I say no more. NIAGARA FALLS: 1842. C. D. to J. F.

"I do perceive a perplexingly divided and "subdivided duty, in the matter of the book of "travels. Oh! the sublimated essence of comi-"cality that I *could* distil, from the materials I "have! . . . You are a part, and an essential part, "of our home, dear friend, and I exhaust my Looking forward. "imagination in picturing the circumstances un-"der which I shall surprise you by walking into "58, Lincoln's-inn fields. We are truly grateful "to God for the health and happiness of our in-"expressibly dear children and all our friends. "But one letter more — only one. . . . I don't "seem to have been half affectionate enough, but "there *are* thoughts, you know, that lie too deep "for words."

CHAPTER XXIV.

NIAGARA AND MONTREAL.

1842.

NIAGARA FALLS: 1842.

Last two letters.

MY friend was better than his word, and two more letters reached me before his return. The opening of the first was written from Niagara on the third, and its close from Montreal on the twelfth, of May; from which latter city also, on the 26th of that month, the last of all was written.

Dickens vanquished.

Much of the first of these letters had reference to the international copyright agitation, and gave strong expression to the indignation awakened in him (nor less in some of the best men of America) by the adoption, at a public meeting in Boston itself, of a memorial against any change of the law, in the course of which it was stated, that, if English authors were invested with any control over the republication of their own books, it would be no longer possible for American editors to alter and adapt them to the American taste.

NIAGARA FALLS: 1842.

This deliberate declaration however, unsparing as Dickens's anger at it was, in effect vanquished him. He saw the hopelessness of pursuing further any present effort to bring about the change desired; and he took the determination, not only to drop any allusion to it in his proposed book, but to try what effect might be produced, when he should again be in England, by a league of English authors to suspend further intercourse with American publishers while the law should remain as it is. On his return he made accordingly a public appeal to this effect, stating his own intention for the future to forego all profit derivable from the authorized transmission of early proofs across the Atlantic; but his hopes in this particular also were doomed to disappointment. I now leave the subject, quoting only from his present letter the general remarks with which it is dismissed by himself.

C. D. to J. F.

"NIAGARA FALLS.
"*Tuesday, Third May*, 1842.

Two obstacles to international copyright.

"I'll tell you what the two obstacles to the "passing of an international copyright law with "England, are: firstly, the national love of 'doing' "a man in any bargain or matter of business; "secondly, the national vanity. Both these char-

NIAGARA FALLS: 1842. C. D. to J. F. The first obstacle.

"acteristics prevail to an extent which no stranger "can possibly estimate.

"With regard to the first, I seriously believe "that it is an essential part of the pleasure "derived from the perusal of a popular English "book, that the author gets nothing for it. It is "so dar-nation 'cute—so knowing in Jonathan to "get his reading on those terms. He has the "Englishman so regularly on the hip that his eye "twinkles with slyness, cunning, and delight; and "he chuckles over the humour of the page with "an appreciation of it, quite inconsistent with, "and apart from, its honest purchase. The raven "hasn't more joy in eating a stolen piece of meat, "than the American has in reading the English "book which he gets for nothing.

"With regard to the second, it reconciles that "better and more elevated class who are above "this sort of satisfaction, with surprising ease. "The man's read in America! The Americans "like him! They are glad to see him when he "comes here! They flock about him, and tell "him that they are grateful to him for spirits in

The second.

"sickness; for many hours of delight in health; "for a hundred fanciful associations which are "constantly interchanged between themselves, and "their wives and children at home! It is nothing.

NIAGARA FALLS: 1842. C. D. to J. F.

"that all this takes place in countries where he is "*paid:* it is nothing that he has won fame for "himself elsewhere, and profit too. The Ameri- "cans read him; the free, enlightened, indepen- "dent Americans; and what more *would* he have? "Here's reward enough for any man. The na- "tional vanity swallows up all other countries on "the face of the earth, and leaves but this above "the ocean. Now, mark what the real value of "this American reading is. Find me in the whole "range of literature one single solitary English "book which becomes popular with them, before, "by going through the ordeal at home and be- "coming popular there, it has forced itself on "their attention—and I am content that the law "should remain as it is, for ever and a day. I "must make one exception. There *are* some "mawkish tales of fashionable life before which "crowds fall down as they were gilded calves, "which have been snugly enshrined in circulating "libraries at home, from the date of their publica- "tion.

Value of literary popularity in America.

"As to telling them, they will have no litera- "ture of their own, the universal answer (out of "Boston) is, 'We don't want one. Why should we "'pay for one when we can get it for nothing?

NIAGARA FALLS: 1842.

C. D. to J. F.

A substitute for literature.

"'Our people don't think of poetry, sir. Dollars, "'banks, and cotton are *our* books, sir.' And "they certainly are in one sense; for a lower "average of general information than exists in "this country on all other topics, it would be very "hard to find. So much, at present, for interna-"tional copyright."

The same letter kept the promise made in its predecessor that one or two more sketches of character should be sent. "One of the most "amusing phrases in use all through the country, "for its constant repetition, and adaptation to

"Yes, sir."

"every emergency, is 'Yes, Sir.' Let me give you "a specimen." (The specimen was the dialogue, in the *Notes*, of straw-hat and brown-hat, during the stage-coach ride to Sandusky.) "I am not "joking, upon my word. This is exactly the "dialogue. Nothing else occurring to me at this "moment, let me give you the secretary's portrait. "Shall I?

The secretary.

"He is of a sentimental turn—strongly sen-"timental; and tells Anne as June approaches that "he hopes 'we shall sometimes think of him' in "our own country. He wears a cloak, like Ham-"let; and a very tall, big, limp, dusty black hat, "which he exchanges on long journeys for a cap "like Harlequin's. . . . He sings; and in some of "our quarters, when his bedroom has been near "ours, we have heard him grunting bass notes "through the keyhole of his door, to attract our "attention. His desire that I should formally ask "him to sing, and his devices to make me do so, "are irresistibly absurd. There was a piano in "our room at Hartford (you recollect our being "there, early in February?)—and he asked me "one night, when we were alone, if 'Mrs. D' "played. 'Yes, Mr. Q.' 'Oh indeed Sir! *I* sing: "'so whenever you want *a little soothing*—' You "may imagine how hastily I left the room, on "some false pretence, without hearing more.

NIAGARA FALLS: 1842. C. D. to J. F.

Frightful suggestion.

"He paints. . . An enormous box of oil co-"lours is the main part of his luggage: and with "these he blazes away, in his own room, for "hours together. Anne got hold of some big-"headed, pot-bellied sketches he made of the "passengers on board the canal-boat (including "me in my fur-coat), the recollection of which "brings the tears into my eyes at this minute. "He painted the Falls, at Niagara, superbly; and "is supposed now to be engaged on a full-length "representation of me: waiters having reported "that chamber-maids have said that there is a "picture in his room which has a great deal of "hair. One girl opined that it was 'the beginning

Mr. Q's paintings.

The lion and ——.

NIAGARA FALLS: 1842.

C. D. to J. F.

"'of the King's-arms'; but I am pretty sure that "the Lion is myself. . . . .

"Sometimes, but not often, he commences a "conversation. That usually occurs when we are "walking the deck after dark; or when we are "alone together in a coach. It is his practice at "such times to relate the most notorious and pa-"triarchial Joe Miller, as something that occurred "in his own family. When travelling by coach, "he is particularly fond of imitating cows and "pigs; and nearly challenged a fellow passenger "the other day, who had been moved by the dis-"play of this accomplishment into telling him "that he was 'a Perfect Calf.' He thinks it an "indispensable act of politeness and attention to "enquire constantly whether we're not sleepy, or, "to use his own words, whether we don't 'suffer "'for sleep.' If we have taken a long nap of "fourteen hours or so, after a long journey, he is "sure to meet me at the bedroom door when I "turn out in the morning, with this enquiry. But "apart from the amusement he gives us, I could "not by possibility have lighted on any one who "would have suited my purpose so well. I have "raised his ten dollars per month to twenty; and "mean to make it up for six months."

Suffering for sleep.

The conclusion of this letter was dated from

"Montreal Thursday, twelfth May;" and was little more than an eager yearning for home. "This "will be a very short and stupid letter, my dear "friend; for the post leaves here much earlier than "I expected, and all my grand designs for being "unusually brilliant fall to the ground. I will "write you *one line* by the next Cunard boat—re-"serving all else until our happy and long long "looked-for meeting.

MONTREAL: 1842.

C. D. to J. F.

"We have been to Toronto, and Kingston; "experiencing attentions at each which I should "have difficulty in describing. The wild and rabid "toryism of Toronto, is, I speak seriously, *appalling*. "English kindness is very different from American. "People send their horses and carriages for your "use, but they don't exact as payment the right "of being always under your nose. We had no "less than *five* carriages at Kingston waiting our "pleasure at one time; not to mention the com-"modore's barge and crew, and a beautiful govern-"ment steamer. We dined with Sir Charles Bagot "last Sunday. Lord Mulgrave was to have met "us yesterday at Lachine; but as he was wind-"bound in his yacht and couldn't get in, Sir "Richard Jackson sent his drag four-in-hand, with "two other young fellows who are also his aides, "and in we came in grand style.

Toryism of Toronto.

Canadian attentions.

MONTREAL: 1842. C. D. to J. F.

"The Theatricals (I think I told you* I had "been invited to play with the officers of the "Coldstream guards here) are, *A Roland for an* "*Oliver; Two o'clock in the Morning;* and either "the *Young Widow*, or *Deaf as a Post.* Ladies "(unprofessional) are going to play, for the first "time. I wrote to Mitchell at New York for a "wig for Mr. Snobbington, which has arrived, and "is brilliant. If they had done *Love, Law and* "*Physick*, as at first proposed, I was already 'up' "in Flexible, having played it of old, before my "authorship days; but if it should be Splash in "the *Young Widow*, you will have to do me the "favor to imagine me in a smart livery-coat, shiny "black hat and cockade, white knee-cords, white "top-boots, blue stock, small whip, red cheeks and "dark eyebrows. Conceive Topping's state of "mind if I bring this dress home and put it on "unexpectedly! . . . God bless you, dear friend. "I can say nothing about the seventh, the day on "which we sail. It is impossible. Words cannot "express what we feel now that the time is so "near. . . . ."

Proposed private theatricals.

His last letter, dated from "Peasco's Hotel, "Montreal, Canada, twenty-sixth of May," described

* See *ante*, p. 128.

the private theatricals, and enclosed me a bill of the play. MONTREAL: 1842. C. D. to J. F. Last letter.

"This, like my last, will be a stupid letter, be-"cause both Kate and I are thrown into such a "state of excitement by the near approach of the "seventh of June, that we can do nothing, and "think of nothing.

"The play came off last night. The audience "between five and six hundred strong, were in-"vited as to a party; a regular table with refresh-"ments being spread in the lobby and saloon. "We had the band of the twenty-third (one of the "finest in the service) in the orchestra, the theatre "was lighted with gas, the scenery was excellent, "and the properties were all brought from private "houses. Sir Charles Bagot, Sir Richard Jackson, "and their staffs were present; and as the military "portion of the audience were all in full uniform, "it was really a splendid scene. The private play.

"We 'went' also splendidly; though with no-"thing very remarkable in the acting way. We had "for Sir Mark Chase a genuine odd fish, with "plenty of humour; but our Tristram Sappy was "not up to the marvellous reputation he has some-"how or other acquired here. I am not however, "let me tell you, placarded as stage-manager for "nothing. Everybody was told they would have

Montreal: 1842.

C. D. to J. F.

"to submit to the most iron despotism; and didn't "I come Macready over them? Oh no. By no "means. Certainly not. The pains I have taken "with them, and the perspiration I have expended, "during the last ten days, exceed in amount any-

Stage manager's report.

"thing you can imagine. I had regular plots of "the scenery made out, and lists of the properties "wanted; and had them nailed up by the prompter's "chair. Every letter that was to be delivered, "was written; every piece of money that had to "be given, provided; and not a single thing lost "sight of. I prompted, myself, when I was not "on; when I was, I made the regular prompter of "the theatre my deputy; and I never saw anything "so perfectly touch and go, as the first two pieces. "The bedroom scene in the interlude was as "well furnished as Vestris had it; with a 'practi-"'cable' fireplace blazing away like mad, and "everything in a concatenation accordingly. I "really do believe that I was very funny: at least "I know that I laughed heartily at myself, and

Mr. Snobbington.

"made the part a character, such as you and I "know very well: a mixture of T——, Harley, "Yates, Keeley, and Jerry Sneak. It went with a "roar, all through; and, as I am closing this, they "have told me I was so well made up that Sir "Charles Bagot, who sat in the stage box, had no

MONTREAL: 1842. C. D. to J. F. The lady performers.

"idea who played Mr. Snobbington, until the piece "was over.

"But only think of Kate playing! and playing "devilish well, I assure you! All the ladies were "capital, and we had no wait or hitch for an in-"stant. You may suppose this, when I tell you "that we began at eight, and had the curtain "down at eleven. It is their custom here, to "prevent heartburnings in a very heartburning "town, whenever they have played in private, to "repeat the performances in public. So, on Satur-"day (substituting, of course, real actresses for the "ladies), we repeat the two first pieces to a pay-"ing audience, for the manager's benefit. . . .

"I send you a bill, to which I have appended "a key.

Private Theatricals.

COMMITTEE.

MRS. TORRENS.	MRS. PERRY.
W. C. ERMATINGER, ESQ.	CAPTAIN TORRENS.

THE EARL OF MULGRAVE.

STAGE MANAGER--MR. CHARLES DICKENS.

QUEEN'S THEATRE, MONTREAL.

ON WEDNESDAY EVENING, MAY 25TH, 1842,
WILL BE PERFORMED,

A ROLAND FOR AN OLIVER.

MRS. SELBORNE. —— Mrs Torrens
MARIA DARLINGTON. —— Miss Griffin
MRS. FIXTURE. —— Miss Ermatinger.
MR. SELBORNE. —— Lord Mulgrave.
ALFRED HIGHFLYER. —— Mr charles dickens
SIR MARK CHASE. —— Honorable Mr Methuen
FIXTURE. —— Captain Willoughby.
GAMEKEEPER. —— Captain Granville

AFTER WHICH, AN INTERLUDE IN ONE SCENE, (FROM THE FRENCH,) CALLED

Past Two o'Clock in the Morning.

THE STRANGER. —— Captain Granville
MR. SNOBBINGTON. —— Mr charles dickens

TO CONCLUDE WITH THE FARCE, IN ONE ACT, ENTITLED

DEAF AS A POST.

MRS. PLUMPLEY. — Mrs Torrens
AMY TEMPLETON. — Mrs charles dickens!!!!!!!!
SOPHY WALTON. — Mrs Perry.
SALLY MAGGS. — Miss Griffin
CAPTAIN TEMPLETON. — Captain Torrens
MR. WALTON. —— Captain Willoughby.
TRISTRAM SAPPY. —— Doctor Griffin
CRUPPER. —— Lord Mulgrave
GALLOP. —— Mr charles dickens.

MONTREAL, MAY 24, 1842. GAZETTE OFFICE.

MONTREAL: 1842.

C. D. to J. F.

"I have not told you half enough. But I "promise you I shall make you shake your sides "about this play. Wasn't it worthy of Crummles "that when Lord Mulgrave and I went out to the "door to receive the Governor-general, the regular "prompter followed us in agony with four tall "candlesticks with wax candles in them, and be-"sought us with a bleeding heart to carry two "apiece, in accordance with all the precedents? . . .

A touch of Crummles.

"I have hardly spoken of our letters, which "reached us yesterday, shortly before the play "began. A hundred thousand thanks for your "delightful mainsail of that gallant little packet. "I read it again and again; and had it all over "again at breakfast time this morning. I heard "also, by the same ship, from Talfourd, Miss Coutts, "Brougham, Rogers, and others. A delicious letter "from Mac too, as good as his painting I swear. "Give my hearty love to him. . . . God bless "you, my dear friend. As the time draws nearer, "we get FEVERED with anxiety for home. . . . "Kiss our darlings for us. We shall soon "meet, please God, and be happier and merrier "than ever we were, in all our lives. . . . Oh "home—home—home—home—home—home—

www.ingramcontent.com/pod-product-compliance
Lightning Source LLC
Chambersburg PA
CBHW030630030726
47497CB00006B/1717
* 9 7 8 3 7 4 2 8 5 4 9 7 1 *